THE CENTAURI SURVIVORS

THE CENTAURI SEQUENCE
BOOK 1

ANDREW J CHAMBERLAIN

ISBN: 978-1-8384480-1-1
Published by Resolute Books
www.resolutebooks.co.uk

For D.A.C.
Per Ardua Ad Astra

THE CENTAURI SURVIVORS

By Andrew J Chamberlain

1

Colony Ship *Aspira*
Alpha Centauri 'B' System
2125CE

GRACE MCALLAN WOKE TO A COOL, blue light. She twisted and felt the restraints trapping her limbs. Pushing out her right arm, she forced the muscles to stretch until a sharp sting made her gasp, and the sound of her voice triggered a memory; distant and abstract; but it was enough. She knew where she was.

"Okay," she said, "I'm okay." It sounded like a stranger was speaking. She shivered, and the sting in her arm receded into a dull ache.

She took a deep breath, and drew the moist air into her lungs, then she forced her eyes open, trying to find some point of reference.

This was her cryopod, on the colony ship *Aspira*, and along with two hundred other colonists, she was on her way to the planet Zera in the Alpha Centauri 'B' system. The sting was from the cannula in her right arm, and the restraints were part of the cryopod harness that supported and protected her body while she slept.

The harness allowed freedom of movement, giving it the ability to exercise the subject and preserve muscle tone. An intravenous feed provided nutrients and removed waste. In the final stages of the journey, it delivered a cocktail of immune system enhancements, stimulants, and nano-machines.

Grace was awake, that meant their sixty-year journey was over, and they'd arrived. She calmed her breathing and listened, reaching out beyond the dark cocoon of her pod.

The deep thrum of the ship came to her. The sound was in her bones, chest, and the space between her ears. She lay still for a while, letting it move through her.

That's the fusion engines, she thought, *we'd only use them for adjustments in orbit. We must be here, at Zera.*

Now she could taste adrenaline as the disorientation gave way to excitement. She had arrived at Zera, her new home. All she wanted was to see the planet in all its blue and green splendour.

She stretched out again, her left hand brushing the side of the cryopod. Far above her, she heard the clear chime of a bell. The pod hissed, a gentle release of air that signalled it was ready to open. But the restraints still bound her.

"Okay, what did they say in the training?"

The pod hissed more loudly, like a balloon losing air.

Grace imagined the intravenous feed and a cluster of other monitors, threading their way back to the pod's central processor, providing a range of data on her physical state, recording everything passing into and out of her body.

Then she remembered she wouldn't have to get out of the pod alone. Rebecca, her key worker from the Transit Team, would be there to help her.

But Grace didn't want to wait. She knew that if she unlocked the restraint clips, the pod would open. She reached down to the release catch.

The clip wouldn't budge. She pulled harder until her fingers hurt, then she lay back down, frustrated, panting. What was it the trainer said? Snatches of memory came back to her, and she reached down again. Instead of pulling on the catch, she twisted it.

The harness unclipped easily and fell away from her arms and legs; as it did so, the light in the pod strengthened and the pale shapes of her limbs appeared before her.

Then something above her clicked, and a fierce white line appeared around the rim of the pod as it lifted. The warm moist air fled into the light and a cold dry breeze blew across her, making her shiver.

The pod lid lifted, and she squinted at the grid of lights far above on the roof of the cryohall, the brilliant white dots making her eyes water.

"I must get out, I must..."

Something jolted backwards; the cannula had pulled on her arm, sending a jab of pain up to her shoulder.

She stared at the transparent and black tubing of the connector, still fixed to the inside of her forearm, linking her to the pod systems. The needle had become loose, and a circle of blood gathered around it.

"Get out," she hissed, taking hold of the base on the cannula and easing it out of her flesh. "Get out!" With a final sting, the needle was gone, she was free.

Her whole body shivered again. Her throat felt dry and thirsty, and she needed to pee.

Bracing her fingers against either side of the pod, she pulled the bitter cold air into her lungs and fought down the dizziness. The bass rumble of the ship's engines was louder now that the pod was open, and she imagined little groups of colonists emerging from their pods, with their assigned Transit Team helpers moving between them.

Her parents would be there, and Dan, her family.

Other pods clustered around her; everyone from her sixteen

and seventeen year old age group. None of the others were open yet.

Rows of pods extended across the cryohall in all directions, clean and ordered, like the headstones in a war cemetery.

She scanned the vast room until her head pounded with the effort. Then she collapsed back into the pod.

There was no movement, no Transit Team members, nothing.

Where are they? Why aren't they here, and why is no one else awake?

"Hello?" she croaked, listening for something more than the hum of the engine. A steady green light shone out from her own pod, across the hall, where all the lights were amber. Amber meant the other colonists were still asleep, all of them. She was the first one up.

"Alone or not," she whispered to herself, "I need to pee."

She pulled herself onto the broad edge of the pod, fighting a dizziness that made the entire room tilt away from her, then swung her legs over the edge and slid down onto the floor. Immediately, her knees gave way, and she clutched at the side of the pod to stop herself from collapsing onto the hard rubber floor of the cryohall.

Cursing, she pulled herself up and, hanging on to the edge of the pod, she stood and breathed deeply. Now she could feel the spin of the great ship mimicking gravity, gently tugging her towards the hull beneath her feet.

Directly behind her were the sky-blue painted doors of the changing rooms and showers. She padded off towards them.

By the time she reached the doors, she was gagging on the dry cold air. She glanced back at the hall. There was still no movement, no Transit Team helpers, no signs of life, nothing; just a sea of pods with a cloud of amber lights hovering above each one. She opened the changing room doors, and the lights inside flicked on.

Inside, she could see the cubicles, sinks, and showers. By each sink, there were stacks of transparent plastic boxes, each holding toiletries, toothbrushes, and water flasks. She turned on a tap, letting the water run for a minute before she drank from it, greedily, swallowing the cool water, letting it moisten her mouth and throat.

She peeled off her bodysuit, and stepped into one of the showers. The control turned on with a shriek, and she waited for the water to run clean and hot.

The jets stung her skin, but the sensation made her feel alive and she scrubbed every part of herself, washing away sixty years of sleep.

Clean and dry, she pulled on her new sky-blue and emerald colony uniform, which still looked as fresh as the day it had been packed for her sixty years ago. Then she put on the St Christopher pendant her parents had given her; an appropriate gift for anyone going on the journey of a lifetime.

Every colonist would have a uniform waiting for them in their own locker, together with the few personal effects they could bring with them. Her younger brother, Dan, would have his beloved tin whistle waiting next to his uniform.

She opened her locker and picked up her the sky-blue and emerald colony uniform, which still looked as fresh as the day it had been packed for her sixty years ago. The material felt warm and comfortable against her skin. When she was dressed, she put on the St Christopher pendant her parents had given her; an appropriate gift for anyone going on the journey of a lifetime.

She strapped on her colony watch, designed for the slightly shorter Zeran days, and then finally, she reached into the locker to pick up her shoulder bag, which would contain her own comm unit, and some of the protein bars Rebecca had given her before she went into the cryopod.

As she picked up the bag, she noticed a plain white envelope at the back of the locker. She recognised her father's writing and frowned. He must have put it there after she had gone into her pod.

She picked it up just as her watch turned on, telling her the time on Zera, and on Earth. Back on Earth it was 11.43 am GMT on Monday, October 1st in the year 2125. With a jolt of adrenaline, she realised that she'd been asleep for just over sixty years. That was the expected travel time to Zera, and Grace felt anticipation within her; maybe they really had crossed the forty-one trillion kilometres and completed their journey.

She walked back into the cryohall, still holding the letter from her father. She was running her finger under the flap of the envelope when a clear chime rang out in the cool air. The envelope went into the inside pocket of her uniform jacket and a green light flickering across the ceiling. It was near her pod, so one of the other teenagers was waking up. She took three quick steps and then broke into a run.

When she reached the pod, the control panel shone out a clear green light, but there was also a message scrolling across the screen beneath it:

Immunity protocol error: stage J4-C warning: administration incomplete.

Immunity protocol compromised.

She frowned, and looked at the nameplate on the side of the pod.

Kellerman, Brandon Max Jr.

Oh great, she thought, *that's all I need.*

The pod opened.

BRANDON KELLERMAN SAT UP, burped, and then looked around.

He squinted at Grace and blinked. "You don't look like Arjun."

"That's because I'm not Arjun," said Grace, "I don't know where he is."

He stared at her.

"So who are you?"

She returned his gaze for a moment.

"I'm Grace, remember? Grace McAllan."

"Oh yeah, Grace, you're that English girl."

"My family is from Scotland. I'm from Stornoway on the Isle of Lewis."

"Right, well, that's good."

He scratched his armpit and looked over the edge of the pod.

"I feel like death on a stick. Weren't the Transit team supposed to be here to help us?"

"I don't know where they are, but if you get out of that pod now, you'll beat the rush for the showers."

"My thinking exactly," said Brandon and hauled himself up from the pod. The restraints pulled him back.

"Ow!" he said as the cannula tugged at his arm. He stared at the needle and swore.

"Just wait a moment," she said. "First, let's sort these out," and she reached over and snapped the restraint clip open.

"Thanks," said Brandon, looking down at the canula his arm. "I should get rid of this thing."

"Let me do it; this will sting."

He was quiet, but she could feel his body tense as the needle slid out.

"Careful when you stand," she said. "The gravity feels weird."

He swung his legs over the rim, slid down, and placed both feet on the floor, then he straightened up, took a deep breath, wobbled slightly, and winked at her.

"Okay, this isn't so bad." He looked down at the body suit. "Except I've got to get out of this stupid onesie. I look like my little brother when he's ready for bed."

Grace smiled despite herself.

"Seriously though, this place should be buzzing. What do you think's going on?"

"I don't know. We've arrived at Zera, but I don't know why we're the first to wake. It should have been the adults."

"Well, I'm going to get changed. I'll see you in a few minutes. I'm sure more people will wake up soon."

"I hope so."

Brandon made his way towards the changing rooms, pulled on the door, and slipped inside. Even from a distance, she could hear him clattering about, trying to get a shower started.

She looked at the rest of the pods, all showing a steady amber glow. Something didn't feel right. People should be waking up; there should be chatter and life and bustle.

She walked over to where her parents were still sleeping and rested her fingers on the brushed steel exterior of her mother's pod.

"Come on, Mum," she whispered, "wake up."

She was looking at her father's pod when a clear chime rang out, and another pod light flickered green.

Joshua Mandela North became conscious and immediately willed himself to relax, slipping into the meditative routine he sometimes used when he needed to calm himself and focus. He took a deep breath, drawing in the warm damp air around him, and tasted just a hint of something metallic within the moisture. His body felt the desire for action now he was awake. He tried whispering a quick prayer, expecting to hear his voice, but all that come out was a breathy wheeze.

A soft blue light filled the interior of the pod, giving his dark limbs a strange smoky colour. Outside his private world, he heard noises: a chime, and more faintly, footfalls, coming quickly, someone running towards him. The sound stopped right next to him. He thought about his Transit Team buddy Arjun, who would be there to help him. His body tensed as the mix of chemicals from the intravenous feed changed, and he tasted adrenaline, the pod giving him one last kick towards wakefulness.

There was a scraping sound, and the lid lifted. He felt an icy breeze blow over his skin, raising the tiny hairs on his arms and legs. He looked up at the person standing over him, but it wasn't Arjun.

"Grace," he said. "It is Grace, isn't it?"

She smiled. "I'm glad somebody knows who I am."

"I know who you are, you are Grace McAllan, Amber and David McAllan's daughter. I guess Arjun's busy with someone else."

"He isn't here. None of the Transit Team is here. Not yet anyway."

She eased his pod open fully and the ceiling lights shone down on him.

"Wow, that is bright," he said, blinking. "So, is anyone else up?"

"Only you, me, and Brandon so far."

"Brandon Kellerman?"

"Yep."

Josh laughed. "So, no adults, and no Transit Team."

"Nope, just us kids at the moment."

"Did you say Brandon?"

"Yep."

Josh smiled and shook his head. "Of all the people."

"Yeah, I know, and I can tell you that sixty years in a cryopod hasn't changed him a bit."

He lay still and looked at her.

"What?" she said, frowning.

"I forgot about that extreme haircut they gave us all. It hasn't grown back, of course."

"It will," she said, running her fingers over the light covering of ginger on her head.

"Well, I'd better get up."

"Yes. But let me help you first."

She leaned forward, unclipped the restraints, and then eased the cannula out of his arm.

"How do you feel?"

"I'm fine, if you need to check the other pods…"

"I'll wait until you're on your feet. Brandon and I were pretty wobbly to start with."

"Okay, thanks."

After another deep breath, he lowered himself to the floor. He remained motionless for a moment, breathing slowly before stretching each part of his body: arms, torso, legs, easing each group of muscles back into life. These were steady, precise movements, in time with his breathing.

"Is that some kind of warmup routine?" she asked.

"I use it for BCT."

"Blended Combat Training," said Grace, nodding. "I never learnt anything like that. You ever had to use those skills to defend yourself?"

"Not yet. I prefer to avoid trouble if I can."

He finished the routine and was just about to move towards the changing rooms when the doors swung open and Brandon strode out, wearing his new uniform. He glanced across the hall.

"Josh!" he shouted, "I thought I heard your smooth voice out here."

"Brandon Kellerman. You always were first to the party."

"Up before all these old guys," said Brandon, waving at the other pods, "and there's a planet to explore."

"Well, I'll see you guys in a minute," said Josh. "I'm going to get cleaned up."

"Check these outfits," said Brandon, swivelling from side to side, showing off the uniform. "They show off muscle contour nicely. What do you think?"

Brandon strode away from them like a model on the catwalk.

Grace let out a long breath.

"I'm sorry, Brandon, I wasn't paying attention, what did you say?"

"Ouch! Get you," said Brandon. "Seriously though, you will love these outfits Josh, they suit that 'group' thing you were always going on about."

"Group thing?" said Josh.

"You were always telling us to 'come together as a team'," Brandon air quoted the phrase, "and work with the planet to survive. Remember that?"

"I do, and it's true. We've got to work as a team, and we have to work with whatever's down there."

"Well, I hope the planet wants to cooperate with us," said Brandon, "because my aim is to survive, and I'll do whatever it takes to achieve that."

"Well, don't go shooting things until someone says you can," said Josh.

"You're hilarious. I assume we have arrived at Zera, I mean, do we know that for sure?"

"I'm pretty sure," said Grace. "We've arrived."

"What makes you think that?" said Josh.

"Well, just listen."

They were all silent for a moment.

"I can hear the engines," said Brandon.

"Yes, but which engines?" said Grace.

"The big ones?" suggested Brandon.

"I don't think they're the main engines," said Josh.

"No, they're not," said Grace, "which means…"

"Go on," said Brandon, "you're dying to tell us."

"That's the fusion engines," said Grace.

"Ah yes, of course," said Brandon. "And?"

"And the ship wouldn't use them unless we were in system. We got here on the optimised EmDrive. Those fusion engines are there just to help us park the ship."

"So, we **have** arrived," said Josh.

"Either that or we haven't ventured out of our solar system," said Grace, "but we've been travelling for sixty years, so I'd say that's unlikely."

"Does that mean we're in orbit above the planet?" said Josh.

"I think so," said Grace, "when everyone's up, we'll travel to the landing zone and set up a base there."

"At least we know what we'll find when we make landfall," said Josh. "That will give us some advantage over whatever we meet down there."

"Be prepared," said Brandon. "You're sounding like me now."

"Of course, we need to be prepared," said Josh.

"Yeah," said Brandon, "but I thought you loved Zera, and we were going to hug the trees and make beautiful music."

"I'm not naïve," said Josh. "I know we have to be careful."

"Yes we do," said Brandon, "but first, we," he let his arm sweep across the cryohall, "need to wake up."

"True," said Josh. "Well, I'm going to get showered. See you guys in a few minutes."

OWEN MORTIS SNIFFED the air and tried to suppress the feelings of disgust that rose from deep within him.

He sat at the end of the table, like the head of the family, and looked across the space they'd shared all these years.

This was the Transit Team mess room, and in the latter years of their journey, it had more than lived up to its name. The table bore the stains of ground-in food and drink. One chair leaned at an odd angle, but all the rest of them were occupied. An air-conditioning vent above the table rattled once as it turned on and then settled into a moaning hum.

On his right sat Dr Amelia Villiers, the *Aspira's* xenobiology specialist. She'd had the chance to be a colonist on this mission, but instead joined the Transit Team. It would cost her ten years of her life, but it gave her the two things she desired most: a life with Owen, and the chance to prepare for power when they reached the new planet.

Next to Amelia was Dr Goran Maric, the man who had woken them all when the pods had malfunctioned. Thickset, sweaty and nervous; Goran survived by holding on to the symbols that confirmed his identity as a true scientist: the white lab coat now frayed with use, and the Voss and Winkelman bow ties he habitually wore.

Facing Amelia and Goran were two other men, heads shaved to match their stubble. On the right was Ray Merritt, 'reliable Ray' as Owen's father called him, the man who appeared on the payroll as Mortis's driver, but had in fact been his Close Protection Officer, or CPO, for ten years before the *Aspira* launch. Ray had originally trained as an engineer in the British Army. As Callum Mortis's CPO, he'd put his life on the line at least twice to protect his boss, actions that had earned him the respect of the old man.

Next to him was Patrick Cullen, stocky, stubbled and wearing a stained blue overall. Patrick was the team's maintenance guy, he fixed things, patched things, and kept it all running on a ship that was slowly breaking down.

Goran picked at one of his fingers, while the rest of them stared at him in silence. The engines rumbled and the Transit Team's air-con moaned above their heads. The only other sound was the gentle tap, tap, tap of a Walther PPZ semi-automatic pistol as Patrick rocked it back and forth on the table.

Owen turned his attention to Goran. "So, what's going on in the cryohall, why you've woken us up at this god-forsaken hour?"

Goran looked at Owen, then the rest of them.

"Yes, of course," he picked furiously at a loose fingernail. "There has been a slight timing problem with the euthanasia protocol, I felt it was prudent to advise you all."

"I thought the timings were all worked out," said Owen, "so what exactly happened?"

"WE CAN'T DEAL with this on our own," said Brandon. "We have to find the transit team."

"When Josh returns, we'll go and find them, maybe…"

She stopped in mid-sentence as a high-pitched whine sounded across the hall. Red lights flickered to their left.

"What the hell is that?" said Brandon.

"Pod malfunction, come on."

They ran, dodging between rows of pods, footsteps thudding on the floor.

A red light flickered above one pod and Grace glanced up at the diagnostic readout on the console.

Warning: Myocardial infarction detected

"That sounds bad," said Brandon

"It is, we've got to open this thing."

They gripped at the lid and pulled, but it wouldn't move.

"Is there a manual override?" said Brandon.

"Under there," said Grace, pointing to the lid, "there's a catch you push."

Brandon felt the edge of the pod; something clicked. The lid slowly lifted, and he forced it up. The alarm stopped, but the red light continued to flash.

Inside lay a man, seemingly asleep, his arms at his sides. Grace glanced at the pod nameplate.

Johnson, Travis Ethan

She put her ear to Travis's chest and listened.

"He's not breathing," said Grace. "We need a defibrillator."

"There must be one in the medical area," said Brandon. "I'll find it."

He ran across the hall, towards one of the med bays, crashing into a gurney as he entered the room. He found cupboards and drawers full of supplies, but none of it was any use to him. He stared helplessly at an unrecognisable machine bristling with probes and wires.

"Come on…" he said to himself.

He scanned the shelves; on the wall to the left, he saw a red box with a heart symbol on its front.

"Got you!" he yanked the box off the wall, and ran back to Grace.

"Do you know how to use this?"

"I think so," said Grace. "We covered it on the First Aid course."

"Well, this is your show, then."

She flipped open the lid. "Okay, rip that body suit open."

Brandon pulled hard at the light material, lifting the man as he did so; the suit snagged and ripped in his hands. Grace flicked on the power button, and the machine whined. She picked up the two small paddles attached to the machine.

"Stand back!"

Brandon backed away and stared as Grace pressed the paddles against the skin above Travis' heart.

I'm glad I'm not doing this, he thought, as he waited for the current to jolt through Travis Johnson's body.

The machine discharged, and the body jerked.

She bent over and listened to his chest again.

"Well?" said Brandon.

"No good, we do it again."

The machine whined as it recharged.

"Let me try some CPR," he said, "mix that with the defibrillator."

"You know CPR?"

"Of course, it's a survival skill."

He tipped Travis's head back slightly, opened his mouth, and then leaned over, placing one palm on the other. He repeated the CPR routine, thirty compressions and two breaths, over and over.

"Try that again," he said, pointing to the defibrillator.

They worked for three minutes, until Grace's hands were shaking and Brandon was leaning on the side of the pod, breathless.

"It's no good," she said finally, "we're done." She switched off the defibrillator.

"Damn it," said Brandon, whacking the side of the pod. He slid onto the floor as she came and sat beside him.

"This is crazy. What if a load of these pods goes off like this at once? We're screwed."

"We need help, now," said Grace.

"They must be monitoring the pods. Surely an emergency will bring them here?"

He stood up and stared around the hall.

"Hey!" he shouted at the ceiling, waving his arms. "Hey, Transit Team, get down here now."

Grace stood up beside him.

"One of us has to get them," she said.

As she spoke, another chime filled the hall, clear green light splashed across the hall from where the children's pods were located.

"Dan!" said Grace, and she ran towards the light.

Then another chime rang out, another green light flickering near to Grace and Brandon's pod.

"I'll get that one," Brandon called to Grace, but she was already gone.

Grace skidded to a halt just as the lid opened.

"Hey, bro," she said, trying to disguise her breathlessness. The boy inside blinked and stared at her.

"Grace?"

"Yes, it's me."

"I thought Darren was going to help me."

"Change of plan," she said, "Darren hasn't arrived yet. We're the first people awake. Let's help you get out of this thing."

Dan looked away, confused, "I don't feel right."

"You've been asleep for sixty years, you're going to feel rough."

"No, there's something else."

She unclipped the restraints, and he sat up.

"Just relax," she said. "Let's get this needle out; it's going to hurt, okay?"

He held out his arm.

"You do it, Grace."

"Hold still." She felt him tense as the needle slid out of his flesh.

"Now get yourself..."

"What's that?" said Dan, pointing over to Travis's pod where a red light still flickered.

"There was a problem with one pod," said Grace.

"What kind of problem? What happened?"

"One colonist didn't make it."

"You mean they're dead?"

She hesitated for a moment.

"Yes," she said. "We knew it might happen."

Dan frowned and looked around the cryohall. "That was it, that's why I didn't feel right."

"Maybe it was," said Grace. "Now get yourself washed and changed." She held out a hand as he clambered over the edge of the pod.

"Go on, everyone else will be up soon."

"What about Mum and Dad?" said Dan.

"They'll be up soon, go on."

"Okay, I'm going." He wandered towards the changing rooms. When he was gone, she glanced back at Travis's pod, red light splashed, brutal and raw across the ceiling.

"You're right," she whispered to herself, "there is something wrong here."

Brandon arrived at the other pod to see the lid rising. He glanced at the nameplate.

Wong, Chi-Ping

He couldn't remember much about Chi, except that he paid more attention than Brandon did at all the briefings.

The pod lid opened fully, and Brandon peered in. Chi looked about the same age as him, but slimmer, wiry and determined. Chi opened his eyes and stared at Brandon.

"Hey," said Brandon. "How you doing, Chi, rise and shine, yeah?"

"Hello," said Chi, squinting at him. "Who are you?"

"I'm Brandon Kellerman. Sorry if you were expecting one of those Transit guys, they're all AWOL at the moment. You got me instead."

Chi blinked twice and uncurled himself, pulling against the restraints. Brandon came forward to help.

"I can do it," said Chi, pulling away.

"Fine," said Brandon, and he watched as Chi pulled against the restraints before he stopped and looked at Brandon.

"I'm sorry, please, can you help me?"

Brandon leaned in while Chi lay perfectly still and watched him.

"You're the Kellermans' son, aren't you?" said Chi.

"That's me. So, who did you come with?"

"My mother," said Chi. He looked at the needle in his arm and pulled it out himself. When he was free of the restraint, he lifted himself out of the pod and onto the floor. His legs bent as they hit the rubber, and Brandon offered him a hand.

"I'm okay," said Chi.

"Okay, well, you know where the changing area is."

Chi nodded, turned and walked towards the doors, disappearing into the room beyond.

Brandon stood and watched the changing area doors shut behind him.

"How about, 'Thanks Brandon'," he whispered to himself. "What an idiot."

Grace appeared beside him.

"So who was that?" she said.

"Some Chinese guy, Chi," said Brandon. "You know, the one who joined the program late."

"I think his mother's one of the software engineers."

"Whatever. Who was in the other pod?"

"My brother, he's gone to get changed."

"Is he okay?"

"Yeah, he'll be fine, but he spotted Travis's pod. When Josh and Dan are back, we'll find the Transit Team."

As she was speaking, the changing room doors opened and they could see Josh, clean and dressed, looking at them.

He jogged up to them and then glanced over at the splash of red light from Travis's pod.

Grace was about to tell him what it meant when another pod alarm broke out. A red light flickered about twenty metres away from them, then two more came on.

Within a few seconds, the entire hall was ringing with the sound of pod alerts. Red light flickered across the ceiling, the noise building and building as more pods wailed.

"What the hell is happening?" said Brandon.

"I don't know," said Grace, "mass pod malfunction maybe." Amongst the chaos, a small voice in her mind cried out to her.

Mum. Dad.

She moved towards their pods, side by side. Red lights appeared above both of them, and for the first time, she saw how much like a coffin these pods were.

DAN CAME BACK into the hall. He still had his bodysuit on, and as he looked out across a sea of flashing red, he saw his sister bent over their mother's pod, trying to force the lid open, frantic. He watched her thumping the console, and then finally the lid rose, slowly, slowly, and Grace was shouting and pulling at their mother, the harness tugging back at the limp body, pulling it back into the pod.

2

———

Finally, finally, everything was silent.

Grace took her hands away from her ears and looked up. The murmur of ship engines came to her again, as if nothing unusual had happened. Red light still flickered across the roof of the hall, but the alarms had stopped, their silence recording the end of each life.

Her mother and father were gone.

Brandon's parents and his brother were gone.

She couldn't remember anything about Josh or Chi's family at that moment, but she knew they were gone as well.

She shut her eyes, and her brain filled with the sounds and images of the desperate actions they had all taken as the alarms had started.

Between them, they'd opened as many of the pods as they could: family, friends and strangers, men and women and children. They'd tried to save them, raiding the med bays, pumping drugs and electricity into the dead and dying, doing whatever they could. The machines had spewed warnings and emergency codes, consoles had flashed with messages about immunity complications, organ failure, cardiac arrest.

And it had all been for nothing.

They hadn't been able to save any of them, not one; and Grace wasn't sure if they'd ever had a chance. All of them had died. As she contemplated the futility of their actions, the questions surfaced in her mind.

Why did this happen?
What went wrong?
Why did we survive?

She had no answers to these questions. She didn't know where the Transit Team were, and she didn't know why they hadn't come to help. The horror of it all left her feeling lost, broken, and alone.

The boys came silently and sat with her. They slumped onto the floor, stunned by the enormity of it all, confronted with their own powerlessness. But even now they were strangers to her, all of them apart from Dan, who was sitting next to her, his head resting on her shoulder. She felt Dan lift his head and watched as he looked out at the pods, now filled with the dead. His eyes were open, and he was not crying, not speaking, not moving; and at that moment, she felt such love and responsibility for her brother that her eyes stung. She put her arm tight around his shoulder and grieved for his loss, as much as her own.

And that was how they sat until Brandon's voice broke in.

"What the hell happened? I mean, what the hell just happened?"

No one answered.

He stood up and stared around the room before turning back to the four of them huddled on the floor.

"Where is the Transit Team?"

"Where are you?" he shouted. The question echoed around the hall. "Where were you when we needed you?"

"Maybe they're dead too," said Josh. "We might be the only ones alive on this ship."

"We have to find them," said Chi, "and then we can establish what's happened here."

"All of us should go," said Brandon. "I'm not staying here."

"Grace," Dan spoke so quietly she almost didn't hear him, "Grace?"

She turned to him, but he was silent.

"Come on," said Brandon, "let's get out of here."

"I agree, it's the most logical thing to do," said Chi, "there is no need for us to wait here."

"Wow," said Brandon, "you seem pretty calm about all this."

"I am calm," said Chi.

"Yeah, so you are," said Brandon. He looked down at Dan, "you'd better get washed and changed."

Dan stared at him.

"Like now, come on, move."

"Hey," said Josh, "go easy on him." He reached a hand down to Dan, who took it and stood up.

Dan looked at Grace. "Go with him," she said. "I'll see you in a few minutes."

Dan looked out at the rows of pods, some with their lids open, others still sealed, he frowned. "There's something wrong with what happened here."

"Wrong?" said Brandon, staring at him. "Of course there's something wrong, they're all dead."

"That's not what I meant."

"There are two hundred dead people here, our families. The Transit Team hasn't even shown up, and everything has gone to hell. You want to know what's wrong? That's what's wrong!"

Josh frowned. "That's enough. Shouting at Dan isn't the way to deal with this. We're all upset."

"Right," said Brandon, running his fingers across the stubble on his head, "you're right, it isn't his fault." He stared at Josh.

"You're angry," said Josh, stepping up to Brandon. "That's fine, be angry, but don't take it out on Dan."

Brandon swore, loudly. The words echoed around the hall. He turned back and pointed a finger at Josh's chest. "If this turns out to be someone's fault, someone's stupid mistake, so help me..."

Josh stared at him as he pushed his finger away. "We all want to find out what's happened".

Brandon took a deep breath.

"Sure, you're right." He looked at Dan, "Hey, look kid, I'm sorry, okay? I know this is rough on you as well."

Dan nodded at him.

"Come on," said Josh, laying a hand on Dan's shoulder.

They headed for the changing rooms.

"I need to have another pee," said Brandon, and he followed Dan and Josh, leaving Grace and Chi alone.

She stared at the ceiling lights and listened to the insistent hum of the engines.

"Grace."

She jumped at hearing Chi's voice.

"What is it?"

"Have you looked at the time?"

"What?"

"The time, I don't mean earth time, I mean ship time."

She checked her watch. "Yeah, it's just after two o'clock in the morning, so?"

"You remember what they said in the orientation sessions? They were going to wake us between seven and nine in the morning."

"Yes, I remember that, so we've woken up too early, yes?"

"Yes, I think we have. That is why the Transit Team hasn't arrived. They weren't expecting any of us to be awake yet."

"But there are alarms, they'd have had some kind of warning?"

"That, I don't understand. They can't have missed this unless the ship communications are damaged, or they are also dead."

"Oh, dear God, if it is just us, if we are alone, then we'll have to dispose of all these bodies."

Chi stared out at the pods, and then he frowned.

"Look over there." In the far corner of the hall, tucked in next to one of the med bays, a single amber light flickered above one pod. "Do you see that? I know who that is."

Grace followed him past the pods and on towards the end of the hall.

They arrived at the pod to find it sealed, the occupant still asleep. Grace tried to run a diagnostic programme from the control panel, but it wouldn't give her access. She looked at the nameplate.

Mortis, Callum Primo

"I've heard of him," said Grace, "the man with the money. He bankrolled this project. His estate back on earth is so large, they say you could spend a week walking around the edge of it and still not complete a lap."

"It's true he financed part of it, but a lot of the money came from a consortium of governments."

"How do you know that, Chi?"

Chi didn't answer.

"Do you think we should try to revive him?"

The changing room doors banged open and Brandon, Josh, and Dan came back into the hall.

"No, Grace, we should rejoin the others and leave this place."

When they were all together, Grace and Chi picked up the shoulder bags they had with them. Brandon pushed one of the water flasks into his jacket pocket, then he sniffed the air.

"This place is beginning to stink," he said. "Let's go."

They walked to the main door in one corner of the hall. It had a large steel bar across it. As they gathered together, Brandon placed a hand on the bar.

"It should be open," said Grace. "We just need to push hard."

Brandon gripped the steel and leaned on it. "Damn thing is stiff, can someone give me a hand?"

Grace pushed against the bar with him. It squeaked and then slammed down with a sharp bang that echoed around them. The door gave way, sucking frosty air into the hall. A crosshatched metal floor stretched out to their left and right.

"Where are we?" said Josh, looking around.

"Port side of the *Aspira*," said Grace, "near the stern. This corridor will take us around the circumference of the ship."

"How do we get to the Transit suite?" said Brandon.

"We need to take the monorail. We follow this corridor around the perimeter until we get to the terminus, and then we take one of the cars up to the bow of the ship."

"You lead the way," said Josh.

"The floor feels weird," said Brandon, putting out his arms to steady himself.

"Gravity replication," said Grace. "We're standing with our feet on the rim of a giant spinning cylinder."

They followed the corridor around the circumference of the ship towards the monorail station. The air grew even colder, their breath coming out as steam in the dim light of the corridor.

Ahead of them, on the left, was a set of large red double doors, with the words "PRIMARY LANDING PARTY STORAGE BAY G2" stencilled in white across them.

Brandon stopped and pointed at the door. "If it's just us, I mean, if the Transit Team are dead too, and we have to survive on the planet on our own, we will need to raid this place."

"What's in there?" said Chi.

"Rations, water purifiers, generators, medical kits; the things we need to keep us alive."

"We shouldn't need to leave the ship," said Chi.

"We'll have to go down to the planet eventually," said Brandon, "assuming we've arrived."

"Checking the ship comes first."

"Survival comes first."

"Okay, you two," said Grace. "Let's see if there are any of the Transit Team left."

Grace led the way, and they passed another corridor, heading off to the right.

"That leads down to one of the shuttle bays. We can go there once we're ready to leave."

The corridor they'd been following broadened out to reveal the monorail station they'd used sixty years ago to get to the cryohall. A dark tunnel stretched away to their left, heading towards the bow of the ship. One of the monorail cars sat with its doors open, the green and blue livery of the colony logo visible on its side. A faint breath of air blew in from the tunnel, heavy with a metallic smell.

They huddled into the car. Grace pressed a button on a panel next to the doors, which hissed, and then rolled shut.

The car lights flickered on and they made their way to the seats at the front. The carriage juddered as first one end and then the other lifted itself onto its rail, and then the whole thing vibrated.

"Why didn't they put this monorail through the centre of the ship?" said Dan. He looked at Grace, because she knew stuff like this.

"It's Zero-G through the core, they only have engines and fuel in there. They kept us near the hull where the artificial gravity would have the most effect."

The surrounding hum intensified, and the carriage jolted forward. It paused for a moment and then shunted forward again, and picked up speed as it headed towards the tunnel.

"So, if it's just us, we're the ones who have to deal with the bodies," said Brandon.

"We will have to eject them from the ship," said Chi, "push them out towards Zera so that the atmosphere takes them, burns them up."

Brandon swore and shook his head. "That's two hundred bodies, plus maybe the Transit Team; what's that, twenty more? And we have to load them up and shoot them out into space?"

"There is no other way to deal with them," said Chi.

Grace stayed silent. She knew Chi was right. No more than three bodies could be held in the ship's morgue. Colony protocol said that ejecting the bodies to burn up in the atmosphere was the only solution. She turned her face towards the window so that the others could not see the tears in her eyes.

The car passed into darkness, rocking them back and forth as it picked up speed. Grace turned back and looked at Dan, who was staring ahead into the tunnel, his eyes fixed. He had said nothing since they'd left the hall.

The car wobbled again as it passed back into light and space and carried on moving.

"Mid-ship station," said Grace. "Another minute and we'll be at the bow."

The car plunged on into darkness again, rattling them along before they emerged into another station and glided to a stop, settling on its rail. They were closer to the engines here and could feel their power through the floor.

The doors opened to warmer air.

"If there's warmth," said Josh, "then there's life."

"Unless what just happened in the cryohall also happened here," said Brandon.

They walked out of the station, Grace taking the lead, and made their way around the perimeter of the hull. They came to a junction, passageways leading left and right; Grace took the right turn. "Transit Team quarters, ahead and up one level."

"Look at that," said Dan, pointing along the corridor where a faint glow came up from the floor.

"It's one of the external viewing ports," said Grace. "This might tell us if we really have arrived."

Dan ran ahead and peered down through the port. A scattering of stars came into view as the ship spun on its axis.

"Where's the planet?" said Dan.

"Just wait a moment," said Grace.

They stood in silence for a few seconds, and then the edge of the viewing port brightened, and finally, a clear blue curve slid into view.

"Wow, is that it?"

"That's it," said Grace, staring through the port. "We really are here."

They could see textured cloud spun into a great whirl over a vast expanse of ocean.

"That's Zera. And it looks as if they're having quite a storm down there."

"Look," said Josh, "there's land; that's one of the main continents, isn't it?"

At the edge of the hurricane, they could see the pale green of a land mass, its coast tapering to a point near the equator, with a spray of tiny dots shooting from its northernmost tip.

"The Queloz Archipelago," said Grace. "The landing site is near the coastline."

"It's just like the pictures from the probes," said Dan, then he pointed. "What's that?"

To the left of the planet, Grace saw a thin sliver of light, a tiny part of one of Zera's moons.

"That's Alexandria, Zera's lighter coloured moon. I'm guessing Nyx, the dark moon, is behind the planet somewhere."

Brandon looked up and scanned the corridor again. "Okay, that's enough astronomy, we need to find these Transit guys."

Ahead of them was a stairwell spiralling up towards the centre of the ship.

Grace glanced up the steps. "They're on deck one, just above us."

They had slowed down, and as they approached the Transit level, the air grew warmer, and there were the smells of occupation: stale coffee, reheated food, human bodies.

"They're not dead then," said Brandon, "just a bit older."

"They weren't awake for all the journey," said Grace.

"They weren't? So, who was looking after the ship?"

"They took it in turns. There were twenty-four people, six teams of four, each team taking two five-year shifts."

"So, they only did ten years each? They'll have only aged ten years, and they spent the rest of the time in cryopods like us?"

"That was the plan," said Grace. "I think Owen Mortis, the Transit Team's head, and his group were going to do the last shift."

"Owen Mortis, you mean Callum Mortis's son?"

"That's him."

"So where did the rest of them sleep for the trip?" said Brandon. "They weren't all in the cryohall as well, were they?"

"No, they were all in there."

Grace pointed ahead. The corridor curving gently upwards, and on their right was a pair of double doors with TRANSIT TEAM CRYOROOM stencilled on them.

"So they had their own place," said Brandon.

"Yes, but let's not go in there now. Let's see who's up and around."

They walked on along the corridor, and without knowing why, started whispering rather than talking to each other.

Dan stopped. "Listen," he said.

Beneath the noise of the engines they could hear voices, a conversation.

They crept forward, the curve of the corridor gradually revealing a spill of light from a doorway about ten metres away. When they'd covered half the distance to the open door, they started to make out the words. An older man, with a thick Serbian accent, was speaking.

"And when I realised it had started, I woke Owen, and then the rest of you."

"So, it's done." Another voice, male, calm, assured. "We'd better get to work shifting these bodies."

"I know him," whispered Brandon, "that's Ray Merritt, Mortis's security guy. My father worked with him on the colony survival plan."

"They know about the bodies, and yet they haven't come to investigate, why is that?" said Chi, frowning.

"We should tell them we're here," said Brandon, straightening up.

"Wait," said Dan, taking hold of Brandon's sleeve, "can we just listen to what they have to say for a moment?"

IN THE TRANSIT TEAM MESS, Goran continued to pick at his moist, grubby fingers.

"So why did the revival process start early?" said Owen.

"Because," said Goran, glancing down at the chipped surface in front of him, "we miscalculated when we would arrive in orbit. After sixty years, we arrived four hours earlier than planned, that is all; it is not a problem." He shrugged. "The virus has done its job; it will have killed them all. It's just the process happened a little earlier than we expected."

Owen shook his head. This was a surprise, and he did not like surprises.

"You sure they're all dead?" said Patrick, still rocking the gun.

"The virus is lethal in all cases, they are dead."

"Well then," said Patrick, "it looks like we got ourselves a lot of dead bodies to deal with."

"Then we'd better start dealing with them," said Owen.

"Are we going to wake up your old man?" said Patrick, flicking at the safety catch on the pistol, "assuming he survived."

"I will deal with my father. We stick to the plan, and that means we deal with the bodies first. Two teams working in shifts. We use the gurneys to wheel them to the port-side evac tube. Amelia will launch them into the gravity well and Zera's atmosphere will do the rest."

Patrick nodded. "Job done."

"You'll be able to take two or three bodies at a time if you strap them together," said Owen, "and maybe four or five when you're transporting the children."

"That's still a lot of work," said Ray.

"I know, that's why we have a plan, and why this needs to be an efficient operation."

He turned to the only woman sitting at the table.

"Amelia, you and Patrick to go down to the cryohall and check the place over. Ray and Goran, you can prep the evac tube. We'll draw up a schedule to work through the colonists. I want us ejecting the bodies into Zera's gravity well in the next thirty minutes."

OUTSIDE IN THE CORRIDOR, they all stared at each other in stunned silence.

"They're talking like they expected us to die," said Dan.

Brandon frowned. "What did he mean, a virus? What are they talking about?"

"They were trying to murder us," said Chi. "They have killed the other colonists, and they will think we are dead too."

Brandon shook his head and swore.

"No, no, no, that's not right. That can't be right. Why? Why would they do that?

"Maybe they want the planet for themselves," said Chi.

"They wanted to kill us all," said Brandon. "I don't believe it."

"Why would they do that?" said Grace.

"They've murdered everyone," said Brandon, ignoring Grace's question. "That's why they wouldn't have come to help us, because they wanted us all dead, anyway."

He moved towards the door, but Josh put a hand on his shoulder. "Where are you going?"

"Where am I going? I am going to kill them. I will go in there and kill every one of those murdering scum."

They could all still hear Owen's voice over the grind of the air-con, going over the plan to throw the bodies into Zera's atmosphere.

"We all want vengeance," said Josh, keeping his hand on Brandon's shoulder, "but we shouldn't just charge in there."

"He's right," said Chi. "They may be armed."

Brandon stayed still, staring at the doorway. Josh kept his hand on Brandon's shoulder. "You need to think about who you are."

"What? What are you talking about, 'who I am'?"

"Aren't you our survival expert?" said Josh.

"Yes, what of it?"

"Then think like a survivor."

"He's right," said Grace. "Help us work out what to do next. Keep us alive, Brandon."

Brandon frowned, he glanced at Grace, then Josh.

They all stared at him. Grace was about to suggest that they move when he spoke again.

"Okay. Okay, we need to collect supplies and get down to the planet, that's our best chance of survival." He took a deep breath. "We need to retreat and then regroup. Let's get back to the monorail car."

"Good plan," said Grace. "Let's go."

They walked back down the corridor for a few metres before breaking into a jog, the voices behind them fading as they reached the stairwell. Then they made their way back to the monorail.

Once they were in, Grace smacked the request button for the aft station.

"I'm going to make them all pay," said Brandon, as they sat down.

"Sure," said Grace, "but first, keep us alive. Then you can deliver on that promise."

"And I'm going to go down to the planet. I haven't come all this way not to set foot on Zera, even if my family can't be there."

"We'll all go," said Grace, "we can't stay here with these murderers."

Then she remembered Brandon's pod, and the console warnings she saw before he woke. "Brandon, there's something I have to tell you."

"What?"

"A warning code came up on your pod when you revived, something about the immunity protocol being compromised."

"What does that mean?" said Brandon.

"It means that you didn't get some of the immunity treatments that the rest of us got," said Grace.

"So if I go down there, I could catch a Zeran cold or something?"

"Or worse," said Chi. "If you haven't had the proper immunity treatment. You'll go the way of H. G. Wells' Martians."

Brandon was silent for a moment. Around them, the car rattled as it picked up speed again.

"I don't care," he said. "I've said I'm going to the planet, and that's what I'm doing. I'm not staying here, I will walk on that planet if it kills me."

"Which it might well do," said Josh. "You understand that, don't you?"

"Of course I understand. What, do you think I am stupid?"

"No, I don't think you are stupid, but you are angry and that doesn't always make for good decisions. Think about what this means."

"Don't lecture me," said Brandon. "I know what I'm doing. They think we're dead, so we can use that to our advantage and get ourselves off this ship."

"I think we're being hasty," said Chi. "We need to consider our options. The ship might be the best place to hide, and anyway, how would we get down to the planet? Can any of you fly one of those shuttles?"

"Grace could fly," said Dan.

They all looked at him.

"Well, she could, couldn't you, Grace?"

"I..." Grace paused and stared at their faces in the half light of the tunnel. "If I needed to, if there was no other way."

"There may be no other way," said Josh. "If we stay here, they'll track us all down."

"I don't agree," said Chi. "You talk about survival, but we don't know what's down there. The threat might be much greater than the one we face here."

"I'd love to stay," said Brandon, "just so I can pick off those murderers one by one."

He made his right hand into a gun shape and mimed out the shots with the last three syllables. "But if you want me to help you survive, then you need to listen to what I'm saying. If we stay on the ship, we might take one or two of them down, but they'll get us all in the end. They'll pick us off and push us out of their evac tube into space. So we need to get off this ship."

Chi turned and faced Brandon. "That's fine for you," he said, "but you are not in charge of me, and I will do as I wish."

No one spoke and the car jolted, bumping from side to side as it continued to make its way down the length of the ship.

"No one will force anyone else to do something against our will," said Grace. "You do what you think is right."

"I understand your fear," said Chi, "and I'll help you get away, but I'm staying on the *Aspira*."

"You're crazy," said Brandon, "but whatever. It's even more stupid to stay when everyone else is going."

"That is my decision," said Chi.

Brandon grunted and then turned to the others. "So, here's what we need to do. You remember that storeroom we passed, the one with the red door? We need to go back there, grab some essential kit, and then," he paused, "we find out just how good a shuttle pilot Grace is."

He smiled at her and winked.

"Any of you should be able to fly a shuttle as well as me," said Grace. "I mean, we all worked on the simulations, didn't we?" She looked at each of them. "You did do the shuttle training, didn't you?"

None of them spoke as the car broke into the light of the midship station and then plunged again into the darkness of the tunnel.

"Oh, yeah, sure," said Brandon, waving a hand, "but flying the real thing? That's different."

"I did the training," said Josh.

"Okay then," said Grace, "you could do it."

"But I also saw the simulation assessment marks," said Josh, turning to her. "You were the best of all of us."

"I did okay," said Grace.

"You did okay? Came out on top of everyone. You're the best person to fly the shuttle."

"It's true," said Dan.

"It's your gig, Grace," said Brandon. "Either you get us down to the planet successfully or we crash and burn. No pressure, by the way."

"Thanks," said Grace.

"So you'll do it?" said Josh.

"Yes, I'll do it."

"If we go down to the planet, will they come after us?" said Dan.

"What do you think?" said Brandon.

"They will," said Dan.

"You just answered your own question, kid," said Brandon. "They will come. At least, I hope they do."

They were silent for a moment before Dan spoke again.

"Why?" he said, looking up at Grace. "Why did they do this?"

"I don't know," said Grace. "Maybe we'll find out if they come for us."

"I'd like to ask them that question myself," said Brandon, staring out into the darkness, "before I kill each one of them."

3

<hr>

"ONE KIT BAG EACH," said Brandon, "that's all we need."

"I assume it has to have the right things in it," said Josh.

"Of course it does, but don't worry, I know exactly what we need."

"Will you have time to get off the ship?" said Chi. "When these people find the empty pods, they're going to come after you."

"What's it to you? You don't even want to come with us."

"I want to help, but I don't want to get caught doing it."

"I know what we want, and I know where it is," said Brandon, "and we have time to get it."

"So, what do we need?" said Grace.

"Solar still, netting, binoculars, a decent knife, maybe two knives, water purifiers, a hook and line, lightweight containers and water bags." Brandon paused for a moment and looked around the room. "Yes, and a rechargeable firelighter, and a battery and some fine grade steel wool. It's always good to have the basic stuff, less chance of it going wrong."

"What if we get sick?" said Dan.

"We'll need the best medical kit we can find. I'm not just

talking about a box of plasters here; we'll need dressings, antibacterials, a transfusion kit, anti-allergy medicine and antivirals; all essential stuff for a trip to sunny Zera."

The car flooded with light as it whistled into the aft station.

"And all of that can fit into one bag?" said Josh as the car slowed to a stop.

"Sure, and they're not that heavy, we should be able to manage one each, apart from you." He looked at Dan. "We'll find something else for you to take."

"Okay then," said Grace, nodding to Brandon, "you lead the way."

They broke into a jog as they made their way back around the perimeter corridor to the storeroom. Lights flickered above them as they pushed the door open, and the air smelt of plastic. They were in a long, high-ceilinged room like a warehouse, with rows of metal racks to the left and right, and a single aisle stretching in front.

"That is a beautiful sight," said Brandon, staring at it all.

As they walked in, Dan paused and cocked his head to one side.

"Guys," said Dan.

"What is it?" said Josh.

"Listen."

In the silence they could all hear it: a whistling sound, faint but growing beneath the muffled roar of the engines and their own breathing.

"That's the monorail car," said Grace. "They must have called it back to the bow station."

"We had better get on with it then," said Brandon.

The broad central passageway ran off into the distance, with aisles leading off on either side. Brandon jogged forwards, pausing by a set of racks that held vacuum-packed jackets and rows of hardwearing boots, stacked by size.

"This stuff is beautiful," he said, "I wish we could take it all."

"What about these boots?" said Josh.

"We get those on the way out. Don't put them on now. Dan can carry them for us, that way, we each have two sets of shoes."

He moved on past the first set of aisles before taking a left turn at the second set. He ran down the aisle, stopped, retraced his steps, and turned right instead.

"Are you sure you know where these survival kits are?" said Grace as Brandon pushed past her.

"Are you sure you know how to fly a shuttle?"

"Point taken, Brandon." She followed him down the aisle to where he was looking at a stack of dark brown rucksacks. Chi, Josh, and Dan followed behind her.

"Now this is what I'm talking about," said Brandon, looking at the rack just above him. He clambered up, using the shelves as rungs until he was two metres off the ground. Then he pulled at one of the large rucksacks, tugging at it until it was clear, and dropped it onto the floor with a dull thump. Three more followed.

He jumped back down, opened one rucksack and rummaged through it.

"What are you looking for?" said Grace.

Brandon grunted and then pulled out a battery about the size of a burger box and a thick plastic packet full of silvery coloured wool.

"Each of you grab a jacket as well, and don't forget those boots."

They all put on a jacket and then Brandon, Grace, Chi, and Josh shouldered a rucksack each. On the way out, each of them picked out a pair and gave them to Dan, who clutched them in his arms.

"Okay," said Brandon, looking at Grace, "let's find ourselves a shuttle."

They walked out of the stores and back along the corridor; the rucksacks bobbing up and down, and Dan holding tight to the armful he was carrying. They took the right turn that led down to the shuttle bay entrance, where they found the main door of the shuttle bay locked.

"Any ideas?" said Josh, looking at Grace.

She put her rucksack on the floor and examined the lock.

"It uses a retinal scanner," she said, "probably registered to the shuttle pilots. I'll see if I can open it."

She stared at the scanner, pressing the entry button. A red light flicked on above the panel, and the door remained locked.

"Great," said Brandon, "so what are we going to do now?"

"Can we open it with a comm unit?" said Josh. "Override it somehow?"

"Maybe," said Grace.

"They're coming," said Dan.

Everyone stopped and looked at him.

"I can hear them coming, the people who are after us."

Out of the silence, the faint but distinct whine of the monorail car could be heard, arriving at the aft station. Then the car door opened.

"They'll be heading to the cryohall first," said Josh. "We need to wait until they've passed the top of the passageway."

They stood still, listening to the sound of brisk footsteps and voices. Patrick and Amelia were arguing about something as they walked along the perimeter corridor, past the turning for the shuttle bay entrance.

"...control yourself, that's all I'm saying," said Amelia.

"I'm telling you," said Patrick, "if any of them are still so much as twitching, I will kill them, no questions asked, okay?"

"That's what I have the inoculation gun for, don't go firing that gun in the cryohall. In fact, don't fire it anywhere on the ship unless you absolutely need to."

They couldn't make out Patrick's response and then the footsteps faded and their voices faded to echoes.

"Whatever you're going to do," said Brandon, "do it now."

Grace dug the comm unit out of her shoulder bag and searched through the menus. She shook her head.

"I know how the functions work on this thing, but I don't know if we can override the shuttle bay doors with it."

She flicked through the menus while Brandon paced up and down. "They're going to end up walking down here and finding us at this rate."

"If you've got any better ideas Brandon, I'd love to hear them."

"May I have a look please?" said Chi.

"Sure, if you think you can do something with it."

She passed the device to him.

"You are Grace Ellen McAllan, yes?"

"Yes," said Grace.

Chi called up a colony list and spun through the names, then he made a few more quick taps on the screen and handed it back to her.

"Try the retinal scanner now."

"But it didn't work before."

"Just try it, please."

She stared into the scanner, and immediately the light above the panel turned green. The door opened with a loud clunk.

"Game on," said Brandon.

"How did you do that?" said Grace.

"It was easy," said Chi.

"Really? Tell me."

"Guys, can we discuss this later?" said Brandon. "We're kind of up against it here."

It took Brandon, Josh and Grace all their strength to push the door open, the hinges grinding as a space opened up for them to go through.

"That was a beast," said Brandon.

"It's designed to hold if there's a breach on the other side," said Grace, "come on, shuttle number four should be in here."

The bay itself was dark, and the air bitterly cold. A light frost glittered on the floor. Ceiling lights winked on as they entered, illuminating the grey bulk of a shuttle, a number '4' emblazoned in red on its side.

They carried the rucksacks through, and Chi laid his on the floor.

"You can take this now, I need to go."

"You sure you don't want to come with us?" said Josh.

"Yes, I'm sure, but I wish you all good fortune, and I hope we meet again."

"I'm sorry to see you go, good luck," said Grace. They all paused, Dan shivering whilst he clutched all the boots.

"You want to take your pair?" said Josh.

"Please," said Chi. He slipped off his soft-soled shoes and put on the boots. "And there's one last thing I can do for you. Once I'm on the other side of the bay door, I will try to lock it. That will keep the Transit Team out of here while you all figure out how to get this shuttle working, and the bay open."

"And what are you going to do?" said Josh.

"I will hide, and hope they think we've all left. Then I will deal with them, just like Brandon intended to."

"You know sometimes I almost like you, Chi," said Brandon. "a bit of me wishes I could stick around to watch the show."

"Well, if I miss any of them, and they come down to the planet..."

"Don't worry, I'll finish the job for you."

Chi nodded, then slipped through the heavy door, and into the corridor that led back to the ship.

"I'll try to get the shuttle started," said Grace. "You guys get this door shut."

She hitched up her rucksack again and looked at Dan. "Come with me, bro."

Grace and Dan walked across the bay floor towards the shuttle, the icy surface crackling beneath their feet.

"There's a bulkhead door at the back of the shuttle," said Grace. "We go in that way."

Dan stared through a porthole. He could just make out shelving on one side beyond the entrance; they pushed against the door, which was unlocked and opened easily.

Inside the shuttle, there was a small lobby with storage racks and webbing on each side. Most of the racks were empty, whilst some held booster cushions for the younger colonists, who would be too small for the standard shuttle seats. A bulky looking yellow bag sat on the top shelf of the racks.

Grace let the rucksack slide to the floor.

"If you get this bag and the boots stowed away, I'll see if I can get this thing started."

Ahead of her she could see two blocks of green and blue seats, with an aisle down the centre of the shuttle. At the front of the craft was a pilot's chair.

She jogged down the aisle and looked at the controls. When she flicked on the ignition switch, the pilot's console lit up with an array of dashboard readings in orange and turquoise.

Then a message in large red letters appeared at the centre of the screen.

Pilot authorisation required.

"Okay," she said, "let's see if I can persuade you that I am the pilot."

She hovered over the console, trying several codes. Nothing worked. She dug out her comm, and for a moment she thought about asking her father what she should do next. The thought paralysed her, and immediately a new word entered her head.

Orphan.

Orphan.

It hadn't occurred to her until that moment, but she was an orphan, and so was Dan; they all were.

"Not now, please." She pushed the thought away, suppressing the emotions that were welling up within her.

She checked the override menus on the comm unit. There was one for the shuttle, but it only activated in an emergency. She ran the emergency routine from the comm, and on the shuttle console, the message changed:

Override requested.

A calm female voice filled the air.

Override request denied. No emergencies at this time.

"This is an emergency!" she thumped the control panel.

OUTSIDE IN THE BAY, Brandon and Josh had dropped their rucksacks next to Chi's, and had their shoulders against the bay door. They nearly had it shut, with Chi on the other side, when they heard him shout.

"Wait!"

"What?" said Brandon.

"Please open the door now."

They pulled at the door and Chi squeezed back through into the bay.

"What's happening?" said Josh.

"They are here," said Chi.

He stepped back into the bay and a couple of seconds later, two figures appeared in the doorway.

"Uh-oh," said Brandon. "Show time."

The woman was slim, almost skinny, with jet black hair tied back in a ponytail. She had dark brown eyes and a lean, hungry look on her face.

The man next to her was broader, and heavy. He had a shock of curly ginger hair and a face covered with stubble. He wore a Transit Team uniform, spattered with black oil stains.

"My name is Amelia," said the woman, "and I'm so glad we've found you." She smiled and laid a hand on Patrick's arm, restraining him. "I know you three have had a terrible time, but you'll be safe now."

Chi, Brandon, and Josh looked at each other.

"How did you find us?" said Chi.

"These bay doors make a lot of noise when you open them," said Amelia. "the sound echoes right through these corridors. We wondered whether some of you had survived. We're here now to help you."

"You need to come with us," said Patrick.

Amelia kept her hand on Patrick's arm.

"This is my friend Patrick. We are both here to help you."

"Hi kids, nice to meet you." Patrick grinned at them.

"I expect you saw what happened to the other colonists, to your families," said Amelia. "I know this has been a terrible shock. It has been for all of us, but you're safe now."

She focused on Brandon.

"Now, young man, why don't you come with us?"

Brandon looked up at Amelia and then glanced at Josh who was gazing intently down towards Amelia's right hand where she held a tiny inoculation gun, partially concealed by her sleeve.

"Well, thanks for the offer," said Brandon, "but we'll be looking after ourselves from now on."

"That won't be necessary," said Amelia.

"Actually, it will. We're just going to hop on this shuttle and go down to the planet on our own, thanks."

Amelia stared at him for a moment. "I don't think that would be a good idea." She sounded genuinely disappointed, as if he'd somehow let her down. Patrick moved his hand just inside his jacket.

"And how do you propose to fly down there?" said Amelia, "are any of you qualified shuttle pilots?"

They were all silent.

"I thought not. Now, you've had a terrible shock, and it has clouded your judgement. That's understandable. You need to come with us and we will look after you."

You'll look after us all right, thought Brandon, *just like you did all the other colonists.*

He clenched his right hand into a fist and reminded himself that he had made a promise to seek vengeance. Maybe the shuttle bay was the place to start.

4
———

INSIDE THE SHUTTLE, Dan finished strapping the webbing around the rucksack and the boots.

He was looking to see what else was on the racks when he heard voices he didn't recognise out in the bay. He crept over to the door of the shuttle, which was standing ajar, and peered out.

"This is bad," he said, stepping back, "very bad."

He heard footsteps behind him and turned to see Grace walking back down the aisle. "What's going on? I thought..."

She stopped mid-sentence when she saw Dan put a finger to his lips and wave frantically at her. "Those Transit Team people are outside, they've seen the others."

"Oh no, no, no," whispered Grace. She tiptoed over to the door and leaned out. She recognised Amelia and Patrick from her introductions to them sixty years before. They were saying something to Brandon.

"We need an emergency," she said, "now."

Dan glanced from his sister to the equipment racks, then he walked over to the survival rucksack and slowly unclipped the top flap.

"What are you doing?" said Grace.

"You wanted an emergency." He pulled out the firelighter and then reached down to the bottom of the storage racks and took one of the smaller shuttle seat cushions.

"You aren't going to start a fire in here, are you?" said Grace.

"More like out there. Hopefully, something in this bay will detect the smoke."

She reached out to take the firelighter.

"I can do it," said Dan. "Just get the shuttle started."

She stared at him for a moment.

"Go on, Grace." He flipped on the firelighter and pointed the flame at the cushion, touching it to the edge of the material, "get this shuttle started."

Grace stared at the smoke and then at Dan, and then she willed herself to run back to the pilot's console.

AMELIA FROWNED at the boys standing in front of her.

"So you want to fly this shuttle down to the planet," she said. " Why do you want to do something as foolish and dangerous as that? You won't be able to start it, and even if you did, you won't be able to get it out of this bay."

She took a step forward, and Patrick stepped up with her.

Josh and Brandon instinctively took one pace back. But Chi stepped forward, he was now right in front of Amelia.

"And who are you?" she asked.

"My name is Wong Chi-Ping."

"Well, Wong," said Patrick, "why don't you and your friends behave yourselves and come with us now?"

"I think the correct form of address would be Chi-Ping, or perhaps just Chi," said Amelia. "Wong is your family name–that is correct, isn't it?"

"That is correct," said Chi.

"Well, Chi," said Amelia, "Please come with us and we'll look after you. That's what we are here for."

"Sorry," said Josh, speaking for the first time, "but we are leaving."

Even as he spoke, he shuffled back, edging nearer to the shuttle.

Amelia glanced at him. "I am NOT talking to you."

She turned back to Chi.

"Thank you for addressing me correctly," he said. "But as my friend says, we are leaving."

"You'll do what you're bloody told," said Patrick.

"Now, now, Patrick," said Amelia, turning her head toward him. "Remember, these boys have had a nasty shock."

She turned back to face the three of them. "We don't want to upset you, but the time for games is over, and I will not ask nicely again."

"You can't just kill us," said Chi calmly.

"We've no wish to kill you, but we will take whatever action we consider necessary to protect you. I'm sure you realise we have an emergency here. This is for your own good. Patrick, could you give our young friends some encouragement, please?"

"With pleasure," said Patrick. He removed the gun from his jacket and grinned. "You *boys*," he emphasised the word, and looked at Josh as he did so, "should just come along with us now."

He was about to speak again, but then he sniffed the air and frowned.

"Can you smell that?" He turned to Amelia. "Something's burning."

He looked across the bay to where a thin wisp of smoke was rising from the stern of the shuttle. "What the hell? One of them is in the shuttle."

Amelia turned to the shuttle door. "You in there, out now."

In the shuttle lobby, Dan pulled the door open just a little further, then tossed the heavily smoking cushion out into the bay.

It skittered over the icy floor and landed just behind Josh. Smoke rose in curling wisps towards the ceiling.

Amelia cursed under her breath. "Patrick, put that thing out and drag whoever is in the shuttle over here."

Before Patrick could move, a piercing wail ripped through the bay.

In that moment, Josh turned, scooped up the smoking cushion and threw it into Patrick's face. Patrick jumped back, and the gun fired, the bullet smacking into the bay wall behind them.

Then it started to rain.

Grey metallic water cascaded down onto them all, covering the floor with a sheen of icy slush.

The water provoked Amelia into action. She stepped towards Chi and brought her right arm down.

He had been watching her, and even as the needle of the inoculation gun fell towards him, he twisted his body away from the blow. The needle passed just in front of him, and as Amelia tipped forward with the momentum of the attack, he pivoted on his left foot and kicked out with his right, connecting with her wrist. Amelia screamed, and the inoculation gun skittered across the floor.

Patrick let out a stream of curses and levelled his gun at Josh's head.

***

GRACE COULD SEE the water streaming down onto the cockpit window in front of the pilot's console.

"Surely now," she said, keying in the override request again.

The calm voice spoke over the thrash of the water.

Override request denied. There are no emergencies at this time.

"You have got to be kidding me," she pounded a fist on the console.

Override request denied. There are no emergencies at this time.

She slumped forward, leaning her head on her hands.

In the shuttle bay, the deluge stopped as suddenly as it started. Patrick blinked back the water and stared at Josh.

"Enough games," he said, "I'm going to take you down, all of you, and you first, you arrogant little..." He squeezed the trigger just as Brandon slammed into him. The gun jerked out of Patrick's hand and bounced across the floor of the bay.

Josh felt a hot sting across the top of his left shoulder as the bullet tore into his jacket and through flesh beneath, before burying itself in the outer bay door behind him. The echo of the gunshot faded and Josh heard a light hiss of air. Hazard lights flashed all over the bay.

A calm but insistent voice filled the whole space.

Shuttle bay breach.

Repeat: shuttle bay breach, emergency lockdown procedure activated. Main bay access door will close in three minutes to preserve ship integrity.

Please evacuate the bay. Repeat: please evacuate the bay now.

Grace straightened up and stared at the console; the shuttle ignition sequence appeared before her as a series of green and blue glyphs on the screen. She turned around towards the back of the shuttle. "Dan, we're leaving."

She stared at the screen options, trying to remember the lessons of six decades ago. Almost without thought, her fingers skittered across the screen, and the little craft shivered and hummed as the engines came to life.

At the rear of the shuttle, Dan leaned out of the door and shouted as loud as he could. "Guys, we're going!"

Amelia was clutching her own wrist as Brandon got to his feet. He saw Josh reaching out his right hand to him, his left shoulder covered in blood.

"What happened to your shoulder?" said Brandon.

"Bullet clipped it, I think," said Josh. "But I'd be dead if you hadn't taken Patrick out."

"Brandon, Josh! Come on," said Chi, over the sound of the shuttle powering up. He ran for the door and Brandon and Josh scrambled after him.

Behind them, Patrick was searching for the gun. Amelia put her good hand on his shoulder. "Leave it. We need to get out of here before the main bay doors open and suck us out into space."

"No," said Patrick, "I want them dead." He glanced around himself, saw the gun and scooped it up from the floor just as Chi, Brandon, and Josh clambered into the back of the shuttle.

The smooth voice echoed across the bay again.

Warning. Main ship access bulkhead will close in two minutes to preserve ship integrity.

As soon as Brandon was through the door, he turned around and started to push it shut. He turned to the others.

"Help me out here, guys."

Patrick glared at the shuttle door, skidded across the bay floor, and slammed his shoulder against the bulkhead.

"You," he said, "aren't going anywhere."

Chi and Dan joined Brandon, pushing from the other side, Josh joined them, leaning his uninjured shoulder against the bulkhead door.

"Come on," grunted Brandon, "push!"

The door gradually closed, Patrick's boots slipping on the wet surface. With just an inch of the doorway left, Brandon twisted his head to look out of the porthole, straight at Patrick's face.

"You're not getting us, murderer."

The shuttle door slammed shut and Josh spun the wheel handle, sliding the bolts into place.

Brandon stared out of the porthole, directly into Patrick's bruised, wet face.

"You come after us and I will kill you!" he screamed at the thick glass. "I will take you down."

Patrick pointed the gun at the window. He leered at Brandon, only stopping when Amelia pulled at him with her left hand and shouted something.

GRACE SCANNED the controls and tried to ignore whatever was going on behind her.

"Ignition sequence, engines and navigation online, okay." Flight control readings blossomed across the console screen. Her fingers tapped through the launch sequence as she sent a command to open the external bay doors.

Outside, the calm intercom voice announced that in just ninety seconds, the access doors to the rest of the ship would close and the external bay doors would open, exposing the bay to vacuum.

BRANDON WATCHED as Amelia pulled Patrick away from the shuttle porthole and towards the exit. He grinned Patrick and Amelia scurried back to the door, and then laughed as he saw Patrick trying to squeeze back into the corridor that led to the rest of the ship.

Next to him, Josh watched them disappear out of the bay.

"That's right," said Josh under his breath, "you run away, *boy*."

"Just a shame about those rucksacks," said Brandon.

Sitting on the bay floor, slumped against each other, were three rucksacks. They'd only been able to salvage the one that Grace had carried onto the shuttle.

"Well, we're going to have to survive with what we've got," said Brandon, then he turned and looked at Josh's shoulder. "Okay, that does not look good."

The jacket at the top of Josh's left shoulder was in tatters, and blood had seeped down into the material.

"Better he got me there than where he was aiming," said Josh, pointing at his forehead.

"True," said Brandon, "but we should deal with that wound."

Josh slumped into a seat.

"You're bleeding," said Dan.

"Ah, he won't die," said Brandon, "and it will leave a scar he can show off to the girls."

"I'll be okay," said Josh, still breathless. "Let's just get out of here."

Brandon raised an eyebrow at him, and Chi glanced over.

"We should treat that wound before we leave," said Chi.

"Don't worry, Mr Planet-lover," said Brandon, "we'll soon have you fixed. Now get that jacket off."

Josh eased his jacket off and sat back in the seat again.

Dan gawped at the blood and tatters of the jacket.

"Dan," said Chi, "get the medical kit. Now, please."

"Sure." Dan pulled the medical kit out of the large rucksack. He handed it to Brandon, who flicked open the box and rummaged through the contents, scattering some of it onto the floor: antibiotics, scissors, and surgical blades.

"We'll need disinfectant and then the skin sealant," said Brandon, holding the canister.

"This is going to sting like all hell," he said, smiling at Josh, "but you'll thank me for it later."

"I'm sure I'll be forever grateful," said Josh.

Brandon sprayed disinfectant on the wound while Josh clenched the arm of the seat with his other hand, then Chi sprayed on some skin sealant and Brandon applied the dressing.

"There you go, as good as new."

He sat down next to Josh, clipped the seat straps over himself, and then passed Josh the flask of water he'd brought from the cryohall.

"Thanks."

"Just don't drink it all," said Brandon. "If we'd had more time in the stores, maybe we could have brought one of those 3D printers and I'd have made you some proper skin. As it is, you'll just have to heal up the way nature intended." He sat down on the seat next to Josh.

"What a mess this turned out to be," said Brandon.

Josh turned to him.

"What?" he said.

"It's a mess."

"No, it's not," said Josh. "You succeeded." He handed the flask back to Brandon.

"You call this a success?"

"Of course, we're alive, all of us; we've escaped, haven't we?"

Brandon shrugged and nodded as the shuttle jolted forward. "Yeah, for now."

"Hey!" shouted Grace from the front of the shuttle, "if you're not strapped in, do it now."

"I mean it," said Josh. "You're the survival guy, and we survived." He looked over at Chi.

"And it looks like you'll be coming with us."

"So it seems," said Chi. "I will adapt to the situation."

"Yeah," said Brandon, "I guess you'll have to."

AT THE FRONT of the shuttle, Grace watched as the bay doors silently opened. Now they would find out if she really could fly this thing. Outside, the air disappeared into the vacuum, and the water on the bay floor whisked out into the void, freezing as it scattered into space.

Grace closed her eyes for a moment, breathed in the smoky air, and tried to remember the simulations she'd worked on. Slowly, slowly, she fingered the touch screen, cycling through the launch sequence. "Okay, this is it."

She slid one finger across the console. The engine roared, and the shuttle lurched forward; she heard Brandon whooping behind her. She pulled her finger back and then eased it up again. The shuttle skittered forward across the bay and toward the expanse before them. As they drew closer to the lip of the bay, the corner of the planet came into view. Grace traced a finger back again, and the shuttle stopped, balanced on the edge.

She took a deep breath.

"And we have lift-off," she said and tapped the screen once. The engine fired again, and the shuttle tipped over, slipping into space, and accelerating so that all of them slammed hard into their seats.

An ocean of sound and vibration surrounded them, and every bone in Grace's body shook as the shuttle sped up, pushed by its engines and pulled in by Zera's gravity. It pitched forward as if they were on some vast fairground ride. Ahead of her, the viewer threw up the tremendous panorama of the planet, a bowed horizon of blue and green. Grace heard Brandon swear and then burst out laughing.

And that was the point when Grace remembered they were sitting at the top of a gravity well that could suck them in and smear them across the surface of the planet like a squashed bug. She remembered that there were four other people on board this ship, and even if she only loved one of them, she had a responsibility to everyone.

She scanned the array of red and orange glyphs on the console in front of her, the readings for velocity and altitude, and then she slid her fingers across the screen. The shuttle slowed, pulling her forward in her seat. The pitch realigned under her direction, and she brought the little craft under control. Then it rolled, turning towards the planet, and they all leaned hard against the left side of their seats.

"Hey, Grace," Brandon called from behind her, "did you really do that shuttle pilot course?"

"Do you want to try flying this thing?"

There was no answer.

"Well? Do you?"

"No, thanks."

She smiled to herself. *I thought not.*

She brought up the shuttle's planetary map and saw that the colony landing zone, or LZ as the pilots would have called it, had already been programmed in. But that would be the first place the Transit Team would come looking for them. She scanned the terrain for somewhere else to come down and keyed in coordinates for a spot twenty kilometres north of the original site.

"Hey, Grace," called Brandon, above the noise of the shuttle engines.

"What now?" *Why is it always Brandon?* she thought.

"Can you get the heating working? Some of us are freezing our nuts off."

"You want me to do inflight service as well?" she whispered under her breath as she searched on the control screen for the environment controls. Eventually, she found the cabin temperature system and turned it up to the max. She felt a twinge of sympathy when she remembered that, unlike Dan and her, they had got a soaking from the sprinklers. She turned her head towards her passengers.

"Next stop, planet Zera!"

BRANDON, Josh, and Dan cheered, and she turned back, took in a deep breath, and then slowly let it go. The air in the shuttle warmed up, and for the first time in a while, she relaxed, and took a couple of deep breaths.

"Grace." The voice made her jump and, turning around, she saw Josh clinging to her seat. Brandon had taped a white dressing to his shoulder, but the cloth of his shirt hung in bloody tatters around it.

"What are you doing up here? Get back there and get strapped in!"

He smiled at her.

"What?" she said.

"I just wanted to say thank you. None of us could have worked out how to fly this thing."

"That's because apart from you, none of the rest of them actually did the pilot training," said Grace.

"Well, there is that, but you were the best of us."

"You're welcome, but we've still got to land yet."

"You'll get us down safely, I know you will."

"Thank me when we're on the ground and not dead."

"I will," said Brandon, and went back to his seat.

A few minutes later, the shuttle rolled as it came into orbit. Tubes of anti-bacterial cream rolled around at her feet.

She leaned over her shoulder to look at her passengers. Dan, Brandon, and Josh were strapped into their seats, eyes half-closed.

Josh opened his eyes, smiled, and gave her a thumbs up.

"Idiot," she whispered to herself, "coming up here just to say thank you."

As she focused on the pilot console and a wave of weariness came over her; the coloured symbols on the screen blurred together, and for a moment she didn't know what she was looking at. Josh's kindness had opened up something she didn't want exposed right now.

"Come on, Grace, get a grip." She reached up to her right shoulder and massaged her aching muscles. As she did so, she felt something in the lining of her jacket; it was the envelope her father had left her.

She pulled it out and looked at his handwriting, staring at her name for a few seconds, and then slowly put it back in her pocket. Grief welled up inside her. This was the first moment she'd had her own space since she'd emerged from the pod. Josh's words had softened her up, and now her mind filled with images of her parents. She buried her face in her hands and rocked back and forth, helpless as the sorrow cut her open, again and again, leaving her raw.

5

———

THE AIR in the Transit Team mess room was heavy with the smell of cold coffee. Owen Mortis's team had gathered around the table, which was strewn with the usual complement of recyclable cups, plates, and food wrappers.

Owen turned to his left, where Goran Maric slumped over the table; the doctor's head was in his hands and tremendous patches of sweat darkened the shirt under his armpits.

"I'll ask again. How did five children survive your killer virus and then get off this ship?"

"It isn't the virus that is a killer," said Goran, "we despatched them with RNA silencing. We use a virus to host a tiny piece of RNA, customised for each colonist. The RNA can..."

"Spare us the lecture, doc," said Patrick. "You heard the man, how come it all went south?"

"I have some theories." said Goran, fiddling with the small bowtie pulled tight against his neck.

"You have some theories," said Owen, "so you don't actually know why this happened?"

"With time, we will discover the cause. The evidence will show which of my ideas is correct."

Patrick smirked. "What happened, Doc, is that you blew it. This fancy genetic killer of yours should have bypassed all the pod monitors and knocked out every colonist with none of us going near them. 'None of the team gets implicated', those were your words. Well, we're all implicated now, aren't we? And we've got these kids running around on Zera."

"Actually," said Goran, sitting up, "there are five colonists running around on Zera because you let them escape, firing your gun in the shuttle bay of all places. You even damaged the ship hull. Only you could be so stupid, Patrick."

"Remember why I was down there?" said Patrick, leaning across the table. "Trying to clear up after your incompetence."

"You call this clearing up? If anyone is incompetent..."

"Enough!" Owen cut through the raised voices. "You squabble like children in a playground. My God, you even live like them!" He swept a hand across the table, scattering dirty plates and cups onto the hard rubber floor.

"We have travelled for sixty years. Sixty years so that we can be the first humans to set foot on a new planet, and now a bunch of *kids* have taken the prize from us."

They were all silent.

"I will continue with my investigations," said Goran eventually. "I am sorry that this has happened." He stared down at the pockmarked surface of the mess table.

Owen leaned back in his chair and stared at the ceiling. "This was supposed to be a fresh start. Ridding ourselves of the political appointees that Earth's governments stuffed into those pods. Then it would be just us and the allies we got onto the Transit team. Our friends who are still fast asleep in their separate pods. Together, we were going to be a new community for a new world. Do you all remember how much we talked about that?"

He looked around the room, but no one spoke.

"Clear out the old, that's what we were going to do. Be rid of those who didn't belong here, those who should never have come to Zera. Just a handpicked group with an entire world to explore. But we needed the rest of the colonists dead, with no evidence that we'd killed them."

"And there will be no evidence," said Goran. "The RNA silencer is still a wonderful creation; invisible, untraceable. None of us was near the cryohall when the incident occurred–it will leave behind nothing to provoke awkward questions."

"Well, those kids might beg to differ," said Ray, speaking for the first time. "They are the issue we need to address now, not theories about why they might have survived."

"Maybe we should have gone down to those colonists soon after we left Earth and done the job properly. That would have been a lot easier than all this fiddling around with this R & B of yours."

"RNA! It's called RNA, and you know well enough why we had to wait until we got here to deal with the colonists."

Patrick looked at him, unconvinced.

"Goran's right," said Owen. "The ship needs four members of the Transit Team awake at any one time, all the time, for the entire journey. If we'd killed all the colonists straight away, we'd have had to kill the rest of the Transit Team to cover that up, and if we'd done that we'd have had to stay awake for the entire journey to run the ship. I didn't want to come to Zera only to arrive as an old man."

"Anyway, it's done," said Amelia, joining the conversation. "Ray is right, we need to focus on the subjects that survived, get down to the planet and terminate them as quickly as possible."

"There is one question," said Ray. "Should we wake Mr Mortis, and tell him what's happened, before we try to deal with this?"

"Perhaps it would be better to wait until we've solved the problem," said Amelia. "I'd rather tell him we've dealt with an issue than ask him to solve it for us."

"It's tempting to solve this ourselves," said Owen, shaking his head, "but no. If he finds out we've been down to the planet without him, he will never forgive us, and we will never hear the last of it. So we will wake him before we take this any further."

Goran spoke, but Owen cut him off.

"You've had your say for now, Goran." He turned to his right. "Amelia, what do you think?"

Amelia leaned forward on the mess table, steepling her fingers and looking at all of them. The air-con, which had been humming throughout their conversation, stuttered and fell silent.

"There are three hypotheses," said Amelia. "First, the toxin didn't work for these five, it just didn't function as it should."

"Impossible," said Goran.

"Unlikely," said Amelia, glancing at him, "but not impossible. The second hypothesis is that the toxin would have worked, but somehow the genetic code records for these colonists didn't map to the RNA."

"I checked each code myself," said Goran. "I cross-referenced each sample with the medical records, and customised each virus with the genetic match of its recipient so it would be undetected by the pod system, invisible within the body after death. The match was perfect."

"I'm sure the match to the records was perfect," said Amelia, "but if we started with the wrong records, then the toxin would fail. But we also have a third option, which I think is the most likely reason for what has happened."

"And that is?" said Owen.

"That the intravenous tech in the pod failed, and so didn't deliver the toxin."

"That's possible," said Ray. "One pod malfunction amongst hundreds after sixty years, I can believe that."

"One yes," said Owen, "but five? Five pod systems failing?"

"The pods did not fail," said Goran. "They have been working with no faults, it should have been a smooth and easy process."

"Death is never easy," said Ray, "not even one death, and

certainly not on this scale. It was always going to be messy, and we haven't started clearing out the bodies yet."

"Something could have gone wrong with the pods," said Amelia. "The thawing process is the most complex protocol we have."

"So, if anything was going to go wrong," said Owen, "it would be just as the colonists were coming back to consciousness. And because they all woke early, it caught us off guard."

"That's the most likely explanation," said Amelia.

"But the pods were all checked," said Owen. "That is the case, isn't it?"

He looked over at Goran. No one spoke.

"You ran the diagnostic routine on each one of them, didn't you?" asked Owen.

"Yes," said Goran, "over the two-year cycle."

"No," said Owen. "We agreed to check all the pods within a thirty-day window prior to arrival. Isn't that what we said?"

"How could I do all of that and pursue my work with the embryos?" said Goran, waving his fleshy arms in the air. "They were my priorities. The embryos are our future on Zera."

"Let me be clear on this," said Owen. "Are you saying you didn't check all the cryopods in the last thirty days?"

The room was silent.

"Maybe ninety percent," said Goran. "It was an impossible regime in the time I had given my other duties. I would never have been able to get everything done."

"But you knew that when we arrived in orbit, our focus needed to be processing the subjects."

"The embryos need my constant attention," said Goran.

Owen slammed the table with his hand.

"The embryos weren't about to go through a complex thawing process, but the colonists were. The embryos weren't going to sneak off this ship, but now we know some *children* have done just that. Didn't you understand how critical this phase was?"

"The old man will go nuts about this," said Patrick, grinning; "who's going to tell him what's happened?"

"I will brief my father when he has woken up," said Owen, "I presume the rest of the Transit Team are dead, apart from our colleagues who will become surrogate parents, or have we killed them by accident?"

"They are fine, fine!" said Goran. "We can wake them when we're ready to bring the embryos to full term in the *Aspira*'s artificial womb."

"Well, raising colony babies will have to wait until we've cleared up this mess," said Owen. He took a deep breath. "Okay, we all have work to do. I want the bodies all expelled within the next twenty-four hours, and I want to be on Zera in thirty-six hours' time."

"We'd better get to it," said Patrick.

"Yes, you had. Goran, Ray, Patrick, you can collect the bodies, and get them to the forward evac tube, I'll join you in a few minutes. Amelia, please calibrate the tube for optimum delivery into Zera's gravity well. The last thing we want is for any of our dead colonists to float off into orbit."

Everyone got up from their chairs.

"We're off this ship in no more than thirty-six hours," said Owen, "so let's go."

They all shuffled towards the door, Amelia standing to follow the others out.

"Wait, Amelia," said Owen.

She paused as the others left.

"Close the door, please."

Amelia pushed the mess door shut.

"I'd better not be long," she said, "or Patrick will complain that I'm not pulling my weight again."

"Patrick can shut up and do what he's told," said Owen. "So, after those kids escaped, did you go back down to the cryohall and have a look around?"

"I did. Five pods are empty. Four of the escapees are in their teens, and there's a younger one. I haven't cross-referenced the pods with the colony records yet, but I will."

"And my father?"

"The only living soul left down there."

"These children, how do you rate their chances of survival?"

"If they put the shuttle on autopilot and tell it to land, then it will do the hard work for them. So they're likely to get down to the surface in one piece. But surviving on the planet is a whole different story. You know what's down there, and that's only what we're aware of. When they've landed and search for food and water, they're likely to fall foul of something indigenous, although if they survive, they might scatter."

"Let them," said Owen, tapping his fingers on the surface of the table. "They won't get that far. We will find them, or what's left of them."

"How are you going to break it to the old man?" said Amelia.

"In the simplest way possible," said Owen. "There's no point in dressing it up."

"That will be an interesting conversation."

"My father and I are due to have a chat, anyway. He can rant as much as he likes when he finds out, but he and I have other scores to settle."

"So you will challenge him before we set down on Zera?"

"Yes. What's happened with these kids doesn't change any of that."

Amelia looked at him.

"What?" he said.

"How many more chances does your father deserve?"

"Just this one."

She sat down next to him.

"Owen, we are on the brink of having everything we wanted. We've made it here. We made it. We've dealt with the colonist problem, or we will have soon. This is our time."

"I know."

"Then don't give the old man any more chances to ruin it. He's no better than the colonists; worse after what he did to you, and to your mother."

"Don't mention her," said Owen, "please."

"It has to be said, Owen, because it's the truth. Every opportunity he got, he just put himself first, over your mother and over you."

"He deserves one more chance."

"No, he doesn't. He won't change. If you offer him your love, a son's love, he will think you are weak, and he will treat you with contempt."

Owen was silent.

"Kill him," said Amelia," like Goran did to the others, and let us be free of him at last."

Owen looked at her and he knew she was right, but didn't think he couldn't do it. This was not another faceless, anonymous colonist, this was his father.

He looked around the messroom, and for the first time, he noticed that one of the ceiling lights was flickering. The air-con shuddered and started up again.

"About the escaped children," he said. "Just how might Zera kill them?"

Amelia looked at him.

"Well, if they survive the landing, predators might eat them, or something might poison them. There will be bacteria, and viruses, of course. They'll be especially vulnerable if the pods didn't deliver all the immunity protocols. There are plenty of ways to die on Zera."

"I bet there are," said Owen, smiling. "I'll remember to tell the old man that when I wake him. It should appeal to his sense of humour."

"Do you want me to come with you when you do it?"

"No, I don't want him to think you're involved. This is between him and me."

"Very well. I'd better get on with it.

Her chair squeaked as she stood, and she bent over him.

"You know, Owen, this problem with the colony kids and your father. None of that matters compared to what we can do, what we can be on our new world. This is our prize, Owen, ours."

"I know, I want it too, all of it for us."

"Then just make sure your misplaced love for the old man doesn't ruin everything." She kissed him on the lips, turned and walked out of the room.

Owen waited for her to go, and then thought about his father. The old man's life was in his hands. He could kill him now or give him that one more chance.

He weighed the options and made his decision. Then he got up and went to join the others to help with clearing out the bodies.

THEY TOOK JUST under twenty-four hours to expel the dead. Strapping them, two or three at a time, to the gurneys, trying to ignore the smell that was now doing battle with the *Aspira*'s recycling systems.

Patrick and Owen, Goran and Ray; two teams of two, wheeling the corpses to the *Aspira*'s evacuation tube, with Amelia pumping the bodies out into the void and down towards a burning end in Zera's atmosphere. They worked two eight-hour shifts with a six-hour rest between them until all except one pod was clear.

When they finished, they powered down the heat and the light in the cryohall to save energy, ate a little more of their pasty rations, showered to rid themselves of the taint of the bodies, and then went to their quarters to sleep.

"A MOTHER'S SON."

Callum Mortis's Estate
Summer 2025

Callum Mortis closed his hand around the soft tangerine and yanked it from the bowl.

He ripped at the peel and crammed the segments into his mouth. Juice spattered onto the blue leather surface of the desk and he smeared it away with his hand.

"Enough of this." He pushed back in his chair, stood up, and paced across the royal blue carpet before slamming his flat hand against the frame of the large window, the triple-glazed panes humming under the impact.

Below him, summer heat lay fat and brooding on the gardens of the villa. The pink bells of the flowers in the bed swayed in the breeze.

"I need air," he said, and gripped the window handle, forcing it up. He pushed hard on the glass, his hand leaving a sticky smudge on the pane. A warm, scented breeze blew into the room. He breathed deeply, rolled his shoulders, and then returned to the desk.

"Screen!"

A panel covering most of the opposite wall flickered from inert grey to pale blue.

"International News, mute."

A talking head appeared on the screen, mouthing away to itself in silence.

He sat down again, and the phone buzzed.

"Yes, Ellen?"

"Owen is home from school, Mr Mortis."

"Send him in."

Mortis reached out for another tangerine, as there was a light tap on the door.

"Come in!"

The door handle turned back and forth, rattling the lock.

"I said, come in!"

The door rattled again.

"Oh, for goodness' sake," he said, pressing a button on his phone, "help him out, Ellen."

The handle was still for a moment and then spun firmly, and the door opened. A boy in a smart school uniform peered in.

"Come in, Owen. How was your school day?"

"Good thank you, Father," said the boy. His face was red with the heat, and dark curls clung to his forehead.

Mortis looked at his son, the delicate features reminding him so much of the boy's mother, the pale blue eyes harbouring resentment and weakness.

"Come here and sit down." He pointed to the chair in front of his desk.

The boy walked in and sat, keeping his eyes on the carpet.

"Head up, Owen," said Mortis, "walk like a man. You're not feeling sorry for yourself again, are you?"

"No, Father." The boy shook his head.

"Good. Now listen, because I have something important to tell you; I've just had some good news. You know those scientists at that big telescope I told you about?"

"The ones who are looking for the new planet?" said Owen.

"Yes. They think they've found something."

"What?"

It gratified Mortis to see that at last the boy was paying attention.

"A new planet," said Mortis, "a very special new planet. At least I hope they have–one of them has promised to write me a report all about it. I just hope he sticks to the facts and doesn't get overexcited."

Mortis leaned back and waved a finger at his son. "You'll discover, Owen, that scientists have a weakness for exaggeration, and an excessive concern for matters in their own field, which I suppose is understandable; but they have to be managed and supervised like children. Now sit down here."

He glanced back at the screen in front of him, which now showed an imposing neoclassical building.

"There might be even more good news for us by the end of the day. Let's see how our philanthropic activities are going, shall we?"

The boy shifted in the seat and then twisted his neck against the collar of the shirt so he could look at the screen.

"Sound!" shouted Mortis as he ripped at the skin of another tangerine.

The voice kicked in, just as the camera panned to a thickset man with cropped grey hair standing on the steps of an imposing building, surrounded by a group of Andean villagers, the men in ponchos and bayeta pants, the women in their monteras. A byline at the bottom of the screen placed this as the Palace of Justice in Lima, Peru. The thickset man waved to a group of journalists and smiled.

"Ah, the reliable Mr Todd," said Mortis. "Let's see what he has to say for himself."

"...after the ruling, we spoke to Baxter Todd, counsel for the FIP."

Mortis shifted in his chair and winked at Owen. On the screen, the man stepped forward, smiling at the assembled *periodistas*.

"This is a great day for the Calichua people," he said, speaking to the cluster of microphones in front of his face. "In fact, it's a great day for indigenous peoples across the world. The court has endorsed the primacy of those who settle on a piece of land first, recognising their right to claim it as their own. The Foundation for Indigenous Peoples has been proud to represent the Calichua people in their fight for justice."

One of the assembled journalists threw in a question:

"Mr Todd, what exactly is your interest in the Calichua people? And who is bankrolling the FIP?"

"Our only interest is in seeing justice done," said Baxter. "This is about the right of people to claim their own land; and that principle should apply anywhere and everywhere." He stressed the last word as he spoke it, leaning forward and looking intently at the cameras. Then he held out his hands, trying to imply honesty. "Look, the Calichua have primary ownership of their homes, they were living on this land before anyone else came along, and we believe that means they have ownership of that land. It's a fundamental principle, and we intend to support them and any other indigenous groups in their fight to claim what is theirs."

Another reporter waved a microphone in front of him.

"Ryan Travers from CTN, isn't it true that one of the FIP's main donors is the media and energy magnate, Callum Mortis? Why is Mr Mortis suddenly so interested in the rights of indigenous people? He didn't seem to care about the rights of people affected by the Marliaté dam project?"

"Now that's an unfair comparison," said Baxter smoothly. "There's nothing sudden about Mr Mortis's interest, he has a well-established record in defending the rights of indigenous peoples around the world. This is an issue that has been close to his heart for many years."

"But why," someone shouted, "is he so interested in this cause?"

"It is the FIP who have fought this cause on behalf of the Calichua people," said Baxter, smiling affably, "and I think we have proved today that this is a cause worth supporting. Now what we should focus on is celebrating this great victory and letting the people get on with deciding how to manage their land for themselves. Thank you, everyone, no more questions."

He gave one more wave before striding towards a waiting limo.

Mortis flicked the screen off, and the room was silent again.

"Not a bad effort from our Mr Todd, don't you think, Owen?" He leaned on the desk again and looked conspiratorially at his son. "You don't think any of the locals noticed him wrinkling his nose at them, do you?"

"I don't know, Father," said the boy, scratching at the edge of his shirt collar.

"What's the matter with you, Owen? You look pale, are you unwell?"

"No, Father."

"Good. Did you watch how he performed?"

Owen nodded.

"Baxter is a perfect example of what I want from one of my staff," said Mortis. He sat back and steepled his fingers, the chair creaking under him. "I try to surround myself with people just like him; competent but not too ambitious."

The boy nodded and eased a small finger under his collar.

"What's that line from Shakespeare?" Mortis frowned, "'Let me have men about me that sleep at night?' Something like that, anyway. I... don't fiddle with your clothes, Owen, remember who you are."

"But it's this shirt, Father, I just..."

The boy flinched as his father raised his hand, but then Mortis remembered himself and the plump fingers landed on the desk.

"Now then," said Mortis, "how old will you be on your next birthday?"

"Twelve, Father."

"Twelve years old," said Mortis, shaking his head. "Do you know, in some societies, that would put you on the threshold of manhood? Are you ready to be a man?"

Owen frowned, his eyes flicking around the room. "I think so."

"I had to grow up when I was not much older than you, didn't I?"

"Yes, you did, Father," said Owen, staring at the carpet.

"I never forget where I came from, Owen, never, and neither should you."

Callum Mortis had told his son the story of his childhood many times, but he never seemed to tire of giving the tale one more airing.

He had grown up in poverty, the oldest of five siblings. Their father had abandoned them when their mother was pregnant with her youngest child, and she had then struggled alone with her children for ten years before succumbing to addiction and despair. When she died, Callum continued to look after his brothers and sisters, first out of a sense of duty and then with simmering resentment as he saw his own life wasting away.

He announced his intention to leave when he reached the age of eighteen and he was as good as his word. He was a man now and needed to make his way in the world–the care system would look after his younger brothers and sisters. He went to the city and earnt the money to ensure that he would never be destitute again.

"You should consider yourself fortunate, Owen," he said. "I never had the benefit of my father's attention."

Mortis's eyes drifted across the surface of the desk.

"I'm sorry," whispered Owen.

"Sorry? You've got nothing to be sorry about," said Mortis, "at least not on that score." He picked up another tangerine and threw it back and forth.

"Don't waste your time being sorry, Owen," he said. "Being sorry is for people who look backwards, I only look forwards."

He was about to continue, but the feeling of warm moisture on his hands distracted him. Looking down, Mortis could see that he'd clenched the now deformed tangerine so hard that it had burst and the sticky pungent juice was running between his fingers and onto his desk.

"Damn it!" He reached for a burgundy handkerchief from his pocket, and as he did so, there was a sharp knock on the door.

"Come in!"

A woman in a tailored grey business suit paced into the room; her brilliant red shoes made no noise on the carpet as she walked towards Mortis's desk. Owen watched her, mesmerised by the fluid grace of her movement, wondering how she could be so self-assured, so brave, around his father.

She gave the boy the briefest of glances before turning back to his father.

"The case went well then," she said.

"Oh, yes, Baxter came through for us, although God knows we spent enough money on it. But yes, we won; as did the Calichi people."

"The *Calichua* people," she said. "I think you'll find it's pronounced, *Calichua*."

The boy flinched slightly as Mortis stared at her, but she kept perfectly still, holding Mortis's gaze.

"Did you want something, Ellen?"

"The report from the observatory at Mauna Kea has come through."

"Ah, my pet astronomer, now let's see what he has to say for himself."

Mortis dropped the flaccid remains of the tangerine into the bin and flipped the document open, scanning the first few lines.

"Where's the summary, Ellen? I told him to prepare one."

"He's put some of the data together and sent it through."

"Idiot, I told him to send me a summary. Have you read it?"

"I scanned through it before I came in."

"And?"

"He thinks this is the planet we've been looking for."

"Hmm." He flipped the file closed and leaned back. "So, at last they think they've found a habitable one," said Mortis, "and practically on our doorstep."

"Apparently so," said Ellen. "It looks nearly perfect."

"It had better be," said Mortis, "for all I want to do with it. Now get Ray to bring the car around and take Owen home, please."

"Yes, Mr Mortis."

Ellen turned and walked smartly from the room. Even under his father's gaze, Owen watched her walk all the way out and shut the door behind her.

"You're quite an admirer of hers, aren't you?" said Mortis.

Owen blushed.

"Oh, don't be ashamed of that, Owen," said Mortis, winking. "She is a handsome woman, and competent. She wouldn't be working for me if she wasn't."

Mortis pushed his chair back, stood, and walked around the desk, bending in front of the boy; one of his knees cracked as he came down and he balanced himself by putting both his hands on the boy's shoulders. Even sitting, Owen swayed slightly under his father's weight.

"I'll tell you a secret, Owen," he said. "You want to know a secret?"

"Yes," said Owen.

"This business with Baxter, and the astronomer finding us a planet, they're connected. Do you know how? I'll tell you, I am going to invest whatever it takes to get to that planet. And I am going to take you with me, Owen, if you prove yourself worthy. We'll take a team, a community, and when we get there, we'll claim it for ourselves." Mortis leaned closer as he confessed this most personal and obsessive ambition, whispering the details, and breathing the smell of orange into his son's face.

"Do you know how I am going to achieve this?"

"No, Father."

"By fashioning the law, shaping it, so it will give me ownership of the land I claim, just as it has today for the Calichi people. Do you see, Owen? Money and patience are the keys to power, and believe me, when I need to, I can use both."

Owen nodded.

"You'll see it more clearly as you get older," said Mortis, standing up, his knee clicking again. "Now we have something to work for, you and I. Your mother would be proud of us."

Owen twitched. His father hardly ever mentioned his dead mother, Owen felt the sting of tears immediately. He sat perfectly still, willing himself not to cry. To show weakness now would only lead to humiliation.

Mortis didn't notice his son's struggle as he walked back to the window.

"You must work hard, Owen," he said, "to fulfil your potential. You know that, don't you?"

"Yes, Father."

"And this is how you can prove that you are a man. I'll buy you the best education I can, but you must play your part."

"What's the new planet called?" said Owen suddenly.

"What?" said Mortis. "I don't know, although if they auction the right to name it, I suppose I might put in a bid."

Owen was about to suggest they name it after his mother, but some instinct told him to keep quiet.

Mortis looked out again onto the grounds below, and away to the green of the lawns beyond. He removed the sticky handkerchief from his pocket and dabbed his forehead; his nostrils filled with the cloying scent of orange. The Mortis estate was impressive, of course. Built by his father, expanded and improved under his management, and a worthy centre for his empire.

But it wasn't nearly enough, and now was the time to do something about that.

"Okay," said Mortis, "let's get on with it. Phone! Dr Sergey Federov, private number."

He glanced back at his son; they could both hear a dialling tone.

"Now that I know this planet is worth the effort, it's time for me to commit to Federov's Alpha Contact project and grab a share before anyone else does."

"Who is Dr Federov?" said Owen.

"That's who I'm calling now," said Mortis. "he is a very clever scientist, and he wants to send lots of little probes all the way to Alpha Centauri, where the new planet is. He is going to push them there with just a beam of light. When they get to the new planet, they're going to send back pictures and video to show us what that place is like."

The phone made a series of quiet ticks and then rang.

"Hello, Callum, to what do I owe this pleasure?"

"Sergey! I'm sorry to call you so late, but I wanted to let you know I've reached a decision on the funding question, and it is good news for you. I'll be coming on board with your Alpha Contact project. All the funds you need. I just wanted to let you know."

"That's wonderful news, Callum," said Sergey, "and thank you for your support."

"Well, thank you for the opportunity," said Mortis, "consider yourself funded!"

Mortis smiled down at his son and closed the call.

"This has been a good day for me," he said, and he turned back to the window. He felt the breeze on his face and he could hear a sprinkler whirring with a rhythmic hiss as it pattered water onto the lawns. Mortis looked up from the flowers to the unutterable blue of the summer sky.

"I have outgrown this place," he whispered to himself. "I have outgrown this place, and it is time to leave."

He'd quite forgotten that his son was still sitting in the room, and only remembered when Ellen called through to say that Ray had arrived with the car to take the boy home.

6

————

OWEN WAITED until everyone else had settled before he made his way back along the length of the ship for the appointment with his father.

The cryohall was dark and cold, but the ceiling lights flicked on when he opened the door. Beneath his feet, he could see the faint tracks of the gurney wheels where his team had spent the last few hours carrying out the dead. The tiny flicker of a console light shone out in the darkness, indicating the one life still left in the vast room.

He took his time, shivering occasionally as he walked amongst the empty pods, reading the names of the departed, reflecting on the enormity of what they'd done, still certain that it had been the right thing.

Owen had always known that the final act, the administration of the virus, would require immense self-discipline, an adherence to their cause. In this, the length of the journey had turned out to be their ally. As the years had passed, all of his team, even Owen himself, had stopped thinking of the colonists as people. Over time, they'd all come to realise the colonists were just pawns, chips in a game, the discharge of all the wrangling governments who'd paid for part of the *Aspira*'s journey and wanted to claim power over the new planet. Neither he nor his father would ever accept such an outcome.

It had taken time, but time had been the one thing they had plenty of. Eventually, they'd all seen the truth that the old man had perceived from the start. These people were just dead bodies in waiting, an impediment to the vision of the real beneficiaries of this trip.

But Owen was glad that Goran had been the one to administer the fatal dose that killed them, he was not sure he could have done it himself. It was a personal weakness of his, and he had not even confessed to Amelia.

He continued to wander between the pods, taking his time, doing the rounds as he'd done sixty years ago just as the *Aspira* set off on her journey. But he was only ever heading in one direction, to that last pod, with its separate life support and monitoring system.

At last, he came to the untroubled world of Callum Mortis. Everything was in order. The revival protocol had started a couple of hours previously, and his father was warming up and gently surfacing from a deep slumber. Owen brought up the console menu and keyed in the last instruction manually. The mix of nutrients and stimulants arrived on cue, and he knew the old man was ready to wake.

"Welcome back, father," he said, and shivered.

The amber console light changed to green and shone out across the hall. Owen hesitated for a moment before he keyed in the final command. Even now he could still return to Amelia with the news she would want to hear: that he'd decided not to give the old man another chance, that instead he'd aborted the final stage of the revival protocol, and had dispatched his father into the void along with the other subjects.

But he could not do it, any more than he could have administered the fatal dose to the colonists, and so instead he watched as the pod lid eased slowly open, yielding its warm, moist air to the surrounding coldness.

Owen looked at his father again for the first time in sixty years. The old man seemed perfectly relaxed, arms by his sides, mouth slightly open. When the lid fully lifted, he heard his father's breathing deepen, and saw the chest rising and falling.

The console above the pod displayed a series of reassuring messages as the old man's eyelids flicked open. He blinked twice before he focused on the face of his son.

"Owen," said Mortis, "God, you look a mess. Have we made it?"

Owen resisted the temptation to adjust the collar of his Transit uniform.

"Yes, father, we've arrived. We made it."

"Ha! How about that, I was right to have faith in you all along. Amazing. Are you sure we've arrived at Zera?"

"Yes," said Owen, "we are in orbit around Zera."

Mortis sniffed. "Smells a little stale in here."

"There have been two hundred bodies in this cryohall for the past sixty years," said Owen, "and I presume you remember the fate we planned for them."

"Of course," said Mortis. "So, did that go smoothly?" He tried to stretch his limbs, but felt the pull of the restraints. "You might need to help me with this thing."

"No, it didn't," said Owen.

Mortis didn't seem to hear his son's reply as he tried to sit up.

He shivered extravagantly in the frosty air. "And what the hell have you done with the temperature in here, Owen? It's freezing."

"Perhaps you didn't hear me," said Owen. "I said things didn't go smoothly with the colonists."

Mortis stared at him. "What do you mean? What happened?"

"Five of the younger colonists were unaffected by Goran's toxin," said Owen. He had rehearsed these words, and he felt no fear as he said them. "They woke early and have escaped to the planet in one of the shuttles."

"What?" croaked Mortis, wriggling and stretching against the harness. "Ow! Damn it!"

Owen moved forward, but Mortis raised his hand.

"Wait, let me get this straight. Did you say children? Five children woke up and then managed to escape down to the planet? What were you all doing, sleeping on the job?"

Owen reflected on the fact that this was actually true.

"We tried to stop them, but we failed."

"How the hell did that happen? What is the matter with you, Owen, can't you organise anything properly?"

"Well," said Owen, ignoring his father's rhetorical question, "either Dr Maric's toxin wasn't as fool-proof as we thought, or the delivery system didn't work. The rest of the colonists died as planned."

"And you let these kids just grab a shuttle?"

"Patrick and Amelia tried to stop them."

"Patrick... you mean Ray's brother?" Mortis wriggled in the pod and pulled on the needle still stuck in his arm. "I'm surprised he didn't just shoot them."

"Well, he tried," said Owen, "and ended up shooting a hole in the shuttle bay wall."

"What a mess," said Mortis. "Patrick is an idiot, but the blame can't fall on him. You make a mistake of this magnitude, and the only people you've talked about so far are Patrick and Amelia, and that fool Maric. Damn it, Owen, you should have woken me first so I could oversee this." He shivered again.

"Calm down, father, you've been asleep for sixty years, you mustn't get stressed."

"What are you talking about, 'I mustn't get stressed'?" said Mortis, pulling on the restraints again as he tried to sit up. "Do you think that's how I got us here? By not worrying about it, by shrugging my shoulders and letting the world push me wherever it wanted to? We need to get this sorted out now. Where's Ray?"

"Getting some rest. We'll follow the kids down to the planet and pick them off from there."

"Ray is resting, is he? I expected better of him than the rest of you, but it seems I'm to be disappointed again."

"He's saved your life twice that I know of," said Owen. "You would do well to show him more respect."

"Respect." Mortis stared at his son as if he'd grown an extra head. "Have you lost your mind on this trip? You'll be asking me to say lovely things about that privileged bitch, Amelia, next."

Owen looked at his father. The surge of passionate anger in him was almost delicious. His fingers twitched. One punch might do it, if it was hard enough, one punch to the face, hard and clean. Up against the nose, with enough force to push cartilage into the old man's brain. And if that didn't work, he could always follow it with another blow and then another. He imagined his father twitching and squirming in the pod under an assault from his fists.

Nevertheless, he did not move.

"We need to get down there as soon as possible," said Mortis, trying to sit himself up.

"We need to load one of the other shuttles with supplies and equipment, and then we can go. It will be a few hours yet."

"A few hours, we'll see about that. Get me out of this."

Owen looked down at the old man.

"No, I think I'll leave you there just for now," he said.

The old man looked at him, mouth gaping open.

"What?" said Mortis.

"I'm not letting you out of here," said Owen, "not yet anyway."

"What are you talking about?" said Mortis, slamming a pale hand against the side of the pod. "Is this some kind of sick joke? Do you fancy yourself as the leader of this crew?"

"I am their leader. I'm the head of the Transit Team, remember?"

Mortis studied his son and frowned.

"What do you want, Owen? I mean, what are you doing here? What is this, a power grab?"

"We need to talk," said Owen.

"Oh, I see it. That bitch Amelia put you up to this, didn't she?"

Owen stared at his father for a long time, smothering his anger, keeping his arms still.

"It's nothing to do with Amelia. And if you call her a bitch one more time, I will kill you, right where you sit."

Mortis stared at his son, but kept his mouth shut.

"This is about you and me, Father," said Owen. "We have some unfinished business."

"What unfinished business?"

Owen shook his head. "Can't you guess? Have you so little imagination?"

"You never could say what you think, Owen, you are just like your mother."

"My mother. Well, we'll come to her in a moment."

"I thought we might," said Mortis, shivering again. "For pity's sake, get me out of this thing so I can sort myself out, then we can talk."

"No," said Owen.

Mortis stared at him and smiled. "Dear gods, you've grown some backbone at last, amazing."

Owen stepped closer to his father. "Do you know what my first memory of you is?" he said. "Terror, pure terror; you getting angry at me, at Mother, at one of your staff. That's my overriding memory, right from the very beginning. An angry person, always angry. You were always shouting at someone, and now I come to think of it, it usually was my mother, wasn't it?" he laughed mirthlessly. "You reserved the worst of your temper for her."

Mortis stared at his son and pulled at the restraints again.

"Now look, Owen, we can talk about this, all of it, but..."

"Which raises an interesting question," continued Owen, leaning over the pod and into his father's face. "What happened to my mother? I'll tell you what, Father, you answer me that question, honestly, and I'll let you out of this thing."

"You know what happened to your mother."

"Do I? Why don't you tell me your version of the story?"

Mortis was silent for a moment and then relaxed. "We haven't got time for this, Owen. You know the story. She fell on the stairs; it was a tragic accident."

"A tragic accident. So, nothing to do with the blazing row you had just before this tragic accident occurred?"

"There was no row."

"Liar!" shouted Owen, leaning in towards his father again. "You're a liar, Callum Mortis. There was an argument, a massive row. I heard it and I saw it."

"You were five years old, Owen, just a small child. You're confused."

"Oh no," said Owen, "no, no, no. You think I can't remember because I was young? I remember all right. I saw it all, and I heard it all, the single scream, the crack of her head on the stairs."

Mortis looked at his son and sighed. "So that's it then, is it, Owen? This is what you woke me for? Did you have to wait until you had me shackled like this for us to have a conversation?"

Owen looked at his father, but didn't speak.

"What are you going to do now, son? Indulge in some monologue? Kill me? Did you bring me all the way out here so you could wake me up and then murder me?"

Owen stepped back, his breath rising as steam in the icy hall. "I'll ask you again and let's see if we get the truth this time: what happened to my mother?"

Mortis's eyes flickered around the cryohall and then settled again on his son.

"Your mother was a very emotional person. My God, Owen, if I'd known you were still angry about it after all these years, I'd have..."

"You'd have what, what would you have done? Brought her back? Apologised?"

"I'd have arranged some counselling for you. Helped you reach some closure."

"Closure? You murder my mother and you want to talk about closure?"

"I did not murder your mother," croaked Mortis. "There was an incident, that's all. Now get me out of this and we can talk. I'll tell you what happened, I'll tell you everything."

"Maybe I'll tell you something first," said Owen, "since you're not prepared to tell me the truth. This one other abiding memory I've got of you, Father. Do you remember those tangerines you used to eat?"

Mortis stared at him.

"You used to pick them up with your fat fingers and smear the juice everywhere? I remember you doing that on the day we first heard about Zera. Do you remember that? How pleased you were with yourself that day, do you remember?"

"I remember," said Mortis quietly. "We won our first land rights case that day, the first of many victories for the people. I remember talking to you about money and patience as well, Owen, and now through our use of both resources we have Zera within our grasp. This is what we both worked for; this is our destiny."

"That's a touching speech," said Owen, "but you don't really care about anyone else, certainly not the people your foundation was supposed to help. It was all convenience for you."

Mortis smiled to himself. "Since we're being honest with each other, I'll admit that is true. But I helped them, I did my bit for the poor and needy. It meant I didn't have to fork out any more of my money for child poverty or some other bleeding-heart cause."

"That was the same day that your pet astronomer told you about Zera, wasn't it?"

"Yes," said Mortis, smiling again. "We had a spy at the observatory, and he told me we'd hit the jackpot with Zera."

"But my mother was dead by then, wasn't she?"

"Okay," said Mortis, "okay. You are right, son, we need to talk about this. There needs to be honesty between us."

"You don't know how to be honest."

"How do you know?" rasped Mortis. "How do you know that when you haven't given me a chance to respond, when you have me bound here like a prisoner?"

Owen looked at his father, looked into his eyes, trying to perceive what the old man was really thinking.

"There's nothing there," he said, "I look at you and I'm looking into a pit."

The old man smiled. "I am who I am, Owen, you of all people should have worked that out by now."

"Tell me one thing."

"What?"

"Why? She was my mother, your wife. Why did you kill her?"

They looked at each other for a moment.

"I keep telling you, it was an accident. Yes, we'd had a row, and things were difficult, but it was just a tragic accident, and that's the truth. And here's another truth, I don't think you will kill me. You haven't got that ruthlessness in you."

"You don't understand what motivates me, or what I am capable of."

"So, it would seem," said Mortis. "You know, I like that you're standing up for yourself here. This might be the most meaningful conversation we've ever had."

"Well, you can make it even more meaningful by telling me what really happened that night."

As he spoke, he removed an inoculation gun from his pocket.

Mortis stared at the device.

"Don't do it, Owen, it's not who you are. In that maybe you are a better man than me. But I think you can handle the truth now, so I'll give it to you; and once we're through that, we'll get this project back on track."

Owen stiffened, and watched as the old man realised that he'd made a mistake, talking as if it was all about the project.

"You think I want you to be honest, just so we can get on with your grand scheme, to make you the King of Zera?" Owen shook his head. "You haven't changed,"

"Owen, for pity's sake, at least let me take a leak before you kill me."

"No," said Owen, looking down at the inoculation gun. He flicked the safety catch off.

"Tell me what happened or die, it's as simple as that."

Mortis shivered and looked directly at his son.

"You know—" Mortis paused for a moment and shook his head. "You know, she never left me, did she, because you have the same eyes as her—" he spoke softly now, almost with regret, "and so much else besides. You remind me so much of her."

"Really? And how does that make you feel?"

"How does that make me feel?" Mortis pulled forward in the pod, as far as the restraints would allow him; then he looked around the cryohall again before settling his gaze on his son.

"All of this makes me realise just how much you and your mother were a pair. You and her, your little confidences, little indulgences. You were your mother's boy, you always were and you always will be."

Mortis nodded, as if suddenly grasping a complex idea.

"I'll tell you the truth about your mother. She was the cleverest person I ever met. She wanted to leave me, of course, and that could have been arranged easily. She could have had money, but she wanted something I would never give her: you. You were, you are, my only son. I needed you with me, to ensure you became the man I needed you to be. God knows what you would have been like if she'd brought you up."

Owen stared at him, the tears forming in his eyes.

"So, you murdered her."

"In a manner of speaking, yes," said Mortis, with a casual nod. "I pushed her, although at the time I didn't intend for her to die, it was a spur-of-the-moment thing." He sighed, and the noise echoed around the cryo hall.

"There's your truth Owen, well done, you bested me, although you did have an advantage."

Owen stared at him, and Mortis shivered.

"God, it's cold in here." Mortis looked at his son, "look, Owen, I'm proud of you, You win. Yes, I pushed her. I didn't mean for her to die, but I can't say I regretted how things turned out, especially after I'd got away with it."

Owen stared at him in silence. "Both of you were all I ever wanted."

"What?" said Mortis, "speak up, Owen; I can't hear you over the noise of the engines."

"All I ever wanted was for the three of us to be together, like a family. Amazing, isn't it? You didn't think I cared about you, but I did, I wanted a mother and a father, all of us, together." He could feel the tears rising, and he knew he could not stop them.

"If you cared about me at all," said Mortis, "you'd understand this one thing about me. I've lived in poverty, and I will never be in that position again, ever. And that means I won't let anyone have power over me or take what is mine. No one. If I hadn't done what I did, if she had taken you, then this project, all I have dreamed of and desired, would never have happened."

He shrugged his shoulders slightly. "I could not let her take you, Owen, I couldn't."

Mortis looked around the cryohall again, seeming to admire the icy cavern they were in. Finally, he stared at Owen and smiled.

"There's the truth you wanted, what are you going to do with it?"

"You," said Owen, shaking his head, "are a cold, vicious murderer. But I can thank you for one thing, at least you've made it easy for me to do this."

"For God's sake, Owen," said Mortis, leaning forward in his pod, "I'm your father."

"I know," said Owen, "but it's too late, I'm sorry."

"So am I, son," said Mortis, and he shut his eyes so that he only heard the blunt object hitting Owen's skull. He opened his eyes again in time to see Owen's head jerk forward and the body slump over the lip of the pod.

Behind him was the impassive face of Ray Merritt. He was holding a hammer in his right hand.

Mortis looked down at his son, and then up at Ray.

"Thank you, Ray. Thank you for waiting and giving him a chance. Now help me out of this thing, I need to use the bathroom."

Ray unclipped the restraints and slid the needle out of his boss's arm. The old man sat up, rubbing his wrists.

"Can you take care of this?" He pointed at Owen's slumped body.

"I'll get a trolley," said Ray, "we left them down here. Then I can take him up to the evac tube."

Mortis hauled himself out of the pod and placed his feet on the ground. Then he bent down slowly and picked up the inoculation gun.

"You'd better get rid of this. And Ray,"

"Yes, sir?"

"Well done, a good job."

"Thank you, sir."

"I mean it," said Mortis. "When this problem with the child colonists is sorted out, you'll have your territory as I promised. All the hunting and walking and fresh air you've ever wanted."

"Thank you, sir, I'll deal with the body now."

Mortis nodded and turned his mind away from the pain of losing his son and towards what he was going to say to the team, especially Amelia.

7

———

Grace heard the boys chattering to each other. Brandon was making some joke about how Chi ended up coming with them anyway, and Chi replied that he had had little choice. Then she heard Josh promising to help Chi get back to the *Aspira* if he ever got the chance.

Their conversation stopped as the shuttle lurched to the left, yanking them over in their seats. One of the boys cried out, a sudden shout. Grace heard that cry, and something deep within her mind discarded it.

It doesn't matter, it's not Dan.

And she realised, again, that Dan was her priority. She believed in Josh's notion of them surviving as a group, but Dan was her flesh and blood. If it came to a choice, she would save him before any of the others.

She checked the coordinates of the new LZ and then, finally, allowed herself to engage the autopilot facility. The shuttle steadied and Brandon's laugh brought her back to the present. She unclipped the buckle, stood up, and stretched.

Josh was right, she had got them off the *Aspira*, and it felt good. But piloting the shuttle had been more than an act of bravery, it had been exciting. When the terror subsided, Grace found she revelled in the experience, being in control, stabilising the craft, and then bringing it into orbit around the cool beauty of the planet.

"Hey," called Brandon, "you're a proper pilot now, McAllan." He gave her a thumbs up, and she returned the favour. She knew that one day she wanted to be a pilot, in a better time than they were living through now, in a time when her parents' death didn't sear her memory, and when greedy and crazy people weren't trying to killing her.

But before any of that happened, they had to survive.

She yawned and dropped back into the chair, clipping the harness buckles over herself again. The shuttle was level, and cruising towards the point where they would make their descent to the landing zone. She gazed out at the delicate whirls of cloud covering a vast curve of blue ocean on the planet below her. The majesty of it brought sorrow up from within her, like a bubble surfacing in oil. All the thoughts of her parents and her friends, the people she had lived with. And the immensity of their loss claimed her, so that hidden away in the shuttle's roar, she cried out. She wept, and wept until her emotions were spent, and she was too exhausted to make sense of anything around her.

Then she looked upon the planet in its radiant beauty one last time before she closed her eyes and went to sleep, joining three of the four boys in a dreamless rest, far away from the trauma of their escape.

But not everyone slept.

Chi did not grieve or dream of family. He did not reflect on loss, or the lessons he might have learnt. He had no desire to reminisce or dwell on the past; rather, he was thinking about the future. Safe amidst the howl of the shuttle, he even allowed himself to subvocalize the questions.

"What must I do now?"

"What steps should I take to achieve the objective?"

And then another thought occurred to him:

"What do I owe to my fellow survivors?"

The first imperative would be survival, and in this he shared a common cause with the others. He considered it good fortune to have ended up with this group. Brandon Kellerman seemed to have some idea about how they would survive on this planet, even if he was impulsive. Chi might take issue with some of his tactics, but the boy knew his stuff well enough for Chi to focus on the job in hand.

And then there was Grace, who had flown them all off the *Aspira*. That had been quite an achievement, and not a task he would have wanted to attempt himself.

But now he needed to decide on his next steps. That brought him to the question of what he would do when they landed. If the Transit Team members came after them, which seemed likely, he would have two options. He could stick with this group, wait for the inevitable confrontation and hope things went their way, or he could go it alone, and try to get back to the *Aspira*. Neither alternative seemed attractive, but he had to work with what was in front of him.

Then there was the question of his fellow survivors. His focus would be the primary objective, but he kept recalling a phrase his mother had been fond of quoting when he was a young boy:

"A candle lights others but consumes itself."

He thought about the self-sacrifice implied in that phrase and wondered whether it would be his destiny to become the candle, either for the mission or for his new friends.

THE SHUTTLE SKIMMED around the edge of the planet, through the frictionless void of space above Zera's atmosphere. They travelled with the planet between them and its star, Alpha Centauri 'B', so that Zera shielded them from sunlight. They continued on in a steady orbit, and soon the darkness at the arc of the planet's horizon warmed to an orange glow, greeting them with their own dawn.

The shuttle adjusted course, and the engines compensated for the move. It was only a subtle change, but it brought Grace back to consciousness. She opened her eyes and looked out at the revolving panorama beneath her, and then she listened.

They were speeding up, dipping out of orbit and into the final descent. As they picked up speed, the craft shivered. It was just an occasional judder at first, but the vibrations came more frequently until the whole craft was rattling. Some object, a tube from the medical pack, rolled out from under the seat beneath her.

A warning glyph flashed up on the screen. They were coming in hard now, too hard, and the pitch of the shuttle was wrong. She was about to make a change herself when the shuttle's automatic guidance systems kicked in and the little craft levelled out.

There was nothing she could do for now; the shuttle was on autopilot and would fly itself to the landing zone she'd programmed in, but she would have to manage the last part of this journey by landing the shuttle, the 'easy part of any flight', as their instructor had often called it with some irony.

The little craft pitched forward again, nose down towards the surface. This time, it didn't adjust itself. They needed to do to work off the kilometres of altitude between them and the land below.

Outside, the atmosphere thickened. The air hummed and then screamed as it scoured the shuttle's hull. The seats rattled, the racks in the shuttle's stern juddered, and Grace could feel her teeth chattering as they continued to plunge downwards.

Through the cockpit window, she could see the terrain moving towards them, focusing in from a grey-green landmass to reveal the forested tip of a vast continent, and an archipelago that scattered out from its most northern point. Even as Grace looked, the view slipped behind an advancing bank of cloud.

Then she felt the engines kick in again, and the shuttle levelled off and slowed.

"Grace!" Brandon's voice.

"What?"

"Is that the worst of it? Are we going to land soon?"

She laughed at the idea. "No, that was just the warm-up act. We've still got thousands of metres to fall yet."

"Great," said Brandon after a moment. "I love it!"

If he spoke again, Grace didn't hear him. Once again, the shuttle dipped in towards the planet and sped up.

The thickening atmosphere battered the underside of the hull, and Grace knew that the highly resistant material beneath them would soon glow with the friction of the atmosphere against it.

She stared down at the approaching planet, watching the horizon expand before her. Beneath them, the upper surface of the cloud bank shone with the reflection of the sun.

She checked herself even as she thought the word 'sun'. This was not their old star, Sol, this was a new sun, a different star, and as if to emphasise its otherness, the light from it shone with a different, more orangey hue.

The shuttle steadied itself before plunging into the disorientating whiteness, tiny droplets of water smeared against the glass panel in front of her.

Her eared popped as Grace watched the numbers on the console spin in front of her, airspeed, altitude and other data, and she wondered when the autopilot would hand over the controls to her. She could feel her heart beating faster now as the moment approached when all their lives would be in her hands.

They cleared the cloud, and she could see that they were flying in a storm. Rain lashed the cockpit window, and the wind buffeted them, shaking the shuttle from side to side.

She checked the onboard map. The original landing zone for the shuttles was about one hundred kilometres north of their present position, but the new coordinates would put them twenty kilometres further on from that, nearer the coast.

She settled back into the pilot's chair and looked out at the view. Beneath them now there was an expanse of dark, almost black foliage, stretching into the distance. She could just pick out the pale line of a river winding its way up towards its tributary.

The screen in front of her flashed a message and offered her control of the craft. The message flickered and then changed in colour from orange to red. Her finger hovered over the main autopilot control for a moment and then she tapped it, and the autopilot indicator winked off.

Immediately, the shuttle dipped forward and rolled to the left. The guidance control environment appeared on the screen in front of her and she moved her fingers, feeling the craft struggle against the wind. She levelled the shuttle, bringing the nose up, and then consulted the navigation map again.

"Just like the training," she told herself. "All I need is a nice flat space to drop her onto."

She thought back to the simulations and her eyes flicked across the panel in front of her and then out of the cockpit window at the view in front of her. She eased on the brakes, reducing their velocity as the ground approached them.

Within a minute, they'd passed over the original landing zone and flew on towards Grace's new coordinates.

The shuttle continued towards the northernmost tip of the great continent, just thirty kilometres away, north by north-west of their current position. Morning light seeped through the clouds, and she could make out the faint line of the coast ahead of them.

She calmed the engines again and eased on the braking control, feeling the pull of the straps as the shuttle's speed decreased.

Just ahead, the forest thinned out and an expanse of savannah opened up. Grace could make out tiny clusters of dark brown objects moving across the land; they could have been grazing animals. The rain slackened, and she slowed the shuttle again, bringing them in towards the flatter expanse ahead of them.

They were heading towards a shallow valley, and she knew that this might be the only chance they had to land on anything like a level surface. She worked off more velocity and began the final descent.

"This is it," she shouted behind her, "brace yourselves."

The little craft dropped again, and Grace watched as more details of the land below them came into view. The valley opened up, and the animals she saw earlier became distinct, scattering in all directions as the shuttle roared overhead.

Grace checked her altimeter; they were about two hundred metres above ground, and still descending as the shuttle lost velocity. The end of the valley appeared ahead of them, rising to a ridge with a gentler rise beyond it. Grace engaged the landing protocol, the engine calmed, and the ship seemed to relax, as if it were just going to drop lightly onto the ground. When they were still about twenty metres clear of the surface, the shuttle seemed to stop and hang in the air; all the surrounding sounds ceased, the rattling, the engines, the vibration, everything was silent for just a second, and then the ground rose towards them one last time and then:

IMPACT

They were all thrown forward, harness straps biting into them, the little craft shaking as its base slid across the ground. Grace watched as mud and great strands of grass whipped against the window.

They came to a halt with a final jolt that felt like someone had smacked the shuttle on its nose with an enormous club. The interior of the craft went dark, save for a strip of light across the top of the cockpit window, just above a line of dirt.

Somewhere at the rear of the shuttle, an alarm sounded for a few seconds before switching off. Then there was silence.

Several lights flickered on the display in front of her, and an ironic message appeared.

Attention: Irregular landing detected.

"Irregular landing," whispered Grace, "you could say that."

"Hey!" shouted Brandon, "breaking news, we're still alive. Good job Grace."

"Thank you," said Grace. "Good morning and welcome to planet Zera. How is everyone? Dan, are you okay?"

Each of them mumbled something, and the shuttle hummed and ticked as metal cooled and core systems settled into standby mode.

Grace unbuckled the harness. She wasn't cold, but she was shivering. She took a couple of deep breaths and stood up, bracing herself on the console in front of her.

A spray of mud covered the cockpit screen, apart from a thin strip of daylight at the top. Zeran rain pattered onto the glass and ran in trickles to the soil below it. Beyond the cockpit window the mud rose again in a bank, which engulfed the nose of the shuttle and rose ahead of her.

Grace could hear movement behind her as the boys stumbled out of their seats. She turned back to see Brandon, Dan, and Chi stretching themselves and stumbling out into the central aisle; Dan was bouncing up and down, the floor creaking as he did so.

"What are you doing?" said Brandon.

"That's weird," said Dan. "I feel lighter."

"You are lighter," said Grace. "Zera's gravity is about ninety percent of what we had on Earth."

"But it didn't feel strange on the ship, and the gravity was all over the place there."

"That was the ship, they trained us to get used to Zera's gravity, but this feels like a proper planet, this feels like..."

She was about to say 'home', but she stopped herself.

"How are you doing?" she said, looking down at Josh, who was still in his seat.

"My shoulder's a little sore, but I'm fine."

"Come on," she reached out her right hand to his. He grasped it and pulled himself up.

"Thanks."

She nodded and then turned as Dan pulled on her arm.

"Do you think we can we drink that rainwater when we get out of here?" he said. "I'm thirsty."

"We're all thirsty," said Brandon, "and hungry, but we'll need to have a look around this immediate area before we do anything else."

"The shuttle has an external diagnostic," said Grace, turning back to the console. "We'll see what the atmosphere is like out there."

She tapped the console. "Assuming we haven't broken it in that landing."

She punched through the menus, called up the diagnostic routine, and requested an external status. The display showed a little spinning wheel as the shuttle extended every probe it could to taste and sniff Zera's environment.

Finally, it gave her a report

"Okay guys, it says the atmospheric composition is within Earth's standard parameters. The air's breathable, and the temperature is twenty-four degrees centigrade. Wind speed six knots bearing forty-eight degrees from Zeran north. There's no movement detected in the contact radius, some precipitation detected."

"What's precipitation?" said Dan.

"It means it's raining," said Brandon, "or it was. It looks like it's clearing now. Come on, let's see if we can get a better view from the back of the shuttle."

He turned and walked to the porthole in the door. The rest of them followed. Through the rain, they could see the trail of earth where their landing had carved a deep gouge through the rich dark soil.

"You know what," said Brandon, "we will be the first humans

to walk on this planet. I hope those murderers are furious about that."

"I'm sure they will be," said Chi.

"So, is it safe to go out there then?" said Dan.

"If we were at the Landing Zone," said Grace, "I could tell you more about what we might find here, but this place, who knows? Anything could be watching us."

"So, we need to be careful," said Brandon. "I am going to have a look around outside, who's coming with me?"

"I will," said Chi.

"Me too," said Dan.

"We might as well all go," said Grace, "then we can find out what this new planet looks like."

"Boots on," said Brandon, "and stay sharp."

He turned to the racks beside the door and pulled down the rucksack. Rummaging through it, he pulled out a pair of binoculars. Then he dug around again and retrieved a thick plastic bag with handles at the end.

"Water bag for thirsty travellers. Okay, we're ready, let's go."

He moved back to the door, spun the release wheel, and pulled. The bulkhead opened with a sharp hiss.

A wave of Zeran air washed over them, warm and moist, heavy with the aroma of grasses and broken earth. Then the sound came to them, the last scattering of rain and the wind whipping through the grass, a steady breeze blowing into their faces and stirring up the stale, still smoky air of the shuttle. Grace breathed in a lungful despite herself and listened to the first natural sounds that she had heard since leaving Earth.

She stepped forward and stared at the world outside. The wind blew on her face and she closed her eyes, thinking for a moment about home and her parents.

She then looked down the steep incline of the hill where they'd landed, to the valley beyond it, covered with purple and dark green grass, damp and steaming after the now clearing rain.

The walls of the valley angled down to a thin ribbon of water. Grace could just see the blue shimmer of a lake in the distance. Dotted across the hillside, she could see trees, their boughs thin and pointing upwards into the brightening sky. Dark maroon leaves fluttered in the breeze. Above them, the rain clouds were clearing and there were glimpses of blue in the sky above.

Brandon pushed past and stepped down from the shuttle, his feet landing on soft, yielding mud.

"Really boggy out here, guys," he said.

Grace stared at him. "That's the first step any human has made on another planet, and all you can say is: 'really boggy out here'. I thought you were going to make some rousing speech, 'one small step for man', and all that."

"If you can think of something better, Grace, you say it. I'm going to look around for any threats."

With that, he lifted a foot out of the mud and stepped towards the incline that led down to the valley floor.

Grace went after him, followed by Dan, Chi, and Josh. When she had found her footing, she looked down the valley, which stretched for a couple of kilometres below them. A river ran along the valley floor, feeding into the lake. To the west, the land rose and fell like a carpet of purple and dark green before disappearing into a jagged horizon of grey blue hills.

To the south, beyond the lake, the land rose again. A forest of spiky black trees engulfed the lip of the far side of the valley, their branches pointing like bony arms into the sky. The trees covered the edges of each side of the valley, thinning out at the northern end where they now stood. She turned around and looked up, beyond the shuttle to the north the terrain rose again, before falling away to the coast just ten kilometres away.

Grace breathed in Zeran's air. The aroma was warm and damp, and the smell of the earth rose from exposed ground.

They walked from the shuttle to where they'd first landed.

Brandon pulled the binoculars from his pocket and took a long three hundred and sixty degree sweep around them.

"Anything out there?" said Chi.

"Nothing obvious," said Brandon, "but that doesn't mean there isn't something watching us even now."

"So, what we do?" said Dan

"We finish identifying any threats. After that, we find food and water. Water shouldn't be a problem, but we also need to look for some kind of fuel. Dry wood, so that we can build a fire."

"What about the Transit Team?" said Dan, "What are we going to do if they come after us?"

"We worry about them when we need to," said Brandon. "They aren't the threat right now. We need to deal with whatever is in front of us."

"If they come," said Chi, "our strategy should be to get to their shuttle and use it to get back to the *Aspira*. I don't think our one will get airborne again."

"Risky," said Brandon. "All respect to Grace, but do any of us know how to fly a shuttle back up to the ship? Do we know how to dock with the *Aspira* when we get there?"

"We will be in considerable danger if we stay here," said Chi, "you especially." He looked straight at Brandon.

"There's no point in speculating about what we'd do if our enemies turned up. Right now, we need to focus on making it work here."

Chi opened his mouth to speak, but then closed it again.

"You okay with that?" said Brandon.

"Of course, so what should we do?"

"Like I said, we scout the area, then look for food and water," said Brandon.

"We should also try to send a message back to Earth," said Grace.

"No one will come and help us from Earth," said Brandon. "It would take a signal four years to reach them and who knows how long for them to get to us."

"It's not about getting help, it's about telling them what's happened here. I want justice, even if we don't survive to see it."

"Okay, if you want to do that fine, but we do survival stuff first. We should split into two teams, one goes north and the other south. We search for food and running water and we meet back here in half an hour."

"What's that noise?" said Dan.

They all paused and listened. At first there was just the wind rustling the tall grasses and the distant call of something unseen from the forest to the south, but within a few seconds they could hear a sound like the fall of heavy rain or a drum roll.

Brandon raised his binoculars and swung them around to look up the incline of the valley, beyond the nose of the shuttle. The rest of them watched him as he stood motionless for a second.

"Well," said Grace, "what is it?"

"Move," screamed Brandon, and started running back up the gulley towards the shuttle door. They all started running. As they struggled through the mud, a noise like thunder sounded in the air.

8

———

B RANDON CLAMBERED IN FIRST, followed by Chi, Grace and Dan, with Josh waiting until they were all in before he leapt up behind them. As they piled into the lobby of the shuttle, the noise grew, and the floor vibrated. Then something landed on the roof. There was the sound of feet, or claws, skittering across the ceiling above them. Then something scrabbled at the edge of the roof before bounding off onto the soil.

Brandon and Josh pushed the bulkhead door shut and peered out of the porthole.

"What are they?" said Josh.

"I don't know," said Brandon, "but there's a lot of them coming down the hill behind us. Some of them must have got onto the roof."

They clustered around the porthole and stared out at the mud where they could see their tracks. The sound intensified, clattering on the roof of the shuttle. The space outside the door filled with dark bodies, moving fast, coming along the sides of the gulley they'd made, and jumping down from above.

The creatures were long-limbed and lizard-skinned, dark and fast. They were about a metre tall and hopped, like kangaroos, on

108

powerful hind legs, which took them swiftly across the mud and down towards the valley. Some paused for a moment, either to clutch at a grass stem, or to pick up something from the ground. One of them found a bright orange worm, trying to burrow back into the mud; it grasped the worm with tiny forepaws and tugged until it was free of the soil. The little creature lifted the worm to its mouth and chewed its prize with enthusiasm. Grace stared at it. She could see now that the dark skin had a light covering of fur. It finished chewing and turned, bounding away with the others towards the valley.

"There're loads of those hopper things," said Brandon. "It looks like they're heading down to the lake to drink. What time is it on Zera right now?"

"Early morning," said Grace.

"I guess 'hoppers' is as good a name as any for them," said Josh. "If they are heading down to the lake, they'll probably be coming back this way later, and we've landed right in the middle of their territory."

"That probably means we've landed in the middle of something else's territory as well," said Brandon, "something that eats those hoppers. We've still got to find food and water. We'll have to be even more careful."

He went back to the shuttle door wheel and spun it open again.

"Come on."

They climbed out of the shuttle again. Paw prints covered the surrounding earth. Grace squinted at the sun, which was just clearing the line of the horizon. Far above them, the two moons of Zera were fading into the searing blue of the sky.

In the distance, the dark mass of hoppers moved down the valley river towards the lake.

"So," said Josh, "do we stick together, split into groups, or what?"

"We stick to the plan," said Brandon, "two teams, one to head south, the other north. We take a water bag each and look out for anything that might be edible. Look for long, straight branches, anything we can carve into a spear. Meet back here in an hour. Nobody eats or drinks anything they find until we get back, and I've had a look at it."

"Can I come with you?" said Dan, looking at Brandon.

Grace was about to protest, but paused.

Brandon looked at Dan. "Okay, but keep up. This is not a sightseeing trip."

"I'll come with you," said Josh.

"Are you up to it with your shoulder?" said Brandon.

"Are you kidding? I'm not just going to sit in the shuttle while you guys risk your lives to find me something for dinner. Don't worry, I'll be fine."

"Okay, well, you can look after the kid here," said Brandon.

"Dan," said Josh, deliberately using his name, "that's who you mean, isn't it?"

"Sure, Dan, whatever. We'll go south, and you guys," he looked at Chi and Grace, "can go north. Let's go."

He turned and strode away along the line of mud towards the incline into the valley.

Dan and Josh followed him. As Josh passed Grace, he whispered to her, "I'll look after him."

She nodded quickly, and he hurried on, catching up with Dan. In a moment, the three of them had disappeared down the hill.

Grace sighed and turned to Chi.

"I'm sorry you ended up here with us," she said. "I know it's not what you wanted."

"It's okay, shall we see what we can find?"

"I'll get one of those water bags." She turned back to the shuttle. Inside the craft, she picked up a plastic tub from the rucksack.

They climbed the bank to the right of the landing site and headed up beyond the nose of the craft until they reached a plateau one hundred metres above.

Looking back to the south, Grace could see the shuttle and the three tiny figures: Brandon, Dan, and Josh, working their way down towards one tributary that fed the river. Suddenly, she wished she was with Dan, looking after him, and her stomach turned as she realised that on Zera she would not be able to protect him.

She forced herself to turn around and look north. The hoppers had pitted the mud with their paw prints. Ahead of them, beyond the rim of the valley, the ground flattened and then sloped down again. She paused and listened to the wind. When she closed her eyes, she thought she could hear water cascading over stones; the sound weaving in between the breeze in the trees and the grass.

"Grace."

She turned to see Chi waving at her, away to her right. He was standing next to a bush of dark purple leaves. Looking closer, she could see that it was covered in bluish-mauve berries, like blueberries but the size of grapes. The sight made her hungry. She ran over to Chi and picked some fruit with him, quickly filling the plastic tub.

"These look good," said Chi.

"We'd better wait and see what Brandon has to say before we try one."

"There's water nearby as well. I think there's some near the treeline."

They headed back to the rim of the valley and then, looking east towards the expanse of woodland, saw the distant glitter of water.

A stream ran down from the edge of the forest. Grace could see the stones on the stream bed. She filled the water bag, sealed it, and they headed back down to the shuttle.

"Why are you so keen to get back to the *Aspira*?" she asked, as they made their way back towards the shuttle.

"It is the safest place for us."

"Do you really think so when there are people on that ship trying to kill us?"

"This planet will be more of a threat than the Transit Team."

"Do you know that for sure?"

He turned and looked at her, but didn't answer. Grace's arm ached from holding the bag of water.

"Well?" she said.

"There's nothing more I can tell you," he said finally, then turned and walked towards the shuttle.

They got back first and placed some seat cushions down behind the chairs of the shuttle. Brandon, Josh, and Dan returned just as Grace was putting the container of berries on the floor.

"We set up the solar still first," said Brandon, "so we can collect fresh water that won't need purifying; and then we try the fruit."

Brandon and Josh set up the still and then came back to review the water and fruit they'd collected. Brandon eyed the collection of alien fruits and frowned.

"Okay, let's see what we've got," he said.

They sat down on the seat cushions and looked at what they'd gathered. Brandon's group had brought back something that looked like a large grapefruit, dark purple, almost black, with a spattering of yellow over its tough skin; they had also discovered some bunches of 'stretched bananas', as Dan called them, a dark yellow fruit, thinner and longer than a banana from Earth. They'd also collected several straight, sturdy branches that they could carve into spears

Brandon held up one of the oversized blueberries.

"And now, let's play: 'good to eat or deadly poison?'," he said, "a game for only one player, that's me, in which I get to guess whether this is a wholesome piece of fruit that could keep us alive, or something highly poisonous that is likely to have me puking my guts up and dying in agony."

"Best of luck to you," said Grace.

Brandon nodded. "Thanks."

He peered at the fruit, cut off a slice and sniffed it, before recoiling.

"Oh no," he said, "no, no, no," and tossed it back into the container.

"Those are not good then?" said Chi.

"Not unless you want to die a painful death."

"Really?" said Chi. "I would have probably eaten one of them."

"Well, I suggest you pick that piece up and smell it. Go on," said Brandon.

Chi picked up the slice of fruit. There was a faintly sharp sweet smell to it.

"That sharpness you smell there," said Brandon, "that's the stuff that will have you saying goodbye to your internal organs."

He wiped the knife and then picked up the Zeran grapefruit. He cut a segment of it and held it up in the dim shuttle light. The flesh was pale green and moist with juice. A sweet, heavy aroma filled the surrounding space.

He sniffed at it and then cut a small piece off, touching it to his tongue. He then bit on and chewed a small piece before spitting it out into the container.

"Not that one either?" said Dan.

Brandon cut another piece and chewed it.

"No, this one's fine, it tastes good and there's lots of fruit sugar in it. Of course, we'll rethink that assessment if I fall over in agony in the next few minutes."

"What about the stretched banana?" said Dan.

"Let's see what effect this grapefruit thing has first," said Brandon.

They sat and watched Brandon, and he passed the time carving the end of one branch into a point, making a little pile of shavings on the floor in front of him. Grace and Josh went outside to look around again, but they saw nothing except the occasional drifting cloud, and grasses swaying in the wind.

Dan took the chance to scurry around the shuttle, picking up stray pieces of the first aid kit and stuffing them back into the rucksack.

"Well, I'm okay," said Brandon finally, "so the giant grapefruit is good."

"Excellent," said Grace. "I fancied a piece of that, so I'm glad it didn't kill you."

She winked at him.

"I'm touched by your concern, Grace." He took one of the stretched bananas and peeled the skin from it. Much to their surprise, the flesh was a deep orange colour. He sniffed it, tasted it, and finally nodded.

"This one is okay too," he said, biting a piece, "um, it's good."

"So, we eat this," said Josh, "and this," pointing to the over-sized bananas and the grapefruit.

"You're okay with the grapefruit," said Brandon, "and I don't think the banana will cause any issues, but let's wait and see."

He picked up the branch and the knife again.

"So, did you boys get as far as the lake?" said Grace.

"Not that far," said Dan, "but we went near it."

"See anything interesting?"

"Well..." said Dan. They all looked at him.

"Well?" said Grace.

"Nothing really happened," said Dan. "We walked down to the river, and we saw the lake in the distance. Those hopper things were drinking like we thought they would be. Then we had a look around and found the fruit, and then we came back."

"We saw some birds," said Josh, "wheeling around above us."

"Yes," said Dan, "three or four birds. They circled the lake and flew off. They were big, though."

"How big?" said Grace.

"Difficult to tell," said Josh. "They were high in the sky so they might have been enormous, but they didn't come near us, and no, we didn't spend long down there."

They all ate the fruit, and no one got sick. Grace started to believe that they would survive, at least for a while. Nothing else approached the shuttle as they ate, either to see who they were or to see if they themselves might be food for a hungry predator.

"So, what do you guys think we should do?" she said when they'd finished eating. "I mean, about the Transit Team coming after us?"

"I think we've got time before we have to worry about those murderers," said Brandon.

"Maybe they won't find us at all," said Dan.

"They will come eventually," said Chi, "All the shuttles have a tracking beacon. They will lock onto our one and find us."

"In that case, I guess we have a choice," said Josh. "Either we wait for them to come and then we confront them, or we leave the shuttle, hide and hope we can evade them."

"That's about it," said Brandon, "I say we wait. If we run, we won't have the shuttle as a base to work from. We'll be exposed out there and die. This is the best shelter we'll find anywhere near here. So, I say we establish ourselves and be ready to face them."

"And when they turn up?" said Grace.

"We kill them," said Brandon.

"And how are we going to do that?" said Chi. "With sharp sticks and knives?"

"Yes, if we have to."

"They have at least one gun between them," said Chi.

Brandon sighed. "Let me explain. This shuttle is the only shelter we have. If we leave it, we will die. Our enemies will probably find us here, yes, but this is our best asset; and we have time to prepare because we didn't land at the LZ. They will have to come looking for us."

"We won't know when they have found us," said Chi.

"I know that," said Brandon, "that's why we need to be prepared."

"And they will have guns," said Chi.

"Look, are you with us or not?"

"Okay, boys," said Grace, "that's enough. I'm sure we'll be fine here while we work out what to do next."

"Yeah, we'll be fine," Brandon stood up, picked up one of the makeshift spears he'd been working on, and headed for the door.

"Just going outside," he said. "I'll be back in a few minutes."

The shuttle door whined as he pulled on it, then he jumped down on the warm soil and stomped away.

"Is he angry?" whispered Dan to Grace.

"He'll be okay," said Grace, "just give him a few minutes to cool off."

Before anyone else could speak, they heard feet running, coming back towards the shuttle. The door squeaked as it opened and Brandon came in, breathless.

"Those creatures," he said, "the ones that ran across the top of the shuttle, they're coming back."

"I guess they must have finished drinking," said Josh. "They probably do this journey every day."

"I want to get a proper view of them," said Brandon.

"How are you going to do that," said Grace.

"Simple," said Brandon, "I'm going to stand on top of the shuttle. Who wants to come with me?"

"What?" said Grace.

"I do," said Dan.

"No," said Grace.

"Why are you always saying 'no' to things? I want to see the hoppers."

"I only say no when it's a crazy idea," said Grace.

"I'll come with you," said Chi, looking at Brandon.

"Okay, if you want to," said Brandon.

"I don't think they'll climb onto the shuttle on the way back up," said Josh. "It looks like they are herbivores or insect eaters, so we should be okay."

"I'm going to watch them too," said Dan, looking at Grace. "You aren't the boss of me."

"What is the matter with you people?" said Grace, feeling like a lone voice standing against an outbreak of boyish stupidity. "Okay, whatever, let's all watch these things walk past, but we stay together."

"Don't worry, Grace," said Brandon, waving one of his spears, "we can take these in case the hoppers mistake us for a bunch of tasty insects."

THEY CLOSED the shuttle door and walked up the incline to where the nose of the craft had buried itself into the grassy hillside. From there, they scrambled onto the shuttle roof, which was about four metres off the ground.

"Here they come," said Grace.

The hoppers made their way back up the hill, stopping occasionally to look around; sometimes one of them would stop to sniff the air, or to dig at something on the ground. They seemed unbothered by the several tons of metal in their path.

Grace was staring at the face of one of them when Dan pulled at her arm and pointed upwards.

"Look, there are those bird things we saw earlier."

She glanced up into the sky where, far above them, three creatures were gliding in a broad arc, sailing on the warm air currents rising from the valley.

"They are big," said Josh, looking up at them.

"They're just birds, aren't they?" said Dan.

"I don't know," said Josh, "look at the shape of them, those wings are quite thin and jointed, and their heads don't look quite right."

"Weird," said Dan.

"Well, this isn't Earth," said Brandon, "and for the record, we're the aliens here."

"True," said Josh, "but they really are big. I'd guess they've got a wingspan of ten metres or more."

"They're circling down," said Grace. "We should get back in the shuttle."

As she spoke, several of the hoppers stopped moving and raised themselves up as high as they could go. Grace could see their noses twitching and their funnel ears swivelling on their heads.

"Something's spooked them," said Brandon.

"There's something in the woods," said Dan, "over there."

As he pointed east to the treeline, there was a crackle in the undergrowth, and then three shapes broke cover, running at them.

They were fast, leaping across the terrain, covering five or six metres with each stride.

They looked like big cats, only with stretched limbs similar to the back legs of the hoppers. They had golden fur, and as they approached, Grace could see the glint of long white fangs, giving them the look of sabre-toothed tigers. The predators ran at the hopper pack with a ferocious pace, scattering the little creatures, who bounded away in all directions.

As they reached the remains of the pack, each sabre-tooth took one hopper in their powerful jaws.

Terrified, two of the creatures ran up the incline and then, in their panic, doubled back and jumped onto the top of the shuttle. One sabre-tooth saw them and then glared at the survivors. It bounded up the hill and leapt onto the shuttle roof. The hoppers leapt off the side of the shuttle, but the big cat ignored them; it had seen the survivors now. It took a pace towards them and let out a throaty growl. Its two companions paused and looked up.

"This is not good," said Brandon.

"Not good?" said Grace; "we need to get off this thing, now!"

She was furious with herself for letting these idiot boys talk her into this situation and putting Dan at risk.

They edged back towards the end of the shuttle roof, and Josh looked behind them at the four-metre drop to the shuttle door.

"One of us could hold them off," he said, "and give the others a chance to get back in the shuttle."

"Are you crazy?" said Grace, staring at Josh, "just jump."

"Those things will only come after us. Someone has to give the others a chance to get inside."

Josh looked at her and then at Dan.

"Go," he said, "get in the shuttle, and shut the door. You can open it for me when I've dealt with these."

None of the rest of them moved. Then the lead predator stepped forward again, keeping its fierce orange eyes fixed on them. The other two moved to keep up with it.

"Okay," said Chi, "come on, we've got move!"

He jumped from the edge of the shuttle roof and landed lightly on his feet. Then he turned around to look up at them.

"Come on," he said, and stepped up to the shuttle door, pushing it open.

Grace and Dan moved to the edge of the drop, but Brandon stepped back and stood next to Josh.

"What are you doing?" said Josh.

"Grace doesn't need looking after as much as you do," said Brandon, "and I'm not going to let you get all the glory."

"You really think you're the man, don't you?" said Josh, smiling and shaking his head.

"Of course I do."

"Well, let's both be heroes, and hope we live to tell the tale."

They heard Grace's voice behind them: "Be careful!"

"We'll do our best," said Brandon, and winked at her.

Grace nodded, and then she turned back to Dan.

"Jump," she said, staring over the edge of the shuttle roof. "Roll when you land and then get on your feet."

"It's a long way," said Dan.

"Just get on with it!" said Grace.

She was about to push him when he jumped, and Grace followed him. She landed and tumbled over onto her back; the wind knocked out of her. When she got to her feet, Dan was standing next to her.

Then she heard Chi's voice. She turned to see him standing just inside the door of the shuttle.

Neither Grace nor Dan looked back up to the roof as they scrambled to the safety of the shuttle.

Josh and Brandon stood, spears ready, as all three of the big cats moved towards them. The lead one was the largest, two metres high at the shoulder. Its mouth opened, showing sharp and jagged teeth, and a low menacing growl made the boys' skin crawl.

Josh watched the creature lean forward as it stared at them, muscles bunching under its sleek golden fur. It cast a glance either side at the others in its pack.

"So, what exactly is the plan here?" said Brandon.

"Do whatever is necessary," said Josh.

"That's it? That's the plan?"

"You wanted the glory, here's where you earn it. At least if you survive this, you will have something to brag about."

High above, there was a raucous cry. Josh glanced up to see that the three birds they'd noticed earlier had glided down and were now circling just above them. Only now could he see how big they really were. The cats glanced up at them and fidgeted.

"Great," said Brandon, "now there's something else queuing up to eat us. This gets better and better."

Twenty metres away, the lead predator backed up a little and lowered itself into a crouch.

"It's going to jump us," said Brandon.

"God preserve us," whispered Josh, and held the spear steady in his right arm.

The big cat pulled itself back and tensed, and Josh leaned forward, the end of the spear braced against the surface of the shuttle beneath his feet.

He watched as the sabre-tooth flicked its gaze upwards again; it hunched down even lower, its ears flattened against its head. A shadow came over Brandon from behind. He felt a wave of warm air blow over him, then something crashed onto the shuttle in front of him, rocking the entire structure. A scaled monster, Josh couldn't think of a better word to describe it, now occupied the space between him and the sabre-tooth, its talons digging into the metal of the shuttle roof.

Beside him, Josh heard Brandon let out a stream of extravagant curses.

The creature steadied itself, stretching its wings beyond each side of the craft, then shook itself, and drew its wings back in with a leathery hiss. Talons on its wing joints clamped onto the shuttle. The monster dropped its gaping beak towards the lead sabre-tooth and lunged towards it. The other cats fled, bounding off each side of the shuttle, while their leader let out a growl of protest, backed away slowly, and then turned and ran.

"We've got to jump," said Brandon, edging backwards, "now."

"Wait," said Josh.

"Are you mad? That thing could swallow you whole."

"No, it will be okay."

While he was speaking, the monster rocked itself from one side to another, shaking the shuttle beneath it as it did. It detached its claws and turned itself around to face them.

Only now could Josh see the bright purple crest of bone running along its head. The fathomless inky black eyes stared at him. Once it had turned, it settled itself and looked calmly down at them both.

Beside him, Josh could hear Brandon swearing under his breath. "It's like some kind of dinosaur. One of those pterosaur things."

The monster continued to stare down, its vast beaked head hovering above them.

Josh slowly laid down the spear.

"What are you doing?" squeaked Brandon.

"It's okay," said Josh, although he thought he was about to die.

He looked up into the eyes of the monster and bowed, slowly and low.

The beast turned its head slightly and then bowed so that its beak hit the surface of the shuttle with a dull *thunk*. The two of them stood motionless for a few seconds, which seemed like hours, human and monster facing each other. A blast of air shot at the boys as it raised its huge head, unfurled its wings, and beat them violently together.

After a few seconds, the talons came free; the shuttle jolted again, and the beast rose into the air, rising above them. As it did so, its compatriots dived and circled. Then all three of them glided around in one more circuit before they flew off south, over the valley, rising into the air and off into the distance.

Josh watched them disappear off towards the blue horizon, and then he winced slightly as Brandon slapped him on his injured shoulder.

"You were right," he said.

"I told you they wouldn't hurt us."

"No, not that," said Brandon, picking up Josh's spear, "I meant about the bragging rights. I'll be able to talk about this for years." With that, he jumped off the end of the shuttle onto the ground.

"We could have walked back along the shuttle and got off that way," said Josh, but Brandon was already calling to Grace and Chi, telling them to pull the shuttle door open.

"Never mind," said Josh to himself, "you have your moment of glory." He walked back along the shuttle, staring at the gouge marks the pterosaur had left in the roof.

9

Callum Mortis watched the gurney carrying his son's body trundle towards the cryohall exit. The wheels hit a bump as Ray pushed it into the corridor, and one of Owen's arms flopped over the side so that a dead finger pointed casually at the floor. Ray continued for a couple more metres before he stopped, stepped forward, and tucked the arm back under one of the restraining straps. Then he turned back and nodded, and Mortis returned a curt nod in response. Ray reached the doors of the cryohall, pushed one of them open and eased the trolley over the edge of the doorway. Mortis watched as the door closed behind them with a *clunk* that echoed across the hall.

When he was finally alone, Mortis walked down to the changing area, through the doors, and then into one of the shower cubicles. He turned the control full on, stripped, and stepped in, listening to the roar of the water as it drummed on the walls and floor of the cubicle.

Satisfied that he was completely out of earshot, he took two deep breaths and let his love for his dear son overwhelm him. Owen had been the only person he had ever loved, his boy, his beloved boy, whom he had fought to protect and prepare for this mission, the only person he had really come here for.

But Owen had turned on him, and if Mortis was honest, he did not blame his son for hating him; he didn't blame him at all. Callum Mortis was who he was. He manipulated and bullied and, finally, killed to get his way. Mortis had always been like this and he knew he always would be. He'd thought himself airtight, sealed against the weaknesses and follies of morality and love, and then his little boy had arrived and all that had changed.

He'd had to discipline the boy to toughen him up, of course, and make him a man in his own image. Now he realised how close he'd been to achieving his goal. Owen had led his team and got the ship all the way to Zera. After that achievement, he had confronted his father, demanding the truth; it was, in Callum Mortis's estimation, the finest moment of his son's life.

And now the realisation gradually came to him, if he had confessed his part in his wife's death to Owen, his son might have let him live, may have even forgiven him. Callum Mortis considered forgiveness to be a weakness, but now he wondered whether it was part of Owen's strength. The boy had wanted that which Callum despised: love, love from his mother and his father. Callum Mortis had spent all this time thinking Owen was fatally flawed, but in fact he possessed the one thing that represented the best of humanity: the capacity to overcome anger and hatred with love and forgiveness.

The old man hung his head, the water hammering down on the top of his skull, and he realised that, up until the end, all the boy had wanted was love, forgiveness, and reconciliation.

But that was not Callum Mortis's way. He wished it had been now more than ever. He wished the kinder, loving, and who knows, stronger way had opened up for him, that he believed in it. But he didn't believe it. He never had. Not when he'd been working to feed all those hungry siblings of his. Not when he'd been fighting his way up to the top of the pile. And not now, when he was on the threshold of being the king of a world.

He sighed and then stood up straight. The shower had hidden genuine tears for the child he loved. He felt the pain of losing his boy, but he could not change who he was. He'd chosen another path, and he was never going back.

He turned off the shower, dried and dressed himself, as the hard purpose in him returned. He thrust his own love for Owen down deep in his heart and sealed it off. His mind turned to the work that needed to be done. First, he had to deal with the crew. He was their leader now, and it was time to remake this group in his own image.

He walked to the monorail. After some confusion about how to make the thing work, the car jerked into life and carried him along the length of the ship to the bow where the Transit Team had lived and worked for the entire journey. He assumed they were probably asleep after a hard shift ejecting bodies into the void.

There were male and female quarters for the Transit team. He wondered if Amelia now had the female space to herself. If his memory served him, she should be the only woman awake on the ship from amongst his team. There were a handful of his people still asleep in the transit team's pod room, these were the workers and surrogate parents who would bring up the colony's babies, his babies.

"Sleep your dreamless sleep for now," he said as he passed the transit team's own cryoroom. "I will wake you when I need you."

He walked on towards the accommodation section and listened outside the female quarter. Then he pushed on the handle, opened the door and looked in.

The room was dark, but with his adaptive lenses, he could make out four single beds, two now pushed together. A person lay on one of the joined beds.

Of course, he thought, *Owen and Amelia have made their nest here.*

He sniffed the air and then walked in, closing the door behind him.

"Owen?" Amelia turned over and stared into the gloom.

"I'm afraid not."

She jerked up at the sound of his voice, and he could see her eyes widen, peering at him through the gloom.

"Who is that?"

"You know who it is," said Mortis, sitting down on the corner of the bed.

"Mr Mortis," she sat up and pulling the covers over herself.

"Yes, Amelia, that's right. I'm sorry to barge in on you like this, but there's been an incident."

"What? What's happened?"

"Something terrible, I'm afraid. This evening, Owen came down to the cryohall to revive me, but after he'd woken me up," he paused here for effect, "after he'd woken me, he attacked me while I was still in my pod."

Mortis was gratified to see her eyes widen at all this talk of violence. He was sure it was pretence, but he enjoyed watching the act.

"Yes, shocking, isn't it? My son, attacking me while I was in a vulnerable state. Fortunately, Ray was there to defend me."

He waited for her to say something, but she stayed silent.

"Now, I know you and Owen were close before we left, and it looks as if you are even closer now." he glanced at the two beds pushed together, "but I'm afraid I have to tell you that Owen is dead."

Amelia let out a slight whimper, she stared at him, and he saw a mixture of shock and hatred in her eyes.

"There was a struggle," he said, "between Ray and Owen, and unfortunately Owen died."

"How..."

He lifted a hand to silence her.

"I don't know all the details. It was dark, it all happened so quickly, and I was still groggy from the effects of cryo sleep." He paused and placed a hand lightly on the blanket, just beside her. "I am sorry to be the one to tell you this."

"So, where is he now?"

"Who, Ray?"

"No, Owen, where is his body?"

"I imagine it's being ejected into Zera's gravity well as we speak. You, of all people, should know the protocol, I understand you've been following it yourself for the past couple of days."

She moved one leg slightly, pulling it towards her.

"But now we have to make the best of things as they are," said Mortis, leaning in towards her. "Speaking of which, I understand that some colonists escaped."

"Yes, they have gone down to the planet."

"That's unfortunate, but don't worry, we can redeem the situation. I am taking charge now. With help from Ray, Patrick, and you, I will resolve this problem. But I need your support."

He looked at her, clutching the bedclothes to herself.

"Do I have it?"

"Yes," she said, without hesitation, "you have my support."

"Are you sure?" he moved towards her so she could smell his breath.

She swallowed and then looked him in the eye.

"You're in charge now," she said, "you always were."

He smiled and moved a hand up to pat her knee with his thick fingers.

"Thank you, that means a lot."

Then he stood, turned and walked out of the room, shutting the door behind him.

When the door closed, Amelia counted a full sixty seconds before she threw off the bedclothes and ran into the restroom that adjoined the quarters. She pulled the partition door shut and turned on the shower to its maximum setting. The steady stream of lukewarm water was enough to hide the noise of her cries as she let out the grief and anger that welled up from within her.

———

AT NINE HUNDRED hours ship time, the Transit Team assembled in the mess room. Patrick, Amelia, and Goran slumped into their seats. Only Ray sat up straight, and only Ray showed no reaction when Callum Mortis walked into the room.

Mortis looked at them, the familiar sense of disappointment washing over him.

Goran and Patrick were surprised to see him, although Patrick seemed more enthusiastic about this development than the doctor. Mortis watched Goran for a moment, fidgeting in his chair, glancing at his colleagues, fiddling with a button on the grubby lab coat he was wearing.

Pathetic, thought Mortis, and then he put on a smile and stepped towards them.

"Good morning, all of you," he said and sat at the head of the table where Owen had been just hours before. "Now I know you didn't expect to see me without Owen at my side, and I am afraid I come to you in sad circumstances." He let out a big sigh, and they stared at him in silence.

"There is no easy way to say this. Last night Owen attacked me, shortly after waking me from my sleep. Fortunately, Ray was there to defend me, but Owen did not survive the incident."

Patrick nodded and twisted his neck until one of the bones cracked. "That's too bad."

"We've ejected the body from the ship," said Mortis, "as per the standing orders of the *Aspira*. We can't allow contamination on the ship."

"Hygiene rules," said Patrick.

"Indeed, but we have unfinished business before us. We have to sort out this minor issue that seems to have occurred whilst I was sleeping."

"I have already..." began Goran.

Mortis raised a hand. "Now, now, there's no need for you to explain, Dr Maric, no need at all." He inclined his head and smiled at the doctor.

"Ray," said Mortis, "how near are we to being able to board a shuttle and go down to our new planet?"

"We need to pack a couple more items of equipment, and I want to make sure the shuttle's got enough fuel for a return trip."

"So, when can we leave?"

"In about an hour."

"Make sure we are ready by then," said Mortis.

"Yes, sir."

"Right, we'll waste no more time." He turned to Goran.

"Doctor, this will be the first time we leave the colony embryos unmonitored. I want you to run a full diagnostic check on them, make sure they are all in tip-top condition. If any are showing signs of weakness or irregularity, just discard them, do you understand?"

"I..." Maric hesitated for a moment and then said, "yes, Mr Mortis."

"Excellent. Now, Amelia, do we know where the escaped children landed?"

"I'm assuming they'll have set down in the designated LZ, but if they haven't, their shuttle will have a tracking device. We'll find them."

"I see. Well, perhaps while Dr Maric is making his checks on the embryos, the rest of us can make final preparations for the journey down. We will leave in one hour.

GORAN MARIC CHECKED the straps of the protective goggles one last time. When he was satisfied, he pulled open the door of the freezer, reached in with a gloved hand and drew out a silver metal canister. He placed it carefully on the steel table in front of him and then slowly unscrewed the lid.

"So, my babies," he muttered, "how are you today?"

Liquid nitrogen bubbled and smoked into the air around him as he took a long pair of tweezers and lifted a narrow container out of the freezing mist. He stared at the glass tube. "You will all grow up to be fine colonists."

"Well, I hope you are right, doctor, I really do."

The voice made Goran jump, and he nearly dropped the narrow tube. He turned, still holding the tweezers. Callum Mortis was standing behind him.

"Mr Mortis. I'm sorry, I didn't hear you come into the room."

"I'm sure you were very busy," said Mortis, "absorbed in your work. So, how are they?"

"They look good, I'm sure they'll all be fine while we are away."

"I seem to remember you were sure that none of the colonists would survive your RNA toxin," said Mortis, "but five of them escaped from us."

"Patrick and Amelia let them slip through their fingers. I do not believe that the virus was at fault."

Mortis stared at him for a moment.

"We are all sorry for this oversight, Mr Mortis," he added.

"Apology accepted."

"I should get on with my work," said Goran finally. "I don't want to make another mistake."

"Don't worry, doctor, you won't," said Mortis. He smiled and patted Goran's shoulder. "We'll find these escapees and kill them. But these," he nodded at the tube in Goran's hand, "these are the children I am really interested in."

"I will check each of them personally," said Goran. "We will only bring the best specimens to term in the on-board uterus."

"My colonists," said Mortis and smiled. He watched as Goran

slid the narrow tube back into its liquid nitrogen and carefully screwed the lid onto the canister.

"You've done some good work here," said Mortis. "I am sure you'll be remembered for it."

"Thank you, Mr Mortis." He slid the canister back onto its shelf and closed the freezer. He turned back to Mortis, but as he did so, he felt a hot sting on his right arm. He looked at his arm, and then at Mortis.

"What is this?" he said. "What have you done?"

"It's not just your incompetence with the virus," said Mortis, holding out the syringe, "it's that we don't really need you anymore. You have done your part for the program, and we are very grateful, but we no longer require your services."

The doctor stared at Mortis and swayed a little.

"Goodbye, Dr Maric. I'm sure Amelia can look after everything from here."

"But my work," said Goran. "I..."

Mortis watched with mild satisfaction as the doctor's eyes flickered, and then he slumped to the floor.

Once the body was motionless, Mortis took a comm unit from his pocket.

"Ray, yes, you can come down now, we'll dispatch the good doctor, and then we can focus our attention on these escaped children."

"I HAVE A SHIP TO BUILD."

Dr Sergei Federov's Alpha Contact Facility
2060 CE

The limo glided through the shimmering air and eased into the parking bay reserved for the sponsors of the Alpha Contact project. Paparazzi clustered around it like flies around roadkill, camera flashes trying to penetrate the tinted windows. A connoisseur of performance vehicles would have seen the quality straight away, holistic sensors, intelligent environment integration, and that ultimate symbol of luxury, a human being could still drive it. For the paparazzi, it was almost worth taking a picture of the car as well as any occupants.

There was, in fact, only one person in the car, and he took a deep breath of the cool quiet air before speaking into his comm implant.

"I'm in place, Mr Mortis."

"Wait there, Ray, I'll let you know when I need you."

"Yes, sir." The driver glanced through the tinted glass, eased the seat back just a few degrees, and gestured to raise the volume on the audio system by one increment.

At that same moment, a red SUV pulled up at the door of the south service entrance for the complex. Callum Mortis turned up the collar of his overcoat, adjusted his aviator sunglasses and got out of the driver's seat.

He strode towards the unattended service door, but before he could handprint the DNA lock, his comm told him he had an incoming call. He checked the ID and sighed, then he accepted the call.

"Callum?" The voice was clear in his head.

"Senator Noonan," said Mortis, "where are you?"

"About a mile off," said the voice in his ear, "still crawling along the main drag."

"Well, you need to get yourself here, assuming you want to be here when the party starts. Be where the success is, Senator." Mortis placed his hand on an ID pad and the service bay door rumbled open.

"What are you, my campaign manager?" said Noonan. "Seriously, my diary's gone all to hell today; I had the President on the line first thing this morning."

"Oh, what did she want?"

"Trying to nudge me into voting for the Energy Unification bill; you know, the usual horse trading. So, are they going to announce a new name for the planet today?"

"Yes. Apparently they're calling it 'Zera'; it means dawn or seed, something like that." He stepped into the service bay entrance and slapped the close button.

"Well, give my apologies to Federov," said the senator. "I'll be there as soon as I can."

"Of course, and don't worry, it's all good news. These pictures will be a sensation."

"I hope you're right. I stuck my neck out arguing for public money on this project; if it all turns out to be all desert and rocks, the voters will have my guts on a stick."

"Marcus, we've all taken a risk here. The private funding has dwarfed anything from the government, but we've spent our money wisely. Just make it here for the press conference afterwards, then you can show me how to really work a crowd."

"Now that I can do, Callum; I'll catch up with you soon."

Mortis switched the comm off and marched down the corridor. This section of the complex was all strip lights and concrete, but as he approached the auditorium, both the lighting and the flooring became softer. The first checkpoint team recognised him and just waved him through. They should have asked for his ID, but walking through the gate without even breaking his stride gave Mortis such a surge of satisfaction that he decided not to have them disciplined.

He passed through two more security checks and then into the auditorium.

The dignitaries had gathered on a viewing platform while the scientists and technicians huddled in small groups on the floor in front of them. Mortis worked his way onto the platform, shaking hands and assuring anyone who asked that the senator would be there in a matter of minutes.

The crowd settled, and with a nod from Mortis, the now elderly Dr Federov, looking tearful, stepped up in front of the technicians and surveyed the room. This was the fulfilment of decades of work, and Mortis knew it was right to give the old man his due.

"Ladies and gentlemen, welcome." His voice was weak, but was amplified to fill the space. "I bid you a warm welcome to the Alpha Contact headquarters. I can confirm that we have now received the first stream of data from the probes sent to investigate the new planet, and edited transmissions of that data, comprising images and film, will begin shortly. Thank you."

As Federov stopped speaking, the screen filled with the sky blue and emerald of the Project logo. The lights dimmed, and the logo disappeared, replaced by a fog of grey static. They all stared at the nothingness. The only noise was the creak of the platform floor and one or two whispered comments.

Seconds passed, and nothing happened. Someone cleared their throat and then, just as Mortis was beginning to feel a prickling sensation on the back of his neck, the screen went black and a sphere of blue light appeared in front of them.

It was both alien and familiar, another Earth, fashioned with the same materials but to a different design. Then another image appeared, the same blue globe but this time with a scatter of land across its surface: a continent shaped like a stretched triangle, with a flat base near the southern pole, and the northern tip tapering off towards the equator.

The image switched again, this time to a view of the edge of the planet, backlit by the orange of Zera's star, Alpha Centauri 'B'. Beneath the protective glow of the atmosphere, a skein of cloud stretched over a vast ocean.

"Ladies and gentlemen," said Federov, his voice quavering, "I present to you, the planet Zera."

There were gasps of amazement across the auditorium, and those closest to him patted Federov on the back. Mortis squinted at the picture.

I hope they show the one with that river running through the jungle; he thought to himself.

Another image appeared on the screen; this time much closer to Zera's surface. Now they saw a great expanse of dark green and purple vegetation, cut through by a bright ribbon of water that opened out into an estuary.

People were talking, commenting on what they were seeing, marvelling at the colours of the new world. The images cycled more quickly now, pictures from different probes that were taken as they fell into orbit around Zera, or broke through to land on the planet itself.

There were tall spindly trees, their tops scattered with purple and ebony leaves, reaching up into the mellow light of the sky. A caramel coloured desert, its sands rippled by a Zeran breeze, the spray of a wave crashing against a black, jagged shoreline.

Mortis stared at it all, feeling the old hunger rising in him. He was so absorbed with his own desire he jumped when someone touched his shoulder, and a breathless Senator Noonan eased in next to him.

"Did I miss much?"

"Just the panoramic shots," said Mortis.

Noonan stared at the screen, "you're right, they do look good."

"You really can own this project now, senator," said Mortis.

They both stared at the stream of images, at once familiar and alien, beamed back from over forty trillion kilometres away.

"Well," said Noonan, "you're right. We can call this a government project now. Time for me to collect my dividend." He looked around at the faces reflected in the light, caught in wonder.

"Game on," he whispered in Mortis's ear, then he took a few paces forward to the front of the platform and turned slightly so he could address the VIPs without wholly turning his back on the project staff.

"My friends, what a sight, what a sight!" Noonan's face beamed with joy and his voice carried loud and clear across the room.

"I would like to extend the warmest congratulations to Dr Federov and his team, a wonderful achievement from all of you."

The images cycled round again, and the room broke up into smaller groups, pointing at the screen and talking to each other.

There were murmurs of agreement, and then the senator clapped. One or two others joined in, and soon the whole auditorium was filled with rapturous applause. The senator smiled, waved and stepped back to his place next to Mortis.

"That's your next term of office, senator," said Mortis, leaning in towards the senator, "and who knows where you might go from there?"

"All the way, my friend, all the way."

"Just remember who your friends are when you get there," said

Mortis, and with that he eased away and walked towards the platform.

"Where are you going?"

"I have things to do."

"What about the press conference?"

"I'll leave that to you, they'll be eating out of your hand after this."

"Before you go, Callum, there was one thing I wanted to ask you."

Mortis raised an eyebrow.

"Now we have this new planet, why don't you help us with the research that might let us there more quickly?"

"Ah, here it is", thought Mortis, and sighed.

"And what particular research do you have in mind?" he said, his mouth twitched into a smile. "Surely you're not short of funds for that base on Mars, are you?"

"You know I'm not talking about that. We've got people falling over themselves for a piece of the action. I'm talking about something a little more speculative, more ground-breaking."

"It's the wormhole project, isn't it?"

"The Einstein-Rosen project to give it its proper name," said Noonan. "I'm telling you, Callum, it's an exciting prospect. There's been a lot of focus on the red planet, but this green and blue one," he waved at the screen, "well, if we can crack this wormhole thing, we can be there by teatime."

Mortis was about to answer when a voice over called their attention to a new set of images that were appearing on the screen above them. More of the trees, the coastline, snow-capped hills along the Western edge of a mountain range.

"And I assume," said Mortis, "that you are expecting some major breakthrough any day now, aren't you?"

Senator Noonan looked at him and smirked.

"I would like to say that cynicism doesn't suit you, Callum, but I'd be lying. I know how you feel about this, but think of the long game here. Within the next thirty or forty years, we won't be satisfied with just looking at this planet, we'll want to go there. If we can build a wormhole to it, it'll be within reach, our reach."

"It's a compelling story, Senator," said Mortis, "but tell me, how long has the government been funding this project?"

"Oh, now come on, Callum," said Noonan.

"How long?"

"Ten years, it's a slow burner."

Mortis smiled. "And in that time, you've spent, what, about fourteen billion dollars?"

"Not quite that much."

"And three trips to the Senate Committee," said Mortis, "and what are the results so far?"

"We think we've moved a particle through time-space. Isn't that fantastic?"

Mortis laughed, his booming voice lost in the room's chatter. The organisers had moved on to the video footage, with five or ten-second clips of trees and grass moving in the breeze.

"You think you've moved a particle through time-space," said Mortis.

"It's almost certain we did so. We're on the threshold of something here; in the next few weeks or months we'll confirm what we've achieved."

"You don't know what you've achieved," said Mortis, "if anything at all. I'd need a lot more than 'we may have moved a particle,' for you to get any of my money. Your engineers don't know if they've achieved a miracle or just built a very expensive piece of plumbing."

"I'm sure we are this close to it," said Noonan, holding up thumb and forefinger, "I can feel it."

"That inch you're showing me will cost who knows how many more billions. And as I recall, you used exactly the same phrase at the last budget review committee two years ago, and three years before that when you persuaded them to keep pushing money at this project."

Noonan leaned in towards Mortis, keeping one eye on the crowd.

"Look, Callum, I'll be honest with you, they'll shut the whole thing down in three months' time if we can't get any more private money. My colleagues have run out of patience. Surely you see how this fits with any ambitions we have for Zera."

"I'm sorry, Marcus," said Mortis, "but I already have a mistress in the form of the Centauri project, and like all mistresses, she is expensive. I can only afford one at a time."

The senator shook his head. "Well, at least you're getting some satisfaction from her," he said.

"And so did you," said Mortis, slapping his associate on the back. "Now cheer up! We've both done well out of today. They'll have a parade for you after this, and a few corporate sponsors will want to share in the glory. Maybe you can persuade one to stump up the billions for your wormhole."

"Believe me, the thought has crossed my mind," said Noonan. He straightened up and turned to look at the crowd. "Well, I'll see you later, I've got to work this room." And with that, he strode away.

"You do that," said Mortis as he watched Noonan prowl around, looking for hands to shake.

Mortis waited a few seconds more before he strolled to the edge of the platform, and then towards the back of the auditorium. He didn't turn as another roar of appreciation filled the room.

As he reached the doors, one of the junior staff from the investigation team offered him a flute of champagne.

"Thank you," he said, not looking at whoever had given him the glass.

He nodded at a security guard but didn't slacken his pace as he walked out into the corridor. Once outside, he quickened his stride, tossing the champagne glass into a recycling bin as he walked past it, spattering the contents onto the carpet.

Two minutes later, he'd reached the service doors and invoked the comm implant.

"Ray."

"Here, sir."

"Are you in position?"

"Just pulling up, sir."

"Any media?"

"One reporter, the boys are dealing with it."

"I'm coming out now."

Mortis touched the exit pad, pushed hard against the slowly opening door and stepped back out into the brilliant sunshine.

He ignored the SUV and watched as the limousine stopped just beside him. The rear door opened with a small snick. Mortis eased himself into the seat, and the door closed. Ray let off the brake, and the limo glided away, picking up speed as it made its way towards the south perimeter gate of the complex.

Mortis made himself comfortable, flicked a switch to smoke the partition glass separating himself from his driver, and pulled a handheld tablet from his pocket. The screen flicked onto one of the news channels. They were showing the pictures of Zera, a voiceover giving a commentary on each image. The news stream shifted to the auditorium, where Senator Noonan was shaking hands with everyone and smiling.

Mortis permitted himself a wry chuckle.

"No wonder you keep getting elected," he said, "but if you think I'm going to fund your fake wormhole, you're more naïve than I imagined."

He muted the voiceover and stared at the images. The only sound around him now was the gentle purr of the limo's electric engine, and the slight creak of his leather seat. He cycled through the pictures and then looked out of the window. They were already accelerating away towards the ring road. He was just reaching into the fridge when a call icon flashed onto the screen.

"Ah..."

He opened a separate link to see a lean-faced man with sharp features and black, sweptback hair appear in front of him.

"How did it go?" said Owen Mortis.

"They loved it." Mortis reached for a bottle of chilled water.

"I assume this is it. We'll throw everything at getting to Zera."

"We've been going to Zera ever since Dr North's team confirmed the planet as Earth 2.0."

"Interesting that we saw no fauna in the images or film, I'd have expected there to be some forms of animal life."

"You've only seen the publicity images," said Mortis.

"There's more?"

"Come on, Owen," said Mortis, "you know we wouldn't show the public everything. I'm inviting a few of the trusted sponsors over to the villa this evening to view some of the unedited material. They'll be seeing more than waves crashing on the shoreline and a few spindly trees."

"Nothing intelligent, though."

"No, thank goodness. The images confirm the conventional wisdom: yes, there is extra-terrestrial life in our galaxy; but no, it is not intelligent."

"Good," said Owen. "I could come up to the villa for the viewing."

"You don't need to be there," said Mortis. "Just concentrate on your part in this. We need a ship to get us there. If I get a chance, I'll get someone to send you the material. In the meantime, build me my ship."

"Don't worry, you'll get your ship on budget and on time."

"Good."

"So, what about the colonists?" said Owen. "Will we have a role in the selection process?"

"Probably, but as long as I have my berth, I don't care who else qualifies. I'll leave that to the government sponsors, it will help them believe they are running this thing. What we need now are the best people to build the ship, and the right team to crew her on the journey."

"Some of the people on our wish list are proving resistant," said Owen.

"Fools. This is such an opportunity."

"Some of them have families, commitments here on Earth."

Mortis sneered at the words. "These people have no sense of history. This will be the project of their lifetimes; they should be begging us to let them play a part in this."

"Take it easy, Father," said Owen, raising an eyebrow.

"Don't patronise me, Owen, and don't worry about the personnel; we'll get our team."

"So, how's your friend Noonan? Basking in the glory, no doubt?"

"Marcus is a good friend of ours. He has put his neck on the line..."

"Noonan is a leech," interrupted Owen. "He has hung on to your coattails for the last fifteen years."

"That man is probably going to be the next president," said Mortis, "and that means he might be in office when the ship becomes ready. He will be our friend and sponsor when we need one, when you need one. Do you understand?"

Owen closed his eyes and ran a finger under the collar of his shirt.

"Frankly," said Mortis, "I sometimes wonder if you've learnt anything about the way the world really works."

"I know enough to get us to Zera."

Callum Mortis looked at his son.

"Well, if you change your mind, and want to withdraw to pursue other opportunities, then you can do that with my blessing."

"Your blessing?" said Owen. "I'm going to Zera, and I don't need your blessing to make that decision."

The link went dead before Mortis could reply. He stared at the blank screen for a second and then flicked the tablet off his lap and onto the floor. He smashed his fist into the soft leather of the seat next to him.

"Arrogant, ungrateful little…"

He knew exactly where this attitude came from. It was that same smug, knowing streak he had never trained out of the boy's mother.

He took a gulp from his water bottle and then grunted as he leaned forward to pick the tablet out of the footwell. When he was comfortable again, he flicked onto a newsfeed.

"…we are also receiving data from probes on the surface of the planet; information about Zera's landmasses, water, even some of the bacteria that might live there. The success of the Alpha Contact project will ignite the debate about the next inevitable challenge: sending people to the new planet. We will have to wait decades for that vision to become a reality."

"The hell with that," said Mortis as he placed a thumbprint on the screen and stared at the tablet's inbuilt retinal scan. The news channel whisked away to reveal an image, a complex schematic of a ship, roughly cylindrical with a convex shield fitted over its prow. He flicked through several screens, looking at images of various parts, being manufactured even now at facilities across the world.

"You wait decades if you want to," he whispered. "I have a ship to build."

10

AT THE EDGE of the treeline, about a hundred metres to the east of the shuttle, *Observer of Small Details* watched as the *Sky Messenger* flapped its great wings and rose into the air.

He put his shoulders back and raised himself to his full height, then breathed in the warm air and focused on the two visitors left standing on their craft.

It had fascinated him to see that one visitor; the most open of the older ones, had dropped his crude weapon and made what was probably a sign of peace to the Messenger. Of course, it had responded in kind. It was possible that this visitor had guessed that the Messenger was there to keep them safe. All of this confirmed in Observer's mind that this particular visitor was the best candidate to give an account for all of them.

He'd been pleased to see something that actually made sense to him. Almost everything these visitors from the stars had done so far had confused him. He assumed they must have some cleverness about them to come here from so far away, but their behaviour had been reckless to the point of sheer folly. First, their craft hadn't landed in a simple and graceful manner, like a bird on a branch. Rather, it had slammed into the lip of the valley, scarring the earth.

Not only that, but they'd landed near the spot where the *Companions of the Hunt* ran out from the cover of the forest to attack the *Ground Leapers* as they had done so today.

The visitors could not have picked a worse place to land their ship. Perhaps they'd had no choice about where they came down, and it was likely that they were ignorant of what they had done, but it was no wonder that three of the Companions had attacked them. He had petitioned the Sky Messengers to stay in the area and keep watch on what happened. The attack had caused no casualties amongst the visitors, but next time, they might not be so fortunate.

There were many unanswered questions in Observer's mind, but the most fundamental was: which of the twin moons inspired their intentions: Aletheia of the Light or the dark sibling, Haserak?

The twins were invisible in the light of day, but they would still be up there, circling the planet, locked in their dance of contention. Aletheia, who sought fellowship and truth, was engaged in a great combat with Haserak, the jealous and greedy sibling. Haserak, the veiled one, the one who deceives and contends in an ancient struggle which, the calculations showed, would one day resolve itself with Haserak being cast out into the void.

If the Siblings taught Observer anything, it was that the balance between them was, in fact, an illusion. There was a struggle as there always is in life, but it was not eternal. At the end of the long age, there would be a final victory. But contention always comes first, and so it was for the moon siblings as in life. Where there is light there is also darkness, and that meant that even if these visitors lived in Aletheia's light, somewhere out there was a counterbalancing force, something that would contend with them, something or someone that bowed to the dark one, to Haserak.

Unless these visitors got themselves eaten by something on the planet in their foolishness, eventually that opposing force, the contention, would manifest itself and come upon them.

11

———

"Massive wingspan," said Brandon as he chewed on one of the banana fruit. "Just massive. At least twenty metres."

"About ten metres," said Josh, "fifteen at most."

"Josh, mate, you're killing my story. Just shut up, okay?"

Brandon turned back to the others.

"Anyway," he said, "that thing was big. I mean, you've seen them in the sky, you heard it land on the shuttle roof."

"And then Josh put his spear down and bowed to it?" said Dan.

"Pretty much so, yes," said Brandon, "but that was only after it had screamed at those sabre-toothed cats and scared them off."

"What made you do that?" said Chi, looking at Josh. "Were you not scared that it would attack you?"

"Something told me I was safe. That creature had protected us from the sabre-tooth, and once it had scared them off, it flew away."

"Well, we're all lucky to be alive," said Grace. "We now know that there's at least one species on this planet that sees us as its prey."

"There will be more," said Chi.

147

"But we need to go out there again," said Brandon, "and get more fruit and water."

"Maybe those cats have gone for the day," said Dan.

"Probably, if we want to get more supplies, right now is the time to do it."

"Okay," said Grace. "We get out there, get what we need, and get back as quickly as possible."

"And another thing," said Brandon. "Did you see the meat on those hoppers? No wonder the sabre-tooths want to hunt them."

"You're not suggesting we hunt them as well, are you?" said Grace.

"I am, they could be an excellent source of food."

Grace just shook her head.

"I keep thinking about grilled hopper," said Brandon. "A piece of meat on a stick, roasted on the fire. Who's not going to love that?"

"Does anyone else think this is a bad idea?" said Grace.

"Look, if you're a vegetarian or vegan, I respect that," said Brandon, "but I need to help us all survive here."

"That's not what I meant. Haven't you learnt anything today? If we go out hunting, we'll become the prey if one of those sabre-tooth things turns up again. And maybe there won't be some enormous bird ready to drop out of the sky and save us."

"Well, tomorrow I'm going hunting," said Brandon. "Anyone who wants to join me can. For now, we'll get more fruit and water."

Grace shook her head. "Idiot," she whispered under her breath.

"No one's making you come along," said Brandon.

Grace didn't answer him. No one said any more about hunting hoppers for the rest of the day.

They made one more trip out, keeping together and taking their spears. There was no sign of the sabre-toothed cats When they returned, Zera's sun was sinking towards the western horizon.

They ate some fruit, drank a little water, and talked about how they might prepare for their human enemies. Brandon declared his hope that their pursuers would get eaten by something on the planet. No one disagreed with him.

They were now exhausted. Each of them created a bed out of shuttle seat cushions and tried to make themselves as comfortable as they could.

THE SCRATCHING CAME FIRST, light but insistent on the side of the hull, and then at the stern. Grace woke up with a jolt when something solid hit the porthole in the shuttle door.

"What now?" she blinked in the half light. "Can't this planet just leave us alone for a few hours?"

She rolled off the cushions, stood up, and made her way towards the porthole. The boys joined her as she peered into an orangey-grey dawn.

She could see figures, shapes outside. She'd just focused on one when she saw something loom towards them and a gnarled forehead smacked against the door.

"Why do half the animals on this planet think we're their food?" said Dan, joining her.

"Because," said Brandon, "we are their food, or might be if they could get at us."

"Maybe it's just curious," said Josh.

"Maybe it's giving itself a headache," said Brandon. He stared out of the window.

"Brilliant, we're being attacked by a troop of heavily armoured emus."

The creatures had crowded around the rear of the shuttle.

Grace joined Brandon and watched as one of them lowered its heavy, stubby beak, and loped towards the shuttle head-butting the door.

"Is that thing going to break in?" asked Dan.

"I doubt it," said Grace, "unless it's got a skull made of titanium alloy."

They were waiting for the next attempt on the door when they heard a thud on the roof of the shuttle, then another. Something was stomping along the hull, pecking and scratching at the skin of the craft.

"Oh, for goodness' sake," shouted Grace. "I've had enough of this."

She turned and strode down the centre of the shuttle to the pilot console.

"What are you going to do?" said Brandon.

"I will bring this ship to life and send these things scurrying back to where they came from."

She dropped into the pilot's seat and tapped the console. A spray of glyphs appeared, some green, some orange and several bright red.

She started the ignition routine; the shuttle let out a low growl, internal lighting flickered and then grew brighter.

"Wow," said Dan, staring at his sister, "are we taking off?"

"No, but we're going to give these creatures the shock of their lives."

"Interesting," said Brandon. "I want to see this."

The engines came online and the whole shuttle hummed. Outside, the creatures had gone quiet except for the occasional grunt and some pattering of feet on the ground.

Grace pulled up the menu on the pilot screen and flicked the virtual switch to turn on as many of the shuttle's external lights as possible.

"See how you like this," she whispered and eased up the engine power.

The plasma engines fired, and light flickered around the porthole. The shuttle jolted as its nose burrowed further into the mud.

Outside, the creatures shrieked, then there were two or three thumps on the ground and scampering noises as they ran back down the gulley and towards the river.

"And stay away," shouted Brandon through the porthole at the retreating creatures.

"Good job," said Josh as Grace re-joined them. They listened to their own breathing, waiting for the silence outside to return.

But the silence didn't return. Instead, the forest was alive with hoots and squawks. Maybe their engine had woken everything up, maybe it was just the dawn chorus. Either way, they had company; something was making its presence known.

"Hey," said Brandon, "maybe we should check the solar still, we might have some actual water this morning."

He spun the wheel lock and pulled the door open, letting the chilly dawn breeze blow in.

The still was untouched and even provided some clean water to complement their breakfast.

When all that remained of the fruit was rind and peel, Brandon retrieved the binoculars from the survival pack and climbed back onto the roof of the shuttle. Josh joined him and they looked out across the valley. The sun was shining just below the treeline, changing the sky from violet to deep blue.

"That's interesting," said Brandon, and he passed the binoculars to Josh.

Out to the west, the hoppers from the day before were on the move, making their way down to the lake.

"They have chosen a different route this morning," said Chi.

"I don't blame them," said Brandon, "but I still want to hunt one of those things."

"What about preparing for the Transit Team?" said Josh. "When are we going to do that?"

"We hunt this morning," said Brandon, "then we eat, then we prepare for the Transit Team."

"You know how hard this shuttle will be to defend when the enemy comes, don't you?" said Josh, passing the binoculars back to

Brandon. "We don't know where they'll come from, or when. We might end up trapped in here."

"You're beginning to sound like Chi," said Brandon. "In case you hadn't noticed, something has attacked us twice now. If we leave the shuttle, we'll just get picked off out there by something."

"I still think we might need to run," said Josh.

"Where would we go?"

"To the landing zone, as Chi suggested. We wait for these Transit Team to land and then try to take their shuttle."

"I don't know," said Brandon. "Maybe we'll do that at some point, but for now this thing," he stomped on the roof of the shuttle, "is our defence and our shelter. So, we stay, okay?"

He put the binoculars around his neck, and then he let out a long sigh.

"You okay?" said Josh.

"A little achy this morning," said Brandon. "Not surprising after yesterday's fun." He searched out the spear he'd used the day before and inspected its point.

"I'm going hunting," he said, turning to the others, "does anyone want to join me?" He turned to Josh. "What about you, is hunting your thing?"

"I'll come with you," said Josh.

"I want to go hunting," said Dan.

"No way," said Grace, "absolutely not."

"I need to go."

"You *need* to go?" said Grace.

"Yes," said Dan, "you know what I mean Grace, I *need* to go."

Grace did know what he meant. Dan had always had a sense of things. He was just her stupid kid brother, but when he said he needed to do something, there was usually a good reason.

"I don't know, Dan," she said. "This place scares me."

He looked at her. She saw the longing in his eyes and knew she had to let him go. If she didn't do it now, she would have to one day soon.

"Let him be a man for once," said Brandon. "Get yourself a spear, junior, and one for your sister if she wants to come with us."

"No," said Grace, "thanks all the same."

She turned to Josh.

"You go, and look after him for me."

"I'll do my best."

"Try to find some kindling for a fire while we're gone," said Brandon to Grace. "Whatever we catch, we're going to have to cook it."

"I'll stay here," said Chi, "if that's okay with you, Grace."

"Sure," she said.

Brandon picked up his spear, his binoculars, and his knife and headed for the door. Dan and Josh set off after him, and once they were outside they heading south towards the slope of the valley and the brown smudge of the hopper herd making its way towards the edge of the lake.

The sun seemed to hover above them as they walked down to the valley floor. The surrounding air was thick and heavy. They headed towards the river and down to the herd.

"The wind's against us," said Brandon. "That's good. If these things get a smell of us, they might just scatter."

"Do we spread out or stick together?" said Dan.

"Stick together. We keep in cover and we get in close, then when we are within throwing distance, we use the spears and all go for the same one."

They made their way along the ground, trying to keep to cover amongst the rocks and the tall spindly grass.

"None of those pterosaur things are flying around today," said Brandon.

"Not that I can see," said Josh, staring up into the sky.

They crept towards the lake, crouching low in the grass. Ahead of them the hoppers snuffled at the water's edge, drinking and nosing around in the mud at the lake shore.

Large boulders poked out of the valley floor. Brandon moved from one to the next as they crept towards the herd.

Two hoppers had broken off from the main group and were drinking at the shore of the river, which was now sluggish and shallow as it fed into the lake. There was a large outcrop of rock about ten or fifteen metres from the pair.

"One of those two?" said Josh.

"Yep," said Brandon.

"They're big," said Josh.

"Good," said Brandon, "more meat for all of us."

Dan followed the two older boys towards the cover of the outcrop, but he froze just before they reached it.

"Did you hear that?" he said.

"Quiet," said Brandon. "Get behind this rock."

They crouched behind the rock, the creatures seemingly oblivious to their presence.

"I heard something," whispered Dan. "I did. Over there beyond the hoppers."

One hundred metres away, at the edge of the hillside, the scrubland was thicker and dotted with tall thin trees.

Observer lay flat on the ground in cover, watching the visitors as they stared back in his direction. He glanced at the boys for a moment, confident they could not see him, then his eyes darted to his left. He only just resisted the desire to move.

"Oh no," he said. "Why do these visitors attract so much trouble?" He took a deep breath and lay perfectly still.

Back at the rock, Brandon squinted into the undergrowth.

"There's nothing there," said Brandon. "Come on, focus on the job."

In the main herd, there was some commotion. One of the hoppers they'd been watching looked up, peered around, and then leaned down again to drink.

"Okay, this is it," whispered Brandon. "We move up to either side of the rock and aim for the smaller one on the left. It will be closer to us. If we get one good hit, we should be able to finish it." He tapped at the knife on his belt.

Josh nodded and gripped the spear in his right hand. Dan fidgeted and looked up at the sky, but Brandon slid closer to the edge of the outcrop, inching his way towards the two hoppers. He was ready to move when he felt Dan's hand on his arm.

"What the hell are you doing?" hissed Brandon.

"There is something there," said Dan, "something dangerous."

Out on the plains, the herd had gone silent. Some turquoise-feathered birds launched out from the trees on the far shore and flew over the lake.

"Shut up," said Brandon, pulling his arm away. He drew back the spear, weighing it in his hand.

Dan pulled at Josh's arm.

"Stop him," he said, "there is something there."

Josh looked at the sheer terror on Dan's face.

"Wait," said Josh.

"Not you as well," whispered Brandon.

"Listen," Josh nodded at Dan. "He has spotted everything that might come after us so far, *everything*. Let's just give it a moment."

Brandon sighed, wishing he'd left both of them back at the shuttle.

"How are we ever going to catch anything," he said, "with you two fidgeting like a couple of..."

His next words were lost, submerged in a shrill scream that echoed up the valley. The lake erupted into a roar as the entire herd took off from the shoreline, thrashing at the water as they went.

The boys flattened themselves against the stone and froze. On the far side of the rock here was a sharp crack, like the shattering of a stick. Just at the edge of their view, a bright red spray flicked across the mud.

Dan shivered; he could hear a moan escape from his mouth, and felt an arm come around him, as Josh whispered in his ear.

"It will be okay."

The air filled with a roar as the main herd thundered away from the lake. After a few seconds, they slowed and gathered again, howling in a mournful chorus at each other.

Brandon edged towards the side of the outcrop again, hoping to get a view of whatever was going on, but he stopped when he heard another scream of animal agony.

For a few seconds, all they heard were the animals settling, and the sound of water flowing into the lake. Then, very close to them, there was a sound like tearing cloth, crunching and guzzling. Something powerful was feeding just metres from them.

Brandon pressed himself against the hard rock and stared upward. A puff of white cloud eased across his vision. He glanced down and saw Josh with his arm around Dan; the kid looked like he'd seen a ghost, and Brandon realised that the boy's instinct had been right, again.

They kept as still as they could while whatever had attacked the hoppers continued with its meal. Again and again they heard the crack of bone, the tearing of skin and flesh, the guttural sound of something gobbling down whatever it had caught.

Brandon raised a hand in front of the other two, one finger extended. This was one solitary predator, feeding on whatever remained of its kill. Dan curled his hand around his spear, pulling it in as tight to himself as he could. The wind continued to blow against the far side of the rock, carrying a different scent to them, warm and fetid. Brandon felt his stomach churn.

And then the feeding stopped, and for a moment all was quiet except for the distant hooting of the main herd that had reassembled on the river shore. Brandon stiffened as he heard something being dragged across the wet mud away from them. The noise faded to silence.

Josh let his arm drop, releasing Dan, who drew in a deep breath. A few metres away, on the glistening mud, the streak of blood was turning dark and seeping into the ground.

Brandon eased himself towards the edge of the rock and peered around the corner.

"Okay," he whispered, "it's gone."

The stain of blood was washing away into the water. Further along the shoreline, Dan could see more blood and a scattering of soft objects, brown and bright blue on the mud.

"I think we'd better go," said Brandon, "now."

The other two followed him with no comment, and they made their way along the valley and back towards the shuttle.

Dan refused to look his sister in the eye as Brandon told the story. They were sitting on one of the mud banks they'd created when the shuttle landed, eating what was left of the fruit. Brandon spared none of the details of the hunt, the ferocity of the attack, the crack of bones, and the blood and body parts on the soft mud.

"It was one of those sabre-toothed things," said Brandon, biting off a piece of the long banana fruit, "hunting alone this time."

"This is crazy," said Grace when Brandon had finished. "We can't stay here."

No one spoke. She turned to Chi.

"What do you think?" she said.

Chi looked at her for a few seconds and she wondered whether he hadn't heard her question.

"Everywhere on this planet is dangerous," said Chi. "We should leave here, but we need to know where we are going. The safest place for us would be the *Aspira*."

Grace glanced at Brandon, expecting him to disagree, but all he did was place his piece of unfinished banana on the floor.

"Aren't you going to finish that?" she said.

"No, I need to get some sleep," and with that he got to his feet and walked back towards the shuttle door.

"I'm going to rest as well," said Chi, and turned to follow Brandon. Dan got up too and followed them in, leaving Grace and Josh alone.

Grace stared at the treeline and wiped the sweat from her forehead.

"Feels like we're trapped here, doesn't it?" said Josh.

"I don't know what to do. I want to take Dan with me and run, but this whole place; I never thought it would be so hostile."

"Well, if we stay," said Josh, "we need to talk about defending ourselves against our enemies. Whatever we do, they will come after us."

"I know they will," said Grace, "that's not my biggest worry at the moment."

"Oh?" said Josh, raising an eyebrow. "What's worrying you the most; is it Dan?"

"No," she said, "it's Brandon."

"I know he's blunt," said Josh, "but that's just his way."

"It's not that," said Grace. "He's sick."

"Is he?"

"His pod malfunctioned before he revived."

"Yes, you said that."

"And now he's tired in the afternoon, and doesn't eat all of his food. What does that tell you?"

"It tells me Zera is making him sick."

"More than that, I think Zera is killing him."

"That means we have to stay here," said Josh, "and help him recover."

"If he recovers," said Grace. It surprised her to feel the tears coming to her eyes. There was no special love for Brandon in her, but she'd had more than her fill of death, and she didn't want to lose anyone else.

The afternoon settled into evening, and Brandon did not wake up from an uneasy slumber. The others settled down to sleep, but Grace could not rest. Her mind was full of conflicting thoughts and worries: Dan, Brandon, and their enemies, both human and alien. She tried to get comfortable, but eventually she sat up and looked around in the shuttle's gloom. Brandon, Dan, and Chi were all asleep, but Josh was sitting up on his bed, staring at the small porthole in the shuttle door where a ray of starlight filtered through.

She pushed herself up from her cushions and padded, barefoot, over to him. He was sitting still, breathing slowly and with a deliberate, steady rhythm.

After a moment, he noticed her.

"Hi, Grace."

"What are you doing?" Her own blunt question surprised her, but she was curious about his behaviour.

"Meditating and praying."

"What, like a Buddhist?"

"Similar," he said, smiling. "It's an Ignatian exercise that helps me process things in my mind."

"Ignatian?"

"Saint Ignatius," said Brandon, "sixteenth-century soldier turned priest. He says that if we want to serve God and help the people around us, we need to know ourselves. And that requires reflection, meditation. I find it useful, especially when there's a lot going on."

Grace laughed out loud.

"A lot going on? Well, based on the last twenty-four hours, you going to have to do a lot of meditating. Anyway, I don't want to disturb you."

"Don't go yet. Come and sit down with me."

He moved up on his cushions and she sat next to him. They were both silent for a few seconds before she spoke, still keeping to a whisper.

"What are we going to do? What are we going to do if Brandon stays sick, and those murderers come after us?"

"Well, there is one option we haven't talked about."

She looked at him. "Go on."

"We could go north to the coast, try to hide up there. It's only about ten kilometres. Not ideal, but nothing looks good for us right now."

"That might work, if we could get to an island in the archipelago. They won't track us there."

"We'd need to get across the sea," said Josh, "and take Brandon with us."

"It's a crazy idea, but we haven't got a lot of options," said Grace, "we can't stay here. We can't let those Transit Team people just walk in and murder us; and I will not let them take Dan."

"I know," said Josh. "I've seen how much you love your brother."

She nodded.

"Let's see how Brandon is in the morning, then we'll make our decision."

"Okay," said Grace, "well, goodnight." She put a hand on his knee and pushed herself up.

"Goodnight, Grace."

For a while afterwards, she lay awake thinking about Dan and Brandon, and Josh, and this beautiful fierce planet that would surely be the death of them all. How were they going to survive? How would they be able to travel if Brandon was sick? What would they do if those murderers found them? Her thoughts revolved around these problems until she slipped into an uneasy sleep.

IT WAS WELL before dawn when Chi opened his eyes and eased off the coat he was using as a makeshift blanket. In near silence, he reached for the clothes he had positioned where he could reach them, the bag that held his few possessions. He picked up his shoes and walked to the shuttle door.

Chi was just about to ease the door open when he saw Dan sitting up, staring at him. He paused and then lifted his finger to his lips, asking Dan to be silent. Dan nodded, but then started to speak into the silence. Chi had to strain to hear the words,:

"You're going, aren't you?"

Chi hesitated and then nodded.

"It's okay," said Dan. "I know you have to."

Chi came over, leaned down and whispered close to him. "Tell the others," he paused, "to stay safe. If it's at all possible, I will come back for them, I promise."

"I will tell them," said Dan, "and I'll shut the door after you're gone if you want me to."

"Thank you," said Chi.

Dan watched Chi rise and step silently to the shuttle door, where he remained motionless for over a minute, as if caught in some internal struggle, before he pulled the door open, stepped out, and slipped away into the darkness.

After a minute, Dan got up and went to the shuttle door. He pushed on it as hard as he could and slowly it shut. Then he turned the locking wheel until the bolts engaged.

No one else in the shuttle moved or woke, so he crept back to his cushions and lay down, but he was awake now and restless.

Far away, something alien was calling out across the valley, and Dan felt alone and the sorrow of losing his parents fell upon him.

He sat up and breathed in the stale shuttle air, still tasting the acrid tinge of smoke from when he'd set the cushion alight. He realised he had not cried yet, and he didn't know why. A sharp spike of grief slid into his guts. Somehow that spike had not surfaced, hadn't come up and out of him, and he couldn't connect with it. Dan didn't even know what he was supposed to feel, nothing made sense to him in this place.

Huddled against the side of the shuttle, he wrapped his arms around himself, and remembered the one thing he had saved from the horror of the Cryohall, the most ridiculous and precious thing he owned, stowed at the back of his locker. In his jacket pocket, his fingers closed around the smooth metal of his tin whistle.

The familiarity of the instrument seemed strange in the burnt odour of the shuttle. He pulled it out of his pocket and looked at the dull gleam of the metal in the starlight, the brass finish with the row of tiny air holes and the green mouthpiece. He put the whistle to his lips and a memory, clear and urgent, overwhelmed him. A memory of music and family, of playing a song with his mother and her brother, his uncle Craig, in their band back on Lewis. With his lips on the mouthpiece, his mind went back to the last time his family had been there, before they'd headed off for colony training.

Dan remembered sitting in the little pub in the village where his mum had grown up and where the band had played. He remembered being perched on top of one of the bar stools, the plastic covering of the stool warm on his bare legs, and the yeasty smell of the beer filling the place, and his beaker of lemonade sitting on the sticky counter next to him, his tin whistle in his hand.

Dan had first picked up the instrument when he was about six, and was too small to play it well, but since then he'd practised and grown in confidence. The whistle was a place where he could do something well, where he had control. When his uncle's band was rehearsing, he'd played along, perched on his stool, picking up the tempo and tune as if it were a conversation with an old friend.

That's when his uncle had called to him.

"Here, Dan," he'd said, "come and play with us."

Dan had looked at his father standing next to him at the bar.

"Go on then," his dad had said.

They put him next to Diarmuid the Bodhran player, an old man with a tremendous moustache and a frayed mustard yellow waistcoat. The pub filled up, and when the band played, Dan played with them. No one told him when to come in or what to play, he just put the instrument to his lips and the music joined him.

And he heard his mother's voice singing *An Innis Aigh*, The Happy Isle. The music filled his mind, and the singing and the smells of the pub, the faces of his family, and he imagined himself playing the whistle as the band played and his mother sang that last time, all the way through to the end of the song to the closing lines:

Mo chadal buan-sa bidh e cho suaimhneach
Mo bhios mo chluasag's an Innis Àigh

My eternal sleep will be so peaceful
If I lay my head in the happy isle.

He thought of his mother, eternally asleep now. He hoped that some part of her was back on the happy isle of her childhood with his dad, and that she felt the peace that this beautiful song had promised to all of them. And when the haunting notes of the song had finished, he laid the whistle down in his lap and imagined the sound of the music again in his mind, and the smell of the beer, and the taste of the lemonade, and the warmth of the room, the sense of belonging and love, all woven together into a tight, sharp point that smote his heart, like a knife making a fresh cut. All the joy and grief flowed out and over him. He felt so loved and so abandoned, that at last the hot, salty tears eased out onto his cheeks and down, to gather at his chin before he wiped them away with the sleeve of his uniform.

As Chi slipped away under the Zeran starlight and Dan reflected on love and losing family, a shuttle flew south over the valley, high in the sky and silent. It was well past the survivors' base when it glided down, taking just a couple of minutes to cover the twenty kilometres to the landing zone. When it reached its destination, it did not ram itself into the earth, but settled into a natural clearing, and then it powered down and became silent.

12

Amelia turned off the engines and stared straight ahead as she heard the thump of Callum Mortis's feet coming up behind her. When he reached her chair, he placed a heavy hand on her shoulder and leaned over her.

"Well? Any sign of them?"

"They didn't land here," she said. "I'll run a scan for the shuttle beacon. If they came down within a hundred klicks of the LZ, we'll find them."

"Damn it." Mortis pushed himself off from Amelia's shoulder and stomped back towards the rear of the shuttle, past Patrick, to where Ray waited for him.

"Was there any weaponry on the *Aspira* they could have got their hands on?"

"No," said Ray. "The only armaments on the ship that were accessible are now on this shuttle with us. There are some other hand-held weapons in deep storage, but they couldn't have reached them."

"So, we have the pistol and your rifle, yes?"

"Correct," said Ray. "I recommend, sir, that you let Patrick and me check the area before you leave the shuttle."

"The hell with that! I will be the first adult to set foot on this planet. That's how history will record this moment."

"We should run a more complex atmosphere analysis," said Amelia, coming up behind them holding her comm unit, "before any of us..."

"Thank you, Amelia, but I'm sure it will be fine," said Mortis, interrupting her. He strode forward to the shuttle door and spun the locking wheel; he tugged ineffectually at it, trying to get the door open.

"Patrick, give me a hand with this."

Patrick and Mortis both pulled on the door, and it swung slowly inwards. Cool, humid air, heavy with the scent of the forest, flowed into the shuttle lobby.

Mortis sniffed and squinted out at the darkness. His adaptive lenses picked out the ring of trees that marked the edge of the clearing. He looked up into the sky, pleased with himself when he found he could recognise the bright hot star high in the sky as Alpha Centauri 'A'.

"Oh, I like this place," he said, reaching for a cigar from the inside pocket of his colonist's jacket. "Yes, this will do just fine."

Ray and Patrick peered out into the clearing where they'd landed. Morning light filtered through to the spiky branches and dark leaves of the trees.

"I've got them," said Amelia, holding up her comm unit.

"How?" said Mortis, "how did you find them?"

"Tracking beacon."

"So, where are they?"

"Twenty kilometres north and slightly west of here, up towards the coast."

"Right then," said Patrick. "Let's do this, shall we?"

"Patience," said Mortis. "I want to savour my first moment on Zera before we go."

"We don't want to hang around too long," said Patrick. "We should..."

"I said," growled Mortis, "patience. Now, let's see what kind of real estate they have here."

Mortis looked out of the shuttle and stared up at the stars. Ray frowned at Patrick and lifted a finger to his lips. Patrick sneered back at him.

A breath of wind gusted through the trees and across the clearing, blowing across Mortis's face and bringing a rich cocktail of scents: the smell of soil and water, and something else, something he could not quite identify; something sharp, an alien smell. From deep within the forest, there came a series of defiant hoots, which lingered on the wind for a moment, before being answered by a similar sound from far away across the canopy.

Mortis stepped down onto the planet's surface, wobbling slightly as his feet hit the uneven ground. He cleared his throat and raised his head, glancing briefly at the others. Then he shouted as loudly as he could.

"I, Callum Primo Mortis, claim this land for the first Zeran colony of mankind."

There was silence around him except for the noise of the wind in the stiff leaves and more hooting from deep within the canopy.

"Be silent, whatever you are," muttered Mortis to himself. "This is my land now."

He turned to the others who were watching from the lip of the shuttle door.

"Come on then, let's have a look around. Amelia, I want you to work out a route from where we are now to where the escaped colonists are. Send it to all our comm units."

"Sure."

Mortis almost reminded her to address him as 'sir', like Ray did, but then he thought better of it; he would try a different approach with Amelia when the time was right.

Ray climbed out of the shuttle after his boss. He took a pair of binoculars from a small pack he was carrying and looked around the perimeter of the clearing.

"Nothing obvious, sir," he said. "Patrick and I can sweep the area."

"Do that," said Mortis.

"I advise you to stay on board for now, Mr Mortis," said Ray. "This area is still unsecured. Patrick and I can put some proximity beacons around the clearing. If anything comes near us, we'll know about it."

Mortis grunted and then pulled a slim metal lighter from his pocket. He put the cigar in his mouth, lit it, and blew the smoke up into the air.

"These aren't bad," he said to himself, "considering they've been in storage for sixty years."

He sucked on the cigar again and looked around, wondering where the best place would be to take a leak.

RAY AND PATRICK wandered out to the perimeter of the clearing, Ray with the rifle, Patrick with a small handgun and a rucksack of sensor beacons.

"You've got to stop arguing with the old man," said Ray when they had gone some distance.

"Whatever."

"Seriously, you need to be careful," said Ray. "He'll…"

"He'll what?" said Patrick. "Fire me? Kill me?"

"Maybe both. You know what he's capable of."

"He's strutting around back there, puffing on his cigar when we should be finding these kids. We could get this done and be back on the *Aspira* within twenty-four hours."

They reached the edge of the clearing, and Patrick spat onto the earth.

"You might think you're right," said Ray, peering into the forest, "you might even be right, but if you cross him, he will cut you down."

Patrick turned and looked at him. "Stop fussing, okay? I'll be fine."

"You sure about that?"

"Yes," said Patrick, as he glanced back at the shuttle. "Look, I know you mean well, but back off, okay?"

"Fine, fine," said Ray, then he was silent for a moment before he spoke again. "You know, Dad asked us to look out for each other."

"Not this again, please."

"I can't forget what he said."

"Who cares about our father, anyway? He's dead and buried. He was gone even before we got on that big ship up there sixty years ago," he pointed into the sky, "and now we're here, and we have some killing to do, and that's fine with me. It's not like we haven't done plenty of it already."

"You need to let the boss take his time," said Ray.

"If Mortis wants to get sentimental about pottering around in his new garden, that's fine with me, so long as it doesn't get in the way of the job."

"He's the boss," said Ray, leaning in towards his brother. "He says what the job is, and he says when it starts. So if he says it starts tomorrow, then it starts tomorrow; and I don't want you on my conscience. You and I are half-brothers, even if you don't like it."

"Our father fooled around with a lot of women, one was your mother, and one was mine. We've probably got a lot of other half-siblings out there."

"But I've only got one here," said Ray, then before Patrick could continue, he paused and raised a finger to his lips.

"Hear that?" whispered Ray.

They were both still for a moment.

"Movement?" said Patrick.

"It's water," said Ray, "a stream nearby; we should try to find it."

"You think we will be here that long?"

"We don't know how long we'll be here, so we need to do this by the book. We establish ourselves, place sensors around the perimeter, locate that water source, find food, you know the routine."

"It's all a distraction," said Patrick. "We've got plenty of rations. We just need to find these kids and deal with them."

"I don't think it will be that simple. So setting out in the morning when we'll have the light is the best option."

Patrick pulled the rucksack off his back and dug out one of the sensor beacons. "If you say so, brother." He rammed the base spike of the proximity beacon into the earth.

<hr>

WHEN THEY WERE BACK, Mortis called everyone together.

"Well, Amelia," he said, "what do you have for us?"

"The map's done," said Amelia, "you should all have a copy."

"And our targets, we have, what, five escapees?"

"Yes, sir," said Ray.

"Interesting that both of the McAllan children survived, that suggests something other than random pod malfunction."

"I'm continuing with my analysis," said Amelia.

Patrick shook his head.

"Who cares why they survived?" he said. "We just need to hunt them down and..." he made the shape of a pistol with his hand, "boom, done."

"Yes, yes," said Mortis, "and we will. But for now, as I told you, a little patience is in order. I want to catch them, but I also want to know why things went wrong."

"I'm guessing we may only have to deal with four of them," said Amelia.

"Why is that?" said Ray.

"Because according to the pod records, one of them didn't get the inoculations or the nanomachine package. It's likely that Zera's viruses will finish him, if they haven't done so already."

"So the bugs here will get at least one of them," said Mortis, smiling, "excellent. But I still want to track them down in daylight. We'll make an early start tomorrow."

Ray stared at Patrick and shook his head slightly.

"Right, I'm hungry," said Mortis. "See what rations we have, Patrick, there's a good chap."

They ate some beef flavoured paste and plain crackers, then Mortis told them to rest for the few hours before dawn. They set out the camp beds they'd brought with them, and the shuttle was soon resonating with Mortis's snores.

But Patrick did not go to sleep. He tossed and turned, convinced he was wasting his time, itching to get his comm out, and start the hike towards his targets.

Eventually, he fell into a fitful sleep, but woke a few hours later, cold, cramped, and in need of a pee. He could just see faint dawn light through the porthole of the shuttle door. He lay on his narrow bed for a few more minutes, and then he got up, quietly picked up his rucksack and slipped on his boots. The handgun was still in his jacket pocket.

He crept to the back of the shuttle. The door wheel squeaked as he turned it, but no one stirred, and he stepped carefully down onto the Zeran earth.

"Right," he said to himself, "let's get this done."

He looked around the landing zone. An orange light was creeping over the horizon, silhouetting the tall trees. The air was cold and sharp with a musty alien scent. He hurried to the edge of the clearing, and for the first time noticed the lighter gravity. He dismissed the experience from his mind, as if it might somehow beguile him away from the purpose.

Patrick thought about the kids he would kill. Amelia had spent hours on the shuttle, poring over the colony record data, trying to work out why they'd survived.

"Waste of time," he whispered to himself, then he opened the front of his trousers and spattered liquid on the ground in front of him.

When he was done, he turned and looked again at the shuttle. There was no movement at the door. He could turn around now and go back, no one would know that he'd been out here, no one would question his actions. But that wasn't how Patrick did things, he turned back and kicked one of the trees. His boot hit the base with a satisfying THUNK.

"Idiots," he whispered.

Somewhere far into the forest, faint on the wind, he heard a noise like the hooting they'd heard before, but this time slower, more mournful, familiar and yet deeply alien.

He looked down at the Honeywell graphene weave boots he was wearing. The ground underfoot was damp and gave slightly under his feet. Ahead was an endless world of trees and darkness, and who knew what? He remembered his brother's comments about being the aliens here. He, Patrick, was the enemy, the stranger, and possibly the victim. He was the threat or source of food for the creatures of this planet. But he was ready for that. He would be the enemy of anything that got in his way.

He pulled out his pistol and checked the safety catch.

"Come on, Patrick," he said to himself. He put the gun in his pocket again and touched the hard outline of the hunting knife at his belt. He was about to step into the tangle in front of him when he felt a slight pressure on his foot.

Glancing down, he saw that a large orange worm had emerged from the soil, inched up onto his boot and was now using one muscular end of itself to push against his shoelaces. The material was sticky where the creature had made contact.

Patrick scraped the side of his boot with his other foot and then brought a heel down hard on the worm. The soft soil gave beneath him, pressing the worm's head deep into the mud.

"Damn!" Patrick stepped a few paces back and stared at the

creature as it eased back into the soft mud. The edge of his boot still glistened where the creature had climbed up it.

He cursed, and then took one long step into the forest, followed by another. He quickened his pace and kept walking, stumbling over tree roots as he went. He resisted the temptation to look back and see if anyone from the shuttle had seen him, and within a few seconds, was gone.

13

He who was known to his own kind as *Singer to the Hungry,* sat motionless in one of the larger trees and watched the male visitor stumble into the forest.

'He' had showed his maleness when he urinated at the edge of the treeline. Now he seemed to have left his group and was venturing off on his own.

This group had emerged from a similar ship to the one the others had brought, and they all seemed to be of the same species. Singer closed his eyes and concentrated as the visitor passed. He gently sought a way in, but there was none. There was no invitation and no openness to the call. The silence in his mind surprised him. Even the Hungry of Eye, the most recklessly aggressive creatures in the whole of Aleth, seemed to listen to him, for Singer could charm all the roving predators of the forest. It was his ability to charm even the 'Hungry' as they were known, that had given him his name when he had come of age.

He waited a dozen breaths, and then a dozen more, before easing his way down the tree. Even now, he could still sense the visitor stomping into the forest. Every footfall betrayed the disorder in the visitor's mind.

And now there was a complication.

The visitor didn't know it, but he was heading straight towards the Sanctuary. If he discovered that place, there was no telling what defilement he might perform there. Singer hoped the visitor would run into one of the forest dwellers and be scared into following another route.

The Zeran picked up the pace, following the visitor as he continued to march across the land, full of self-pity and resentment, still walking straight towards the Sanctuary. And at the edge of Singer's conscience, far away but closing in on them, he knew that the Hungry were coming. That was another problem he might have to deal with.

He had wanted to report back to the First Pairing and tell them of this other ship, and would have done so if this visitor had not disappeared off on his own, threatening the Sanctuary and courting the attentions of the Hungry.

When Singer returned, he would confirm what they had all expected; that after the first visitors arrived, others had followed. These new visitors would counterbalance the first group. There would be light and dark, a dance between opposites, a contention for supremacy. Both of the visiting groups would show their nature soon. Singer thought they probably already had.

The ones that Observer had been watching, the ones that had required the help of the Sky Messengers, were of good character, Singer was sure of it. They had about them a faint reflection of the infinite virtues of Tvorak, the Maker.

And so Singer now had charge of the group that laboured under Haserak's influence. Haserak the deceiver, the liar. He was sorry that it had to be like this, but that was the order of things.

He looked up into the early morning sky where the twin moons, Aletheia and Haserak, were continuing their ancient dance: love and hate, mercy and anger, truth and falsehood.

Singer stopped short, jolted from his thoughts by a sudden powerful scent on the wind.

The Hungry, who had been wandering far across the forest, and far from Singer and his visitor, now decided to come this way. They had probably picked up the alien's bitter alien scent and were curious to see if this was prey for them.

Singer shook his head; his task was about to get more complicated.

14

AFTER TWO HOURS OF HIKING, Patrick stopped and called up the map on his comm unit. He'd walked the ten kilometres he had expected to cover, and even though the ground underfoot had been bumpy, it hadn't presented him with any real problems. He hadn't encountered anything he'd needed to kill, or that wanted to kill him.

He drank some lukewarm water from his flask and checked his location by pinging the *Aspira*, then he set off again, his path taking him along the edge of a large depression in the forest floor.

There was a round bush at the centre of this area and, as he worked his way around the perimeter he looked more closely at it and realised that it wasn't just circular, it was a near perfect hemisphere, as if someone had taken a smooth ball of vegetation and buried it halfway into the ground.

He paused, weighing the desire to pursue his targets against his curiosity. Curiosity won. He stepped off the path and down the incline.

As he approached the shape, he could see that it was not one entity, but a collection of trees and bushes, trained to form an object about ten metres wide. Someone or something had fashioned it into this shape. He stood still and listened, and then he sniffed the air. The wind blew across the structure. He could now make out a warm pungent smell coming from it, like cinnamon and ginger. The aroma reminded him of the cake his mother sometimes made; the memory caught him off balance. He took a deep breath before he looked at the structure again.

"What is this place?"

Patrick could see that whoever had built it had used tall, angular trees that filled the forest to create the frame, bending and gathering the tops of the trees so that they came together to form a dome. A variety of creeping vines had grown around and between the trunks, creating a living circular wall. At the top, the branches and creepers met to form a dome of vegetation in the trademark colours of Zera's flora: purple, dark green, and black.

He stared at it, and a thought occurred to him.

This is a building; it has a purpose.

As he circled the structure, the full implication of what he'd just realised dawned on him. This place meant there was another kind of life on this planet, an intelligent, organised life, not just plants and things that crept out of the mud to bite at his shoes.

He stopped in front of an opening in the branches, a hole in the vegetation leading into the heart of the structure. Here, the smell of cinnamon seemed stronger. He closed his eyes and listened, but all he could hear was the breeze fluttering the leaves of the trees around the edge of the clearing, and a squawking noise that carried on the wind from far away in the forest.

He eased the pack off his back and found his torch. Switching it on, he shone the light into the interior of the structure and peered in.

Most of the internal space was empty. The floor was smooth, compacted earth. In the centre, there was a large flat disc, like a circular table, balanced on three stubby pillars. The disc was a metre across and a few centimetres thick. Unlike everything else he'd seen on the planet, this object looked wholly manufactured.

The disc was made of a dark stone and shone dully in the light of his torch.

Patrick walked over to the table and shone the torch directly onto it. The top of the table formed a perfect circle, and its surface was smooth, charcoal grey without a scratch or blemish. The precision of it frightened him much more than anything else he'd seen so far.

"What is this?" he said, touching the surface with his gloved fingers.

A roughly carved wooden bowl sat at the centre of the table. The wood was a light golden colour and stood out brightly against the surface beneath it.

In the bowl, he could see three objects which looked like pieces of fruit, but Patrick had never known anything like them before. One piece was round and flat like a pancake, dark red apart from some purple streaks on its shiny surface, and then next to it, there was a yellow object that looked like a stretched banana, and finally something like a starfruit with a waxy green colour and light blue at each end.

He turned away from the alien fruit and peered at the wall of the structure. Branches marked off the circumference of the space, stretching up and over him, coming together just beneath the apex of the dome. As his eyes grew accustomed to the light, he saw that each piece of vegetation was unique, and gathered together into a great tuft of foliage above his head. He walked over to the wall of vegetation and ran his hand over the gnarled surface, the leaves of the creepers rustling as he brushed his fingers over them.

He realised that the scent of cinnamon and ginger was coming from the vegetation that made up the wall of the structure. Brushing against it had released a powerful dose of the smell, making his nose sting and catching at the back of his throat.

He sniffed, coughed, and hawked a gob of spit onto the floor. Immediately he felt as if he had violated a principle, or offended a presence of something he'd not previously noticed.

"Sorry," he said without thinking.

Then he thought, *this is a temple. Someone or something comes here to worship.*

He was about to turn to the table at the centre of the space when he noticed a piece of canvas on the wall opposite the entrance. He walked over to it and ran his fingers over the surface, then he sniffed. It didn't smell like the skin of an animal. This was a smooth, odourless material, cut precisely into the shape of a square, and clipped with wooden pegs to the foliage beneath it. On the canvas, he could see distinct images, finely drawn figures in colourful clothing: sunshine yellow and verdant green, sky blue and crimson. The figures looked like stretched humans. Each image showed them in different groups; sometimes many people gathered together, sometimes just two. He could not make out a narrative in the images, but his eye was drawn to the drawing in the centre: a figure seemed to be trapped in mud or rocks and was waving to another figure who looked like they were coming to rescue the trapped one. In the background, he could see the black image of a tower of some kind.

Patrick grew uneasy. The boss would not be happy about this. Mortis was expecting Zera to be *his* planet, but it looked as if it already belonged to others, some intelligent indigenous life. That meant the old man would have to subdue them if he wanted to take this place for himself.

Patrick turned back to the bowl at the centre of the space. He had eaten nothing that morning, and the sight of the fruit made him feel hungry.

The stretched banana seemed like the most familiar item in front of him, and so he picked it out, and with his hunting knife, he carefully cut through the tip of the fruit.

The skin peeled away, revealing orangey flesh beneath; he sniffed at it and his mind expected to sense *banana*, but what he got was something like the cinnamon scent that filled the air. He cut a piece of the fruit, placed it on his tongue and held it there without chewing for a moment. Saliva filled his mouth and at last he chewed; the flesh was salty and sweet, with a smoky aftertaste.

He put the rest of the banana fruit in his bag and picked up the starfruit. He used his knife to slice through a portion, and then again, sniffed.

This time, the smell made him recoil. Beneath the green skin the fruit flesh looked pale pink and moist, but the smell was sharp, acidic, stinging his nose. He dropped the fruit, and it bounced on the edge of the table and rolled onto the floor. He kicked it away and turned back to the bowl.

"And then there's you," he said, staring at the dark red pancake fruit still left in the bowl. He picked it up and with his knife cut through the smooth skin to the dark red and purple flesh beneath.

Immediately, the fruit oozed with a sticky juice. He sniffed at it, but it was odourless. He pulled the fruit open and saw that buried at its centre was a cluster of dark round pips, like black teardrops.

He placed the fruit back in the bowl, wiped the blade of his knife on his trousers, removed the comm from his rucksack, and took some pictures of the walls and the fruit.

"Amelia will love analysing this place," he said to himself.

He took a few more pictures and then stopped himself.

He placed the knife in its sheath and walked back to the entrance, where he peered into the brightness of the morning light of the forest. His gloves felt sticky now, and he decided to look for running water as he headed back up the clearing to the route he'd been following.

The job, he thought. *I need to get back to the job.*

FROM FIFTY METRES, Singer watched Patrick stride away from the sanctuary. He waited for two minutes before he jogged down to see what state the visitor had left the sacred space in.

At first, it didn't look as if there had been any defilement. The guide-image was still in place on the walls, the bowl of offering still sitting on the dais.

But then Singer turned to the share-fruit.

He could see that the visitor had interfered with some of the portions and taken others. One piece was still in the bowl, a large chunk of it now missing, another piece had been tossed onto the ground, and the third piece had disappeared completely. Someone had treated the share-fruit with casual indifference, and the shock of it turned his stomach. He left everything untouched. There would be no point in trying to tidy up; the whole sanctuary would need to be cleansed.

On rare occasions in the past, he'd seen the results of animals entering the sacred space. The aroma deterred most creatures, but it was not unheard of for some hungry animal to enter the sanctuary to snuffle about for food. Sometimes a creature of the forest managed to clamber onto the altar or damage the guide-image by scrambling up the wall to it. Some of his community welcomed these incidents, citing the original purpose of the sanctuaries as a place for travellers who needed some emergency sustenance and shelter. Certainly, no one took offence at the actions of a simple animal.

But the visitor was not one of these. He had tools and a purpose. What that purpose was, Singer could not discern; but the visitor did not seem to understand or respect the sanctuary, and Singer knew this would make their meeting more difficult.

He looked at the mess the stranger had left behind, tears pricking his eyes. He understood that there would be differences between his kind and the visitors, which perhaps could explain this, but still he felt sorrowful and disappointed.

He would have to report this intrusion to the First Pairing as soon as possible, and then the sanctuary would need to be cleansed. But all of that would have to wait while he continued to track the visitor.

Singer slipped out of the sanctuary and up the slope. The man's tracks were clear in the mud, and easy to follow.

As he set off, he tried to discern the feelings inside himself. His father had always reminded him that to know one's own feelings and to identify their source was an essential discipline of life.

He examined those feelings now, expecting to find disgust, anger, confusion, outrage; but all he found was hollow sadness.

After deeper reflection, he realised that the sadness came not from the actions of the visitor, but because he, Singer, could not connect with this visitor from the stars. The visitor's behaviour had been so inexplicable, so blindly disrespectful, that there might only ever be a vast gulf between them. How would they be able to understand each other, and what would these visitors say when the First Pairing asked them to give an account of themselves?

THE BACK of Patrick's neck itched with sweat. He scratched at the skin, then pulled the rucksack off his back. The banana fruit was soft and had leaked over his binoculars. He took it out, ate half of it, and tossed the rest aside.

As he looked up at the tall trees with their sharp angles and dark maroon colours, a vague unease entered his mind. Everything here seemed both familiar and different, like a foreign country where everyone spoke your language. This planet was like the Earth he remembered, but also deeply alien. It was this nearness to familiarity that made Patrick fidgety.

He remembered that Ray had a name for this sensation, for the place where things were familiar and yet strange. His half-brother had once told him that the thing people fear most is not that which is wholly unlike them, but that which is *almost* like them, and he believed it. Part of it was Zera's gravity. Amelia had said that it was about nine-tenths of what it was on earth, but that ten percent mattered. Zera's gravity made him feel too light on his feet. At first it had been a novelty, but now it was just irritating. He felt more likely to fall if he tripped, more likely to end up on his backside if he put a foot wrong. He spat the taste of the banana fruit onto the ground and kept walking.

"Just get on with it, Patrick," he said to himself. "Just do the job."

He carried on through the forest, trying to pick up the pace, keeping his direction as close to north-west as possible. Twenty minutes later, he stopped and listened. Amidst the noise of the wind in the leaves, he could just make out the sound of running water. The noise reminded him of how thirsty he was.

When he found the stream, he stood at the edge, watching the water run strong and clear over a bed of rocks. Still, there was something about the way the liquid moved over the rock that looked slightly off to him, as if the stream itself was being changed and stretched in some uncanny way.

Uncanny valley! He thought to himself as he bent down at the water. That was the phrase Ray used for it, the thing that was both familiar and yet doesn't quite ring true. This whole planet was an uncanny valley.

He dismissed the thought, and plunged his gloved fingers into the stream, then bent down to drink. But he paused with the water flowing just inches from his lips.

Was it *safe*?

He froze, paralysed by indecision, hovering over the stream until his back ached. He wanted to sit up, but instead lowered his head without realising what he was doing. His lips touched the surface, and the water was cool and clean and he drank greedily and freely. When he finished, he took a breath and submerged his head in the stream, then he rubbed the stubble on his face with his gloved hands.

He only heard the noise when he'd finished; something between a growl and a rumble. He stood up and looked around and listened, but it was gone.

"Screw it." He started walking, and then he heard it again, there on the wind, amidst the distant rustle of leaves and the whooping call of a distant bird, there was a growl so deep it seemed to come up from the ground beneath him.

He took the pistol from his waistband and stared around, and cursed. Nothing but the sway of the tall thin branches and the flutter of stiff leaves that clung to them.

He scrambled back up from the stream to the route he'd been taking. When he reached the path, he turned slowly through three hundred and sixty degrees, staring at the foliage, willing whatever it was out there to show itself.

Nothing.

He set off again, still heading north-west, putting one foot in front of the other and glancing down for creatures that might emerge from the earth, for anything that might break cover and run at him.

"Got to get out of this forest," he said, lengthening his stride.

The rumble sounded again, but he thought it was more distant now, and he picked up his pace.

He thought about the gun and wondered how many bullets he could afford to use shooting at things that might attack him. He had six and a packet of nine more. Amelia said there were five kids, so he had to save at least one for each of them.

As he travelled on, the wood became denser, the dark canopy turning the forest floor into a twilight world, with snatches of bright sunlight flickering over the earth. The route took him up a rising bank and into a clearing. Peering ahead, he could make out a lighter patch of ground, maybe a hundred metres ahead of him.

Patrick climbed the bank and pulled the binoculars out of his pack. He raised them to his eyes and scanned the whole area.

He carried on studying the terrain, working out the best route forward, until a prickling sensation on his ankle distracted him. He glanced down and then jumped back as he saw a stream of shiny black ants about a centimetre long scurrying around the side of his boots. He kicked out, scattering the ants onto the forest floor.

Swearing loudly, he jammed the gun back into his waistband, pulled out his knife, and hopped around as he tried to flick the insects away from his boot. When he was done, he jogged over to a large boulder where he leaned against the rock and lifted his foot, pulling the trouser leg up to examine his leg.

Around the edge of his boot, he could see red marks on his flesh where a few of the ants had reached his leg and taken a bite; in one case, it looked as if an ant's jaws were still in his flesh. He picked at the bite on his leg and flicked away the tiny pieces of jaw.

He was so preoccupied with fury he took a moment to realise that someone was standing just to his left, about five metres away, staring at him.

He jumped.

It was definitely male and tall, two to two and a half metres. The face and hands showed pale brown skin, and the figure wore a tight-fitting, sleeved tunic, and trousers that were tucked into brown boots. The clothing was dark purple and black, and blended into the colours of the forest in a way that left Patrick mesmerised. The features were finely drawn, elf-like, with a small nose and large brown eyes set high in the head. Patrick noticed that he was wearing a pendant, a hemisphere of bluish metal, on a thin silver chain around his neck.

The world around them was silent. All Patrick could hear was his own breathing. He thought he could also hear the breath of the man-creature in front of him. He didn't feel afraid, or panicky, he just stared.

After a few seconds, Patrick took one step forward and raised his left hand in what he hoped was a universal gesture of greeting.

The man stared at him and frowned as if it was concentrating, trying to work out some puzzle. Patrick heard a faint echo in his head, as if someone was trying to say something to him from a long way off; he shrugged the sensation away.

"Hi," said Patrick, and then he whispered under his breath, "This is it, this is first contact with a Zeran. The old man will be furious that it wasn't him!" He grinned slightly and then jumped as the Zeran took two long paces forward.

"That's far enough, fella," said Patrick, stepping backwards.

The Zeran stared at Patrick and then down to his side. Patrick glanced down and saw that some tiny piece of the foliage from the building he'd found had caught in his belt. He pulled it free and let it drop to the floor.

The Zeran raised one hand, but then spun around to the left and crouched. Patrick followed his gaze to the trees, but still there was nothing.

Slowly, the Zeran produced a long, thin-bladed knife from his belt. He had almost completely drawn it when the undergrowth about thirty metres away exploded. Patrick stared as something like an oversized emu with a thick, heavy beak crashed into the clearing. It glanced at both of them and, to Patrick's giddy relief, charged at the Zeran.

Even as it closed on him and lowered its heavy beak, the Zeran moved, blending his motion with that of the animal, seeming to climb onto its back, and reach over its shoulder before slamming the hilt of the knife down hard onto the animal's neck. The Zeran and the creature fell. As they hit the ground, the Zeran rolled and stood up in one smooth movement, crouching with his knife held out before him. The stunned animal glanced, shook itself, turned and stared at Patrick as if confused by his presence. It snorted and shook its head.

It was then that the Zeran started to sing.

Patrick stared with his mouth open as the tall guy stood up straight, drew in a deep breath and sang in a clear, deep voice, in a language that was both beautiful and incomprehensible. The beast that had run at them shook its head, stepped back and simply stared at the Zeran, whose voice seemed to gain strength and confidence as the song progressed.

Patrick carried on watching this serenade as he slowly drew the gun from his waistband.

This is crazy, he thought. *When this guy stops singing, that thing is going to head-butt him into oblivion.*

He knew he had to deal with this situation himself. He raised the gun and pointed it at the creature. The beast flicked a glance at Patrick and let out a rasping howl.

Both the creature and the Zeran looked at Patrick. The Zeran stopped singing and raised his hands. The creature jolted, as if woken from a trance, growled at Patrick, and then charged.

As it did, so the Zeran leapt with a balletic grace and slid the knife into the creature's side. The creature screamed, the noise filling the air, visceral and profound, and then Patrick's hand closed on the trigger and he heard a shot.

The beast spasmed and collapsed on the floor; the Zeran falling on top of it, knife still in hand. The creature let out two throaty breaths and then went quiet. The Zeran lay still, sprawled across the creature's back.

Patrick cursed loudly, stared around himself, and then lowered the gun.

"Hey," he said, "you okay there?"

As he drew closer, he saw the wound. Part of the Zeran's skull was scattered across the creature's body. He could see the bullet still lodged in there. He'd shot him instead of the creature.

"Oh great. This is all I need."

He could feel Ray looking over his shoulder, shaking his head, despairing at yet another shambles of his brother's making. The privilege of first contact had fallen to Patrick, and he'd shot the guy, even as he was trying to save his life.

He stared at the body, and again noticed the pendant dangling from the corpse's neck, the chain woven into the fabric of the tunic. Then there was more hooting, from somewhere distant; he looked around the clearing, raising the gun.

He needed to get away from this place, get back to the job at hand, and then report back to the others on his success. He would say nothing about this encounter. He was already telling himself that he hadn't even witnessed this, let alone taken part in it. He would block it from his memory.

He thought about moving the body, maybe digging a shallow grave or covering it, but that was nonsense. Someone, or something, would come, interrupt him, or even attack him. He should go, now.

"This didn't happen, it just didn't happen," he repeated to himself. "The forest is full of predators, creatures who'll treat this mess as their next meal. I just need to tidy up here, and maybe take something for myself, a little memento."

He wanted to run, get away now, but instead he turned once more to the corpse, and took out his knife to cut the thin metal cord holding the pendant around the man's neck. He expected his knife to sever the cord easily, but it held. He hacked at it for a minute, but he just could not cut through it.

He swore and put the knife back in its sheath, then he lifted the Zeran by the shoulder, avoiding what was left of the head, and saw that a simple fastener held the cord together. He unclipped the pendant and eased the cord away from the body, pulling it free.

He was desperate to run now, but still didn't. Instead, he pocketed the pendant, breathed in deeply a couple of times and then went to the Zeran's head and levered the bullet out of the brain and onto the ground. He reached into his rucksack, found a packet of medical wipes, removed one and folded the bullet into it.

"Need to get rid of that later."

Finally, with more discipline than he knew he possessed, he ran back to the stream and let the waters flow over his hands and his knife. He rubbed the side of the blade with his fingers, watching the red smear disappear into the waters.

When he was done, he started off again, walking briskly north west, towards his objective.

CHI WALKED AS QUICKLY and quietly as he could, up the gulley created by their shuttle when it landed and out onto the flat grassland. The dark spikes of the forest loomed before him to the south and east, thin trees pointing into the dawn sky. The calls and hoots were already coming from deep within the canopy: Zera's wildlife waking up to a new day.

He looked back at the shuttle.

"I will come back if I can," he said, his mind jumping again to the image of the candle burning for the benefit of others.

He took from his bag a flat, round object about the size of the palm of his hand and held it up. A panel on the surface lit up and compass points appeared, glowing orange in the pale light as the digital pointer flickered and steadied.

"All shuttles of the *Aspira*," he said to the object, "directional overlay and distances."

The screen went blank, and then the compass needle reappeared in a corner. A scattering of text appeared on the little screen.

Shuttle Armstrong due north, 4.65 degrees 0.034 km.
Shuttle Liu due South by South-East 168.8 degrees 19.89km.

He placed the object back in his bag and strode into the forest, stopping every few minutes to listen and look around. He checked his bearings occasionally and kept a lookout for any water. It would help him stay alert and ready for whatever he might encounter, and he hadn't taken any of the water when he left.

After four hours, he found a broad stream running east to west and drank. He'd covered twelve kilometres, and thought it possible he could meet a party coming the other way. He'd deliberatively incorporated a gentle arc into his route to avoid this happening, but could not be sure that this would avoid an encounter.

Chi hoped they were all together, the more of them hunting for the survivors, the fewer he would have to deal with at their shuttle. He would proceed more slowly, hoping to detect them as they trampled through the forest. He knew it would take a supreme amount of self-will not to attack, or to follow them back to his friends, if he saw them.

Chi had only been walking for a minute when he saw the clearing ahead and to the right. In the centre of the space was a circular structure made of bushes and branches, woven together to form some kind of dwelling. This was not a natural manifestation, and the sight of it made him stop and stare. The consequences of finding a structure like this were enormous. It would delight the scientists whilst his masters, as usual, would be cautious.

He approached the structure slowly, made one circuit, and then paused to look back into the foliage. He could see nothing, but his senses told him he was being watched. That seemed more likely now that he'd found evidence of intelligent construction.

There was an entrance in the structure's side, a simple opening cut into the foliage. He stepped up to the gap, listening as he did so. There was no sound other than the backdrop of forest noise. He sniffed the air: there was an aroma of warm spices coming from inside the structure.

Inside, he took the tracker he'd been using from his bag, spun through the menu, and started the video recording function. He lifted the device and pointed it at the walls, a light shining out from it as he scanned the surfaces and the table.

He focused on the canvas and described what he was seeing.

"These images seem to present a series of tableaux showing bipedal creatures gathered before a bright disk, maybe Zera's star or one of its moons. In one picture, a group of people are clustered behind a figure who is dressed in white, standing opposite another figure of similar size presented in a grey-blue colour. This seems to depict a moment of social gathering, maybe a community meeting or an act of worship, although could also be a conflict of some kind."

He moved forward, still filming.

"The floor is compacted earth but is smooth and level, more so than the terrain immediately around the structure. In the centre of the space is a table, possibly an altar. The top is perfectly flat and has a polished surface. There is a bowl on the table made from a light wood, lighter than I've seen from any of the trees around here. Unlike the table, the bowl has been made using a simple technique, by hand, possibly with a hammer and chisel. It is decorated with images of the fruit we've seen on Zera. Inside the bowl, there's a piece of fruit..."

He picked up the pancake-shaped fruit with his finger and thumb. Something about the way the fruit had been left with a crude gouge in it made Chi think that the Transit Team had been here.

He turned back to the entrance but then paused for a moment as something triggered in his mind; a warning that something, or someone, was nearby. He shut off the device and moved to the edge of the space, away from the door.

He shut his eyes and listened. There was no noise other than the muffled sound of the forest outside. He opened his eyes and stared around. Nothing.

He crept back to the entrance of the structure and looked outside, letting his eyes adjust to the light and listening for any sounds of movement, then he jogged quickly back into the cover of the trees.

In his mind, he imagined the survivors, and he thought especially of Brandon. Chi knew what was coming; there would be no recovery. Rather, Brandon would deteriorate rapidly, and within the next twenty-four hours, their self-proclaimed survival specialist would be dead.

Chi looked from north to south again, sighed, then removed the little console from his pack. Tapping the screen, he scrolled through the menu and called up the colonist's medical records. He skimmed through the data for each of them: Grace and Dan, Joshua, and Brandon. All the details were there: personal profiles, psych reports, congenital illnesses, blood types, and allergies. He stopped on Brandon's file, then flicked forward to Grace's, and then back to Brandon's file, reading the personal data one more time.

"Why," he said, finally looking up to the sky, "do you present me with this choice?" He wasn't even sure who he was talking to, maybe a god, a respected ancestor, or the fates who had given his current dilemma one more twist.

He thought about his mother's candle again, burning for the benefit of others.

"No," he said to himself, "the mission."

But what was the mission? And what action would best serve it? His responsibilities included both the task on the *Aspira* and the welfare of the colonists. And there was no checking with the Central Authority. He really was alone in the field, and he would have to work it out for himself.

He shut down the console and placed it back in his bag. His eyes fell on the bowl and he thought about the large blueberries he'd found when they first arrived. He would have eaten that fruit, and possibly died, had Brandon not stopped him.

Brandon, the arrogant boy, the cocky fool, might have saved his life.

"Very well," he said, "I choose you." He turned to the north, and jogged back the way he had come, towards their shuttle.

15

BRANDON FELT the sickness as he woke.

He had dreamed that he was at the shuttle door, looking out of the porthole, and had seen Patrick grinning at him. The man had run at the shuttle, head down, butting into the hard metal of the hull. He had then run backwards at an inhumanly fast speed, and run again at the shuttle, smacking his now bloodied head against the craft. In his dream, Brandon had seen himself standing at the other side of the porthole and screamed at Patrick.

"I will kill you, I will kill you."

Now awake, he could feel the grip of the illness on him, aching head, tired limbs, sore throat.

He swore, rasping out the words into the dead air around him, then rolled over onto his stomach, got to his hands and knees and forced himself onto his feet.

Standing at the porthole for real now, he could see Zera's sun rising with a new day, and all the challenges it would bring them.

He gripped the wheel lock, turning it easily enough, and then pulled hard at the door, opening it to the cool Zeran air. All the noises of the forest came to him. The wind in the tall grass at the edge of the gulley reminded him of the sounds of waves running along the shoreline.

He stepped down, nearly losing his footing, and looked up at the sky. The palette of colours created by the great star, Centauri 'B', reminded him again that this was not Earth, and they were strangers in a strange land, but if they survived, they would have the chance to make this place their home.

Sharp hoof prints covered the ground around the shuttle. When he walked outside, he could see the mud-smeared dents in the hull, as if someone had taken a dirty hammer and repeatedly hit the side of the craft with it.

He walked through the thick mud, out of the gulley and turned eastwards, towards the edge of the trees where he had set up the still. He would allow himself a little of the pure water before he took it back to the others.

When he got there, all he could see was wreckage.

Something had trampled the still. The tough poly fibre material lay crumpled and covered in hoof marks. The water container was lying on its side, ruined, the water within it now gone.

He had argued with Chi about where to put the still and had insisted it should be here. But maybe Chi had been right, this was not a good spot. Maybe Brandon the survivalist had failed. He had done his best, but now he was sick and he had let the others down. He sat down on the ground and buried his face in his hands.

"I tried, Dad, I really tried, I tried my best." But it was a memory of his mother that came to him now, speaking some of the last words she ever said to him, with the familiar accent and lilt of her voice.

The first rule of survival, Brandon, is to preserve the will to survive.

He took a breath and listened as the words came into his feverish mind again.

The first rule of survival is to preserve the will to survive.

"Yes," he whispered, "yes."

The memory reignited that will in him, rekindled the desire to overcome problems and survive, to master his environment and his enemies. His breathing quickened, and he thought about what it would mean, how his endurance might still be a testament to all of them, his mother and father, even his brother, young Lucas. In that moment he resolved to survive whatever assailed him: sickness, the creatures of this land or the murderers that might even now be hunting them down.

As the will to endure grew, he sought the old anger within himself. He wanted to nurture it again, as he looked at the smashed remains of their still. He pictured his family, hoping that the thought of them would stoke his rage, but to his surprise, he felt not hate but love. In his mind, he saw his father, dressed in the thick navy woollen coat he so often wore. Brandon remembered a camping trip in the woods when he'd been about eight years old, and in one moment his father had picked him up and held him close, and said to him, repeatedly.

"I love you, Brandon, my son, I love you."

Brandon remembered the coarse feel of that coat, the strength of his father's arms around him, the smell of wood burning and fish cooking on the griddle, the sound of his father's voice speaking to him, his mother calling them from their tent as she held little Lucas in her arms. He probably wasn't even walking by then.

Brandon tried to push down the grief because he thought it would make him feel weak. He tried to summon the rage again, blowing on its embers, fanning it into flame, but all he got was a memory of his father, teaching him how to light a fire with a battery and fine steel wool. He knew now that this was the reason he'd made sure that these things were in the survival pack. They didn't really need it; the fire lighter would work perfectly well. But it was wire wool and a battery that his father had used on the camping trips and it gave him a connection with the people he'd lost.

In a moment, that keen sense of loss overwhelmed all the hate and lust for revenge. He cried, and he was glad that the noise of the forest waking to a new day would drown out his pain.

He felt that he was indulging himself with this emotion, but didn't care. He would savour the longing for love and family, and cried out again because it was all he could do, sitting on the planet that his parents had so yearned to visit.

When the grief had subsided, the anger and desire for retribution were still there, smouldering and persistent. He was glad of it because that desire was as much a part of him as the love and loss he now felt.

WHEN BRANDON RETURNED, he sat down on his makeshift bed by the shuttle wall and slipped off his boots. Dan and Josh were up, stretching themselves, Josh massaging his shoulder. Grace looked up at him when he came in.

"Have either of you seen Chi this morning?" she asked.

"I've not seen him since last night," said Brandon, sitting back down on his pile of cushions that were scattered against the side of the shuttle hull.

"Dan," said Grace. She knew when her brother was being deliberately silent, "have you seen him?"

"He's gone," said Dan.

Grace stared at her brother.

"What do you mean, gone? Where?"

"I don't know, he had to go."

"Is he coming back?"

"I don't know."

"When did he go?" said Grace, frustration creeping into her voice.

"In the night, after all that noise, he just got up and went."

"You didn't stop him?"

Dan looked at her.

"Well, did you?" said Grace.

"Grace," said Josh.

"What?" She turned on him.

"It's okay," said Josh. "Dan couldn't have stopped him even if he wanted to."

"Why are you interfering?" she said.

"Hey," said Josh, raising his hands, "sorry."

"This is not your business, do you understand?" said Grace.

"Well, Chi disappearing is my business," said Josh.

Grace stared at him for a moment longer before Dan spoke again.

"Chi said he would come back for us when he could," he said.

Brandon laughed.

"Not much chance of that," he said. "He's gone, deserted us. But we've got something else to worry about."

"What now?" said Grace.

"Those things that attacked us last night," said Brandon, "have trashed the solar still. We will have to drink the water we can find."

"This is crazy," said Grace. "How are we going to survive on this planet?"

"We still have the water we collected yesterday," said Josh.

"Sooner or later, we will run out of purifiers," said Brandon, leaning against the wall of the shuttle. "Then we're going to have to trust Zera's water."

"Then that's what we will start to do," said Josh. "If we can't drink the water here, we'll never build a colony."

Dan had gone to get more water purifiers, but he hesitated, listening to the conversation, and wondering if they wouldn't be needed. He stood in the lobby of the shuttle, looked around, and noticed the large canvas bag strapped onto the top shelf of the racks. He hadn't really paid it any attention, but now he was curious.

He stretched up and unclipped the webbing, pulling the bag down. It hit the ground with a dull thud.

"Wow," he said, staring at it, "it's a lifeboat."

They all turned to see what he was talking about.

A bright yellow canvas bag lay on the floor. It had straps so that it could be carried like a rucksack and stencilled in bold red letters across its surface were the words:

DINGHY: EIGHT (8) PERSONS

Josh looked at Grace and raised an eyebrow.

"If we can carry that dinghy," said Josh, "we can cross water as well as land."

Grace stared at the dinghy for a few seconds.

"Your idea about going to one of the islands," she said, "we could do that now."

"We could," said Josh and smiled.

"That gives us more options," said Brandon, "maybe leaving the shuttle is the right option now."

Dan went back to their rucksack and found a box of water purifier vials. Then he looked through the rest of the pack, curious to see what else was there.

The medical supplies were in a separate compartment. When Dan dug through the rest, he found a box marked "emergency transfusion kit" and a container of red pills marked "NKDC Boost".

"What are these?" said Dan.

"Immune system boosters," said Grace, and she turned to Brandon, saying, "these might help you."

Brandon had closed his eyes.

"Look," said Dan, waving the container at him, "pills that might make you better, do you want to try them?"

"Whatever," he said. "I don't care, let's give it a shot."

They purified the water they had left and Josh sat Brandon up on his bed of cushions.

"Okay, my friend," said Josh, "let's get these down you." He handed Brandon two of the small pills and a cup of water.

Brandon swallowed the pills, took a deep breath, and then he lay down and fell asleep.

"Listen," said Grace, as they watched Brandon shut his eyes again, "if these pills get Brandon back on his feet, even for a few hours, we should take the dinghy and head for the coast. It's only ten kilometres. We can get to one of those islands in the Queloz archipelago from there."

Josh was silent for a moment.

"Okay," he said, "I agree. If Brandon can manage it, we need to collect one last lot of food and water, then go."

"Take Dan to find some water," she said, "and more of that fruit. Maybe this immune medicine will have worked on Brandon by then."

"Sure," said Josh, and he turned to Dan. "You okay with that?"

"Yes," said Dan, "let's do it."

They collected two containers and some water bags. Dan went out first, and Josh followed him.

As Josh passed Grace, she held his arm. "Look after him," she said.

"I'll try," said Josh.

"I know you will," said Grace. "And, Josh…"

"Yeah?"

"I'm sorry I snapped at you, it's just Dan, you know?" she said.

"I know," he said. "You love him and he's all you've got now, I understand that."

Dan appeared at the door.

"You coming, Josh?" he said.

"Yep," said Josh and followed Dan out into the sunshine.

WHEN BRANDON WOKE, Grace gave him the last of the water.

"Thanks." He sat up. "You know what," he continued, shaking

his head. "I knew Chi would bail on us, I just knew it. Selfish and arrogant. I bet he's gone to find that shuttle."

"You think they'll come?" said Grace.

"Absolutely," said Brandon, "it's obvious. They can't leave us down here. They'll get some supplies together, maybe more weapons, and then they'll come and find us. They're probably already here."

"Well then, it's good we've decided to leave," said Grace. "We're going to take that dinghy and make for the coast. How are you feeling now?"

"A bit better actually, I'll be okay once I've had something to eat," said Brandon. "I guess it's more of those banana things for breakfast."

Grace looked at him, then reached into her bag. "Here," she said and took out one of the protein bars.

"Wow," said Brandon, "I've never been so excited to see one of those. How many have you got in there?"

"One less now," said Grace, "so make the most of it."

He ripped at the packaging and put most of the bar in his mouth.

"Oh," he said, "that tastes so good."

He took another deep breath.

"Well, I guess I'd better get up and sort myself out."

While he was pulling on his boots, Grace got her comm and studied the map of Zera. There was little detail, but she could now see how near they were to the northern coast of the continent.

"So, we're going to this island," said Brandon, "and then what?"

"It keeps us safe," said Grace, "for now. Then maybe we go back to the mainland and steal their shuttle. I don't know, Brandon. We haven't got it all worked out, but at least we've survived so far."

"Yes, we have survived," he said, and picked up the spear he'd made the day before. He began sharpening it again.

There was silence between them for a moment.

"You want to fight them, don't you?" said Grace. "You want to take them on."

"Yes, I do," said Brandon. "I want to confront them, fight them, and kill them."

"That's fine for you," said Grace, "and I understand, but I don't want to go out in a blaze of glory. I need to look after Dan, that's what's driving me. But I think you'll get your chance for vengeance, whatever we do."

"I hope so," said Brandon.

"You know," he continued, "even if Chi comes back, you are the only female in the group. You need to think about that."

"What's that supposed to mean?" said Grace, turning to stare at him.

"I'm just stating the obvious," said Brandon. "Maybe those wackos from the Transit Team will let you live. I bet there are more men amongst them than women."

He leaned towards her.

"I'm just saying you need to be careful," he said. "We all need to look after each other."

He placed a hand on her arm.

"I can look after myself," said Grace, pulling away, "a lot better than you can at the moment."

"Whoa," Brandon laughed. "Look, I'm sorry, I am not trying to harass you. I know I can be direct, but I'll always try to be respectful to you, Grace."

"We should get ready to go," she said. "There might not be much time when Dan and Josh get back."

He didn't move.

"Just for the record, I wouldn't hit on you, anyway."

He put down the knife and examined the end of the spear.

"Wow," he said. "I didn't think I'd tell you that." He pulled himself up onto his feet and walked to the door.

"What do you mean, you wouldn't hit on me anyway?" said Grace.

Brandon smiled. "Nothing," he said, "it doesn't matter. I need to go for a pee."

He pulled on the door and stepped onto the earth, Grace followed him out into the morning sunlight.

"Come on, Brandon," she said, "you've always got something to say for yourself; don't hold back now."

"Okay, okay," he said. "I'm just not sure my tastes work like that."

"Okay," she said.

"I mean, I don't know, maybe they do. I just haven't got it worked out like everyone thinks you should by now."

"Well, it doesn't matter what everyone thinks now, does it? I mean, all the people you might care about now amount to, what, three or four of us?"

"Yeah, I guess that's true." He put the spear on the floor and stood up. "I'll be back in a minute."

He turned away from her.

"It's okay," she said. "Really, it's fine."

"Thanks," he said, turning back. "I don't even know why I mentioned it, it's crazy to talk about this now with so much else going on."

"I don't know, maybe it's just the right time to talk about it," said Grace.

"Maybe," he said, and smiled at her. "One thing I am sure of, I will survive."

"I don't doubt it," she said.

"Hey. That is a cue for a great song. I haven't sung anything since we escaped from the *Aspira*; it's time to put that right."

"Really, Brandon," said Grace, "you're going to start singing now?"

He gave Grace a mock bow and launched into a version of 'I Will Survive' as he walked away down the gulley.

BRANDON STRODE to the edge of the forest, feeling more cheerful than he had for a long time. Whatever was in these pills was working.

He carried on singing and chuckled at the line about the villain of the song coming back from outer space.

When he got to the still, he could see that the polyfibre sheet was still in one piece. He picked it up, shook it, and then folded it before turning back towards the shuttle.

When he got back, he saw that Grace was still standing outside the shuttle entrance.

"Hey," he called, "you know that song, there's even a line about..."

He stopped speaking.

Something was wrong. It was in the way she was staring at him; her face was pale.

"You okay?" he said. "You look like you've seen a ghost."

"Not quite a ghost," said a voice, "more an avenging angel."

He spun around to see Patrick standing there, a gun in his hand.

"You," said Brandon.

"Yeah, me," said Patrick. "Did you think we wouldn't catch up with you, eventually?"

"Oh no, I knew you'd come after us," said Brandon.

"Of course we would," said Patrick. "Can't let you lot run around down here, even if we thought the planet would do the job for us."

Patrick glanced around and then looked back at Brandon.

"Where are the others?" he said.

"Gone to find water," said Grace.

"I didn't ask you, bitch," said Patrick. "I asked him." He turned back. "Brendan, that was your name, wasn't it?"

"Brandon, my name is Brandon."

"Brandon," said Patrick slowly. "Bran-don. Well, I recognise you. You're the one who yelled at me through the shuttle door, aren't you? You were feeling brave, weren't you, with a thick piece of glass between us; how are you feeling now?"

Brandon was silent.

"Actually," said Patrick, "you don't look so good. Tell me, have you not been too well lately?"

"What do you know about it?" said Brandon, glancing from Patrick to Grace and back again.

"Oh, quite a bit actually," said Patrick, stepping forward from the shuttle. "You see, we looked at the pods you were in before we came down here. They were all interesting, especially your one. It seems you picked the short straw, Bran-don."

Brandon stared at him.

"The very short straw," said Patrick. "It turns out you didn't get all the boosters. You, my friend, are exposed, compromised. Frankly, I'm surprised you're not puking blood by now."

"Well, I'm not finished yet," said Brandon, trying to sound defiant.

"No," said Patrick, "but I'm sure Amelia's right. It won't be long. I'm almost tempted to leave the planet to kill you, but a quick end is probably for the best."

Brandon moved towards Patrick, but stumbled, coughed, and, with a quick glance at Grace, collapsed onto the ground.

"Ah," said Patrick, grinning, "there it is. You're living on borrowed time, Bran-don."

"Why are you doing this?" said Grace. "Why are you trying to kill us?"

Patrick sighed. "Haven't you worked it out? I thought you were the smart one amongst this lot, but it turns out you're just as stupid. It's simple really," he continued, "we want the place to ourselves."

"That's ridiculous," said Grace. "Other people will come and learn what's happened."

"You think so, bitch?" said Patrick.

Brandon drew a deep breath.

"Don't call her 'bitch'," he said at last.

Patrick laughed at him.

"Oh, how gallant," he said. "What are you, her knight in shining armour? Look at you, it's pathetic." Patrick turned to Grace. "But to answer your question, we took sixty years to get here. Sixty years. By the time anyone else gets here, what happened to the colonists will be a sad episode in Zera's history. A terrible accident that befell all of you, and I mean all of you, before what remained of the Transit Team bravely struggled to establish a colony here."

"You'll never own this land," said Grace.

"Oh, you think so, do you?" he said, grinning at her, "Let me clue you in, little girl. You're not in any position to tell me what I can and can't do, and actually, I will own quite a lot of this soon." His eyes ran over her and he nodded.

"You know what," he said, grinning, "I've changed my mind. I think I'll let you live for now. Isn't that generous of me?" He licked his lips. "Maybe you and I could come to an arrangement."

He stepped closer to Grace and reached out.

Brandon stepped up between them.

"Leave her alone," he said, staring at Patrick.

Patrick turned and raised his eyebrows.

"Now you," he said, "are getting on my nerves."

Brandon grinned at him. "The rest of our group will be back soon," he said, "then you'll be outnumbered. I think you should run while you can."

Patrick laughed.

"I mean it," said Brandon, stepping up in front of Patrick.

Patrick looked at him, shrugged his shoulders, then swung his right hand, slamming the edge of his weapon into Brandon's head. Brandon slumped onto the mud.

"Brave, but so stupid," said Patrick, staring at Brandon's crumpled form.

He raised the gun and pointed it at Brandon's face.

"No!" said Grace, "don't kill him; he's no threat to you."

She felt terrified and exhilarated, angry and defiant. This man was a vicious bully. She resolved, right then, to do everything in her power to defy him, and protect the people she loved.

She realised that it wasn't just Dan who was important to her now; at some point, these other boys had become people who mattered.

"You're right," she said, facing Patrick, "about an arrangement. You and I can work something out." She reached up and unzipped the top of her jacket, exposing the chain of the St Christopher she wore around her neck.

Patrick hesitated and then stepped up to her.

"Perhaps," he whispered, "you're not so stupid after all." He breathed into her face. The gun hovered in front of him.

"Turn around," he said.

She looked at him and frowned.

"I said, turn around."

She shuffled around, so she was facing away from him and willed herself to keep still. For all her determination, she still flinched when his fingers brushed across her neck.

Grace heard him sniffing just behind her ears. She closed her eyes and clenched her teeth to stop herself from running.

"Hmm, that's nice," he said. "It's been a long time since I was this close to a woman."

She turned around to face him, and forced herself to smile, her brain thinking furiously: how to survive, second by second, how to protect Brandon. Josh and Dan needed to come back, but for now, she needed to rely on herself, to think through the options.

He might let you live, but he will kill Brandon, and he will kill Josh, and he will kill Dan.

He will kill Dan.

There was no more time. She'd get the chance for one attack, and would have to make it count. A desperate, reckless idea formed in her mind.

"The thing is, Grace," said Patrick, leaning towards her, "my mercy only extends to you. I can't have young Brandon here regaining consciousness just when you and I are getting to know each other a little better." He ran his tongue over his teeth.

"I mean, it wouldn't do for someone to interrupt us just when we were..."

She punched his nose with all the force she could manage. Her knuckles stung with the impact, and Patrick screamed and stepped back.

"Bitch," he hissed. She swung at him again, but he lashed out at her.

Grace felt the side of her head explode, and then the ground rushed to meet her. She could hear him screaming now, from far away, and through watering eyes she could see the blood on his face coming from his nose. Rather pleased with what she'd achieved, Grace blinked and tried to get up, but the world was still spinning. She saw Brandon next to her, trying to stir.

And then this man was there again, close to her, his stale breath on her face. She could see his eyes, bright and fierce, watering now, the nose seeping blood.

"Here's what will happen, bitch," he whispered, spitting blood onto her face. "First this trash," he pointed at Brandon, "will die. Then as for you, well, we'll see what we can do about you." He leered at her, then he smacked the side of her head with the gun.

She had just a moment to notice a shadow dropping behind him before the blow struck and everything went dark.

CHI JOGGED to the edge of the forest and stopped. He could hear voices, one voice particularly, and it didn't belong to any of the survivors. He peered through the trees, but the bulk of the shuttle and the mud bank it had created obscured his view. Then he heard that voice again. It was one of the Transit Team. He took a few paces forward and saw Grace; she had stepped back and was now in his field of vision. He saw Brandon lying on the ground, panting hard. Then someone else came into view: Patrick, the one with the gun.

Chi turned right and walked swiftly to the top of the mud bank at the front of the shuttle. He crept along the craft to the end. He was padding along the shuttle when he heard a dull smack, and then Patrick screamed.

Chi reached the end of the shuttle and, squatting just above the entrance, he saw Patrick bending over Grace. He seemed to whisper something to her, and he was just raising his hand to her again as Chi adjusted his balance and leapt.

He landed just in time to see Patrick hit Grace again with the gun. He kept moving, running at Patrick, who was now turning to him.

Chi watched as Patrick turned and started to raise the gun, fiddling with the safety catch. The soft earth meant that he couldn't move as fast as he wanted to, and as Patrick's finger pressed the trigger, Chi dodged to his left. The movement almost took him off balance, but when the gun fired, the bullet missed.

Patrick didn't have time to fire a second shot. Chi drove his fist towards Patrick's throat, just above the Adam's apple. It was a good strike but missed its target by a centimetre.

Patrick made a gagging noise and fell backwards, grabbing Chi's arm so that both of them slid around in the mud, each trying to get a grip on the other.

Chi tried to free his arm enough to drive another blow into Patrick's throat, but Patrick brought his gun arm around and clipped the side of Chi's temple.

Chi's head rang with noise and pain; he staggered back and felt Patrick's thick hand close around his neck.

"Got you now, Chinaman," said Patrick. "Looks like you'll be the first."

Even through the pain, Chi felt irritation rise at Patrick's casual racism. It helped him to summon his strength and focus again. He curled his right hand into a fist and drove it into Patrick's gut.

The blow hit home but didn't break Patrick's grip on Chi's throat. His head was swimming now, and he knew he might get one more chance before he lost consciousness. He moved towards his enemy, just an inch, lining up this last desperate move and as he did so, he saw someone picking themselves off the ground behind them. Maybe Grace had recovered enough to attack their enemy from behind.

Patrick took a step away from Chi. "No one sneaks up on me."

As he finished speaking, his body jolted, and his grip on Chi weakened.

"You," said Patrick. Patrick turned his head to the right, and then coughed, a dribble of bright red blood welled up and spilt from his mouth.

"You," he said,

His arms dropped and then he slumped, heavy in Chi's grip.

Brandon appeared at Patrick's shoulder, panting hoarsely.

"Yes, me," he said, whispering the words into Patrick's ear. Chi could see that Brandon had buried his knife, almost to the hilt, deep into Patrick's ribs.

"This," said Brandon, pushing the blade in as far as he could, "is for my family, and this," he twisted the knife as hard as he could. Patrick made a whining noise, and a fresh gout of blood dribbled from his lips. "This is for my friends."

Patrick slumped onto his knees, Chi still holding him.

"And that," said Brandon, twisting the blade in the other direction, "is for all the other people you've murdered."

Patrick swayed and Chi let him collapse onto the mud.

Brandon pulled at the knife, which eventually came free. He

was about to bring it down again when Chi reached out and held his arm.

"What are you doing? I want to finish him."

"He'll be dead within a minute," said Chi. "I need to talk to him first."

Brandon frowned. "Okay then," he said. "You have him."

Chi knelt next to Patrick's ear.

"Where are the others?" he said.

"Go to hell," said Patrick huskily.

Chi ignored the comment.

"Why did they send you alone?" he said.

"Send me?" croaked Patrick. "They didn't send me. Cowards. Wouldn't come after you."

"You came on your own?"

Patrick smiled at him.

"Wanted to finish the job," he said. "Prove I could do it."

Patrick turned away from Chi and looked at the sky above.

"Doesn't matter now," he said. "I made it here. I got here, at least. Oh God, Ray, I'm sorry." He stopped speaking, and for a moment he looked confused, and then sighed and was still.

"Is he dead?" said Brandon.

Chi placed two fingers against Patrick's neck.

"Yes."

"Good," said Brandon. He leaned down and wiped the blade on Patrick's jacket, then turned as Grace got to her feet.

"You okay?" he asked.

She nodded but didn't speak.

"Thank you," said Brandon, "for what you did there."

She smiled.

"We probably all saved each other." She looked at Chi. "You're back."

"Yeah," said Brandon, "I thought you'd abandoned us."

"I came for you," said Chi, looking at Brandon. "We need to find that medical kit."

16

"I don't understand," said Brandon. "You don't care about us."

"You misjudge me," said Chi. "I care about all of you. But to answer your question, I came back because, Brandon, I'm your only chance of surviving."

"What do you mean?" said Grace. "What can you do for him?"

"We all know why you're sick, Brandon," said Chi. "You did not get the immunisation enhancements or the nanomachines in your blood. Your bloodstream is a sea of bacteria and viruses that your body does not know how to fight."

"I was feeling better after I had some of those pills."

"Ah, the NKDC boosters," said Chi, "do you think they will save you?"

Brandon was silent.

"Well? Do you? Or is the effect of them already wearing off?"

"I don't know."

"What I can do is give you some of my blood."

"What?" said Brandon.

"You need to get the immunization enhancements and the

nanomachines into your system. Once they're there, they might self-replicate, or they might not. But first we have to get them into your bloodstream, and the only way we can do that is with a transfusion."

"How much blood are we talking about?" said Brandon.

"If it's going to work at all, it will only need a small amount."

"If it's going to work?"

"This is Zera," said Chi. "Nothing is certain here."

"Okay, but why does it have to be you? Why not Grace or Dan or Josh?"

"Because I am the only one who can give you the transfusion you need, at least with the medical technology we have here on Zera."

"This is about blood type, isn't it?" said Grace.

"Yes," said Chi, nodding. "I'm O negative, and Brandon is A negative. Everyone else is a positive blood type, either O or A, so I'm the only one who can help him."

"Okay, fine," said Brandon. "If it will cure me, then let's do it."

"I'll need your help for this," said Chi, looking at Grace. "We'll do it in there." He pointed to the shuttle.

They sat Brandon in one of the shuttle seats. Grace went off to find the transfusion kit that Dan had shown them earlier.

"I have one more question," said Brandon while Chi sat down in the next seat.

"Are you wondering why I left you all in the first place?"

"That's a good question, but I've got a better one. Who are you? I mean, really, who are you?"

Chi rolled up the sleeve of his shirt.

"That question can wait until after I have saved your life."

"Here," said Grace, "the transfusion kit."

She took out a syringe, some sterilizing fluid, and some antiseptic swabs.

"You must do this," said Chi.

"Okay," said Grace, "you can guide me."

Following Chi's instructions, she sterilized the largest syringe they had. Then she pressed the needle into Chi's arm, drew off one hundred millilitres of blood, and after ensuring there was no trapped air in the syringe, she cleaned the needle again and slid it into Brandon's arm.

"Do it slowly," said Chi, watching her.

She gently pressed the syringe plunger, easing the blood into Brandon's system. He looked away as she did it and closed his eyes.

"Not a big fan of seeing human blood, mine or anyone else's."

Grace eased the syringe down, injecting all the blood into Brandon's vein, then slid the needle out.

"Now rest," said Chi.

"Sure." Brandon took a deep breath and relaxed into the chair, keeping his eyes closed.

Chi rolled his sleeve back and followed Grace as she packed away the transfusion kit.

"Do you think it will work?" said Grace.

"It should help him for a while," said Chi, "but I do not know if the machines will replicate in his bloodstream. This might be just a temporary reprieve."

"Why did you go?" Grace asked, as she wiped the syringe with a swab.

Chi turned to her as if to speak, but held up a finger and turned towards the shuttle door.

"Listen," he whispered quietly.

She strained to hear what had attracted his attention.

Voices.

"It's Dan," she said, "and Josh."

"Are you sure?"

"I know Dan's voice," said Grace. "They'll have seen the body. I need to tell them what happened."

She emerged into the sunlight to see Josh and Dan walking towards the shuttle. Dan carried a handful of banana fruit, and Josh cradled two full bladders of water. They both stopped when they saw Patrick's body, and Dan dropped the bananas on the ground. Grace waved at them.

"It's okay, guys, we're okay."

"What happened?" said Josh.

"The Transit Team has landed," said Grace. "Patrick came on his own and attacked us."

"Are you okay?" said Josh.

"We're all fine; and there's one more thing: Chi has come back."

THEY ALL SAT TOGETHER on the ground, putting some distance between themselves and Patrick's corpse.

"You knifed him?" said Dan to Brandon.

"Yep," said Brandon, "right in the ribs." He mimed his stabbing of Patrick with a theatrical flourish.

"And Chi came back and has given you a blood transfusion," said Dan.

"Yes, and now I feel great. And if any of those other murderers want to come here and point a gun at me, I'll knife them as well."

"What about the body?" said Dan, "are we just going to leave him over there?"

"No point wasting time doing anything else," said Brandon. "There are enough creatures around here that will take care of him for us."

"What happened here means we need to leave as soon as we can," said Grace. She looked at Chi. "We have the dinghy. We have to head north, to the coast. We can use it to reach one of the islands in the archipelago and get away from the Transit Team."

She raised her eyebrows at Chi.

"That's what we're doing, but what about you? What are you going to do now?"

"I will stay with you," said Chi. "For now. I am not convinced

I have saved Brandon. The boost is real, but it might still be temporary."

"Okay," said Grace, "so we have a quick meal, pack up, and go."

They sat at the back of the shuttle and ate some of the banana fruit. While they were still eating, Josh stood up and walked out of the shuttle and over to where Patrick's body was still lying face down in the mud. Already a collection of red and black striped insects was flying around the body and landing on the ground where blood had seeped onto the earth.

Josh reached down and turned the body over; mud clung to Patrick's stubbled cheek and Brandon's stab wound had torn a bloody hole in his jacket.

Now that he was looking more carefully, Josh noticed a thin loop of wire poking out from the top of Patrick's jacket pocket. He reached into the pocket and pulled out a pendant on a thin silver cord. It was a blue metal hemisphere. Josh saw what Patrick, in his haste and guilt, had not seen: an intricate pattern of symbols, grooves and ridges covering the surface of the hemisphere.

"My God," he whispered. "There's something, someone, intelligent on this planet." He looked down at the corpse. "What did you do, Patrick?"

Grace's voice broke in on his thoughts.

"Hey, Josh, do you want to have one of these bananas before Brandon eats them all?"

He heard Brandon's cries of protest as he pocketed the pendant and walked back to the rest of the party.

BRANDON AND JOSH crammed as much as they could into the rucksack: medical supplies, a few of the bananas, the firelighter, and water bags, and Josh shouldered it, wincing as he settled it on his shoulders. Chi volunteered to take the dinghy. Grace took point, navigating with the comm map, Dan took three of the wooden spears, and Brandon brought up the rear, ready to scan the terrain behind them.

"We can be there in three hours if the ground isn't too rough," said Grace. "You all ready?"

They nodded, and set off up the hill, past the nose of the shuttle and on towards the ocean.

They walked for just over an hour before they stopped for a rest. He unshouldered the dinghy pack and let it fall to the ground.

"We're just over seven klicks from the coast now," said Grace, "let's take a few minutes."

Josh put the rucksack down and Brandon lifted the binoculars and scanned across the grassy terrain to the south where they had come from.

"Any sign of them?" said Josh.

"Not that I can see." He handed the binoculars to Josh, who peered through them and turned slowly through three hundred and sixty degrees.

They clustered around the dinghy and the rucksack. Brandon took his knife out of the sheath on his belt and inspected it.

"How are you holding up?" said Josh, turning to Brandon.

"Just peachy at the moment," said Brandon.

"Why did we survive?" said Dan suddenly, "why didn't we die like the rest of them?"

"Wow, where did that question come from?" said Brandon.

They all looked at each other, waiting for someone to answer.

"I think I know why it didn't affect me," said Josh. They looked at him.

"I mean, I may be wrong, but if this virus is genetic, then the Transit Team might have made a mistake with me."

"How?" said Brandon.

"When I was born, the doctors discovered I had sickle cell disease, the anaemia variant."

"Sounds bad," said Grace.

"It certainly wasn't fun. Anyway, as I grew up, they gave me treatments to manage the symptoms, but then when I was about twelve, my parents heard about this revolutionary new therapy a clinic in India had developed, a method for fixing the genetic mutation that causes the disease."

"No way," said Grace. "You mean they could change your DNA?"

"A little bit of it. It was a long course of treatment, but it means my genetic profile has changed since we all signed up for the Zera programme. The last course of treatment was just before we left, and after our DNA check. There would have been a tiny change to the sequence, but maybe that was enough."

"What about you two?" said Brandon, looking at Dan and Grace. "What was your ticket to survival?"

Grace glanced at Dan.

"Tell them," he said. "I don't mind."

"Our biological father is not the person we call dad. It was one of my dad's brothers. They used IVF and, well, here we are."

"Okay," said Brandon, "didn't know that."

"No one knew," said Grace. "Our parents kept it a secret. They only told Dan just before we left."

"That wouldn't have changed the DNA record they had for you though, would it?" said Josh. "I mean, we were all tested, the records would have still shown your correct DNA sequence."

"That's true, but our mother was the chief medical officer. She told me they'd even altered the DNA records slightly to cover our true identity. She didn't want anyone to start asking questions when we arrived on Zera, as far as my parents were concerned, it wasn't anyone else's business."

"But that would have meant you didn't get the immune boost," said Brandon.

"No, that wasn't dependent on your DNA," said Grace. "Everyone got the same dose, but I'm guessing this virus thing had to be unique to each colonist. Whoever administered that virus used the records my mother had falsified, and so the virus didn't work on us."

"So, thanks to your parents covering up who you are," said Brandon, "you guys got to survive all this."

Grace nodded. She thought about her mother, the memories coming upon her suddenly, as they always did, and she felt the grief waiting on the edge of consciousness, pricking at her eyes. She hugged herself tightly to resist the emotion. As she did so, she could feel the shape of the envelope containing the letter her father had written. She unzipped the pocket and pulled it out.

"What's that?" asked Josh.

"It's a letter from my father, I'd forgotten I had it, he left it in my locker."

"Are you going to open it?" said Dan.

"Yes," she slipped a finger under the flap.

"You might want to read that on your own," said Josh, "or with Dan."

"It's okay," said Grace.

She opened the envelope and took out a single sheet of paper, covered in her father's distinctive handwriting. She read the words, whispering to herself.

"It's a list of instructions," she said, frowning, "something he wanted me to do if he didn't survive. There are some unusual codes and a single word at the top of the page here: Project Jemison."

"Jemison?" said Chi.

"Yes, that's right," said Grace.

"Please, can I see?" said Chi, and reached out for the paper.

Grace frowned slightly, but handed it to him. He studied it for a moment and then passed it back to her.

She looked at him. "Do you know something about this?"

"Perhaps you should just follow the instructions your father left you," he said.

"Okay," she rummaged through her bag for her comm.

"Hey," said Brandon, "you got any more of those protein snack bars in there?"

"Later," she said, "I'm busy."

She switched on the comm; her fingers flicked over the command menus.

"Okay," her eyes darted between the paper and the screen, "hold this a moment, please." She passed the letter to Josh.

He took it and stared at the codes.

"Can you read them out?" she said.

He read the numbers, and she tapped them into the comm. Areas of the software system she never knew existed popped up on the screen, guiding her through the menus.

"This has given me secure access, emergency overrides for this Project Jemison, whatever that is."

"There's one more code," said Josh, and he read a string of numbers.

"It's asking for a password," said Grace. The rest of them stared blankly at her. She scanned the rest of her father's letter. "There's something here at the end of the letter, like a clue, 'the Space Administration's first astronaut'. What does that mean?"

"Try typing in: Yang Liwei," said Chi.

"Yang Liwei?" said Grace.

"Yes," he spelt the name for her.

"You're in on this, aren't you?" said Brandon, looking at Chi, "whatever it is."

She tried the word. The console went blank, then two words appeared: "Protocol activated."

"So, what was that?" said Brandon. "You going to spill the beans, Chi?"

"Let's get moving," he said, "and I'll tell you on the way."

"Okay, but no more evasion, I'm holding you to that."

FAR ABOVE THEM, the colony ship *Aspira* floated in silence. Across her decks and in her cargo holds, all was dark. The ship was still, the whole structure cooling and waiting. The rooms that had occupied the business of human life grew cold, as warmth leeched slowly to the edge of the craft and out into space. The great ship carried on her steady orbit of the planet, monitoring systems ticking over.

Within that cooling silence, one receiver, operating on a sliver of energy, noted the receipt of a signal, a small radio wave rippling out from a point on the planet near the northern tip of the main continent.

The receiver sent a short message reporting this to one of the other shipboard systems, and into the stillness came activity, instructions that would move a package out into one of the cargo launch bays at the front of the ship. The package emerged from its berth as a dull grey cylinder and slid with just a little resistance along a launch rail into the bay, airtight doors sealing behind it.

The outer bay doors shuddered, moved, stopped, and then moved again as systems dormant for over sixty years lurched back to life. The doors slid open, exposing the interior of the bay to the void. Targeted jets of xenon gas pushed the package out of the bay and into space.

Moving now in the void, the package ran a series of diagnostic checks on itself before the tiny jets kicked in, moving it away from the *Aspira*, and spinning it sixty-eight degrees clockwise along its lateral plane.

When it was in position, it used the jets one final time to steady itself, and then the cylinder opened at each end, releasing a tight cluster of rods which unfolded and expanded out into a ring of silver metal.

When the ring had formed, the package attempted the most important task of its mission. It generated a field within the ring, which would have been invisible to anyone watching it, and then passed two transmissions through that field, the first a simple test message, just a few bytes, the radio equivalent of "Hello."

The second transmission, longer this time, was a message that contained a summary of the *Aspira*'s condition on arrival, and the condition of her colonists. It was a message full of triumph and despair; beyond all hope the *Aspira* had arrived at her destination, but only a handful of her colonists had survived to witness the achievement.

The radio wave carrying the message winked out of existence and appeared again, instantaneously, within reach of a long-range receiving station in orbit around the Earth. The station received the message and relayed it down to the Zera project monitoring facility, where the jubilation of registering the message was soon replaced by the horror of realising that most of the colonists had died.

Back in orbit around Zera, the silver ring busied itself with its next task, an extensive programme of analyses of the planet and the expected receipt of a return message from Earth.

A reply came within the hour: disengage all research and data collection activity. Divert all resources to the generation and development of the enhanced ER bridge field.

The package duly obliged, switching power away from its onboard scanning devices and powering up the instruments that would create a more ambitious version of the field it had already conjured to send its first message.

Within a few minutes, a portion of space one hundred metres from the package twitched and rippled, the waves of that ripple radiating out in a perfect circle, the circumference of which glowed blue-white against the inky darkness.

As the field gained form, a small portal on the side of the package opened and a rectangular bar comprising a range of alloys emerged, held by a robotic arm. The arm extended away from the package and with expert precision threw the bar into the space towards developing field. As it entered the field, the bar winked out of existence, and appeared again, instantaneously inside a project research station in Chengdu, China. The duty science team analysed the bar. The results showed that even its softest sections it had maintained perfect integrity in the jump.

Without waiting for further instructions, the package proceeded with the final stage of the testing routine. Ejecting a Plexiglas lozenge from itself, containing a series of organic and inorganic substances suspended in an inert gas, this followed the metal bar all the way to Earth.

Even before the lozenge arrived, a search and rescue ship, the *Obama*, was being prepared for the jump to Zera.

17

———

Callum Mortis paced up and down the central aisle of the shuttle, clenching his fists.

"Well, where is he? Do either of you have any idea at all?" He tried and failed to resist his old habit of clenching and unclenching his fists.

"He took the handgun," said Ray. "We haven't seen him this morning, so my guess is that he's gone after these kids on his own."

"What? Did I not say we wait? Did I not say that?"

Both Amelia and Ray had been silent, but now Amelia spoke:

"I imagine that he thinks we have been too slow, and he has taken matters into his own hands."

"Arrogant fool!" shouted Mortis. "What could make him think he knows better than me?" He punched one of the shuttle chairs, rattling its floor fixings.

While the boss vented his anger, Ray tried to contain himself. He was furious with his brother, who had, once more, done the impulsive thing, the stupid thing. It was bad enough on Earth, but here on Zera there wasn't the safety margin for Patrick's brand of selfish indulgence.

To make matters worse, Ray also looked like a fool. Not for the first time, he wondered whether he should have left Patrick behind, whatever promise he'd made to their father.

Mortis took a breath as if he were engaged in some titanic struggle to stop himself from exploding. He looked from Amelia to Ray.

"I dearly hope," said Mortis, "that something in that godforsaken forest finds him and eats him."

"Given what we know," said Amelia, "that's quite a likely outcome."

Ray detected a hint of humour in her comment and smiled despite himself.

"We need to get after him," said Mortis, "right now. If he finds his way through to those brats, they'll scatter before we can deal with them properly." He turned to Ray.

"How far away did you say the other shuttle is?"

"Twenty kilometres by a direct route. It'll be further travelling through the forest, but not much; we'll need to be careful ourselves."

"Of course we'll need to be careful," said Mortis. "Prepare a pack each. All the equipment you think we'll need. And, Ray, I assume you still have your rifle?"

"Yes, sir."

"Good, well, go on, both of you."

ONE HUNDRED METRES beyond the treeline, up high in the canopy, the one known by her people as *Patient in Judgement* watched the three figures as they entered the forest. She had picked up the duty of watching these visitors, a duty the First Pairing considered an essential task, while her brother Singer had taken on the irksome duty of following the other visitor from this group.

Patient had ventured closer to the camp last night to get a better look at them. What she saw tempted her to make a quick judgement, but, as was her name and nature, she held back, wanting to be sure that her assessment was fair and not clouded by resentment. Singer's message about the desecration of the Sanctuary had caused anger among her people.

But for all her patience, she had decided that she did not like the loud one, the one who was always noisy, always waving his arms around. A sense of self-importance boiled off him. It reminded her of the antics of the male Hungry during the mating season, and it was with some regret that she concluded that this loud one was a leader.

In her culture, leadership was a shared calling, and so once she was sure of this conclusion, she looked for other leaders who complemented him, but neither of the others seemed to fit that role. Unable to perceive how this arrangement worked, she'd given the matter no further thought. It was possible that, with the visitors, someone led alone, maybe that was true for this individual.

The other two were, in her estimation, a male and female. The female was perhaps a technician or a scientist. Patient had watched her consult pieces of equipment kept in a bag with her. She also noted that this female sometimes looked at the stars, and there was a sadness deep within her, like the longing for something lost. Patient wondered whether she missed her home, or possibly a partner.

Then there was the other male. He interested her because of the three of them, he paid the most attention to the world around them. He peered into the forest with the look of one searching for threats; he smelt the wind and listened to the noises that the life of the planet made. He was the one who, she thought, might be the most likely to notice her if she was careless. She could not decide what his role was, maybe a tracker or a ranger.

And now they were all running around looking busy, so frantic, and yet they seemed to have little of the wisdom or self-awareness that Patient knew was the stuff of life.

She watched them as they entered the forest; the ranger leading them in. They moved at a steady pace as if this might help them avoid the attention of the Hungry or the Companions, or any of the other creatures of the forest they might come across.

After a few moments, Patient moved off after them, watching the older one at the back with a mixture of distaste and fascination. Even from this distance, she could hear him jabbering away, the anger brimming over in his voice. He was by far the most unaware, unconnected person she had ever encountered.

It was while she was reflecting on these things that she noticed movement from the west. Something was coming towards the three figures. She froze, trying to sense what was coming; probably the Hungry of Eye she'd seen earlier.

She forced herself to stop, breath, and be calm. Should she intervene? She glanced again at the movement; it was definitely the Hungry, and more than one of them. The wind was blowing gently from east to west, so it was probable that the visitors' scent had attracted them.

She forced herself to relax and sense the right course of action, the wise decision. Even as she contemplated the options, she heard the loud person at the back shouting something to the other two.

She made her decision: she would keep her distance and watch.

"GET A MOVE ON, RAY," said Mortis, turning around to scan the forest. "You don't have to go this slowly on my behalf."

Ray looked as if he was about to answer, but then he glanced at Amelia and nodded to his left. She turned the motion tracker in that direction and studied the screen.

"Movement," she said, "something coming this way, directly towards us." She dropped the tracker into her bag and pulled out her Buck hunting knife.

Ray unslung the rifle in one easy move and raised the sight to his eyes, then listened.

"Two." He spoke the words quietly and Amelia moved next to him.

"What's going on?" said Mortis, catching them up and glancing into the trees.

Ray ignored him and stood perfectly still, gun ready.

"Talk to me, Ray," said Mortis, moving up behind them.

"Stay close to us, sir," said Ray.

FROM HER VANTAGE point some fifty metres away, Patient had a good view of the visitors and the creatures who were closing in on them. There were two of the Hungry, an older experienced female and a juvenile learning to hunt. They would be looking for Ground Leapers, but the senior one was teaching her younger charge all the skills of the hunt. Patient knew it was never wise to approach one of these animals when they had a juvenile with them.

The creatures were a few metres from the visitors now. The adult female stopped and sniffed the air and then moved up to the edge of the cover. She flicked a glance at the juvenile, and then she broke cover and charged.

Once the adult was in the open, it gathered speed, and Patient could tell that it had already picked its target. It lowered its head a fraction, readying itself to slam into its prey. The Hungry was fast, but before it had closed half the distance to the visitors, the juvenile exploded from the brush, bounding after its guide, unable to resist the excitement of the kill. Unlike its mentor, its jaws were open and its eyes wide and staring straight at the prey.

RAY SAW the creature break cover, and for a fraction of a second, he stared in wonder. It was built like an overgrown emu with a spray of straggly purple and pink feathers at its neck. It was fast for its size. He remembered that this was a planet with less gravity than they had on Earth.

The bird had covered half of the distance to him in a little over a second, but that was time enough for Ray to bring the Heckler & Koch rifle to eye level and fire off two rounds. The weapon was more suited to long-range shots, but it served its purpose well enough here. He registered the noise of the second creature breaking cover as he was taking aim, but by then, he was committed to taking out the first one.

The 45 mm bullets fragmented on impact. The first was more than enough to remove the top of the creature's head. The second shot ripped through what was, by then, an expanding mass of bone and brain tissue. Ray stepped smartly to one side as the beast crashed into the mud just to the right of his feet, he then swung his attention to the other target.

It was the same kind of creature, but smaller. It emitted a rasping, high-pitched sound, somewhere between a growl and a squeak. It didn't seem to notice or care about the fate of its older comrade; it just ran straight at them.

He fired one shot that grazed the animal's flank, causing it to turn its head. The result was that the animal clipped Ray's side rather than crashing straight into him.

If the larger creature had done this, it would probably have crushed him, but this one was still big enough to knock him off his feet and send the rifle flying.

He tried to roll with the momentum of his fall, knowing he'd now have to deal with this creature using a knife. As he turned, he saw it staggering, jaws open, while it let out an anguished howl. It was bleeding profusely from its flank, but still focused on him. It tensed, ready to attack, but at that moment Amelia leapt towards it and brought her own knife down with all the force she could muster on the back of its head, just behind the skull. Even as he lay prone on the floor, Ray nodded his approval; it was an excellent choice of attack, efficient, precise, and deadly. The animal let out a short, breathy moan, then collapsed onto the ground.

The forest fell silent for a few seconds before the immediate backdrop of distant calls and hooting resumed.

Ray pushed himself up, feeling the pain of bruising and stretched muscles.

Once he was on his feet, he scanned the immediate area.

"Well, that was a hell of a skirmish," said Mortis, stepping behind the pair of them. "Good job, both of you. We'll barbecue some of this later." He pointed at the mutilated animals on the ground.

Ray put his fingers to his lips.

"If I could ask for silence, sir," he said, "in case there are any others."

He gripped his own knife in his hand and listened for a few seconds; then he limped over to the Heckler & Koch.

Amelia took out the comm again and swung it in an arc around them, studying the screen.

"Nothing," she said.

"Can't hear anything apart from some crazy birds up there in those trees," said Mortis.

"I'm sorry to interrupt you just then, sir," said Ray, "but we needed to assess the area for further threats."

"Of course. Are you hurt?"

Ray took a moment to stretch his limbs and flex each finger. He probed carefully with his fingers across his stomach and chest.

"Just some bruising, sir. It will pass. Amelia, are you okay?"

Amelia was wiping the blade of her knife on some leaves on the forest floor.

"I'm fine, we should get moving."

She took up the lead, with Mortis in the middle and Ray bringing up the rear.

"Hell of a beast, that thing was," said Mortis, "Do you think there will be more of them?

"Probably," said Amelia, "although as the heat increases, we're less likely to see them out hunting."

"Either of them could have picked off Patrick," said Mortis, nodding. "All we might find of him is a few bones and some clothing."

"He has the handgun," said Ray.

"Yes," said Mortis, "and I'll want that back."

THEY ARRIVED AT THE SURVIVORS' shuttle in the early afternoon.

The last part of the journey had been slow and tense. Mortis had grown impatient with Ray's methodical process, and his frequent stops to confer with Amelia. The immediate approach had taken over an hour as Ray satisfied himself that the site was deserted and that the survivors had left. As they came closer, they could see the damage that the landing and a subsequent pummelling from one of Zera's creatures had done to the shuttle.

Amelia was the first one to see Patrick's body.

"Ha!" said Mortis, looking at the corpse. "So, he made it all the way here."

"He probably confronted them," said Ray, "and they overpowered him."

"Well, he's lost us the handgun. That makes the job of hunting them that much harder for us, the fool."

"The gun is just there," said Ray, pointing a few metres from the body.

Patrick's handgun lay partially covered in mud, muzzle pointing into the Zeran earth.

"I'll take that," said Mortis, checking the safety catch. He wiped the barrel on his sleeve and slid the pistol into his pocket. "Amelia, come with me. I want to see what you can find in that shuttle."

They left Ray to study the soft mud. The ground was a mess of footprints, human and otherwise. He walked around the perimeter and thought of his stupid brother, who he had loved so much. In the end, he hadn't been able to save Patrick from himself. That failure, and the grief he felt, made his eyes smart. He found Patrick's rucksack a few metres on from where the gun had lain; all it contained were his binoculars and an old water bottle. Ray took the binoculars and tucked them into his own rucksack, then he looked back at the body of his half-brother, took a moment to compose himself, and re-joined the others in the shuttle.

"Well?" said Mortis.

"They went north, towards the coast," said Ray.

"How many?" said Mortis.

"All of them."

Amelia was running a dark plastic wand over the seat cushions scattered across the floor.

"What's that you're doing?" said Mortis.

"DNA check," said Amelia, "I've nearly finished." Ray came over and looked at the results on Amelia's comm.

"Right," said Mortis, "well I don't suppose that will take you long."

"No sir," she said, "probably a good thing, given the amount of patience some of us have today," she added in a whisper.

Ray gave her a half-smile.

"Well?" said Mortis, "what do we have?"

"There are five separate identities here," said Amelia, glancing at the readouts on her comm.

"Okay, we've got them all," said Mortis. "Let's get after them."

"There's something odd about this data, though."

Mortis raised an eyebrow.

"I recognise two of them, but the database doesn't recognise the other three."

"What do you mean?" said Mortis.

"One of those records is an exact match to the records on the

Aspira manifest, the other is a partial match, and then there are three that are just different. It's like they are unregistered passengers."

"How can that be? Explain."

"The one that matches is for Brandon Kellerman. We think he's the one whose pod malfunctioned. The partial match is for Joshua North. Then there are two others, I think they're related. I believe these could be the siblings, Dan and Grace McAllan."

"That makes four of them," said Mortis.

"The last one is the real mystery," said Amelia. "This DNA print doesn't even remotely match what we have on record for Wong Chi-Ping."

"That is interesting," said Mortis.

He was silent for a few seconds, lost in thought.

"I wondered whether one of them might pull a stunt like this."

"What kind of stunt, sir?" said Ray.

"The governments who tried to get their sticky fingers into this project. Well, this changes nothing, we just need to deal with these murderers."

"And preferably before the sun sets," said Ray. "It will be dangerous out in the open after nightfall, and I can't guarantee your safety in the dark."

"Okay," said Mortis. "let's get on with it then."

He strode towards the exit of the shuttle, leaving Ray and Amelia behind him.

FAR ABOVE THEM ALL, in the void, space and time rippled for an instant and a ship emerged, coming to a stop once it was clear of the gate. It hung motionless in space for a few minutes before moving off towards one of the *Aspira*'s docking bays.

18

THEY MADE one more stop at Brandon's request. He was exhausted, far more so than Chi or Josh, even though they were carrying the packs.

The last couple of hours had been slow. They'd all felt weary, and they were stopping every twenty minutes to recover. None of them wanted to talk about whether Chi's blood transfusion might end up being a temporary measure.

Grace knew they should be planning for survival, and talking about what they would do when they reached one of the islands, but the energy and vision required was getting harder to find. She could feel herself getting tired, not just sleepy but exhausted, deep in her bones.

They'd been running for their lives for three days now. They'd been orphaned, hunted down, and they had killed one of their attackers. There had been too much fear, too much blood spilt, and it was getting harder to keep moving forward, to have hope.

These thoughts cycled around her mind, none of them gaining traction. She felt a weight in her body, as if all the tragedy and exertion would catch up with her soon.

And then suddenly, she knew they were near to the sea.

She stopped and listened and breathed in the salty air. The wind was blowing with a little more force and felt cooler, fresher. The grassland included a little sand in the earth, with small hillocks that tested them as they struggled on.

And then, faint on the air, she heard the distant breath of waves breaking on a shoreline.

"We're nearly there," said Josh. He smiled at her. They kept going for another hundred metres and then stopped at the top of a shallow hill that they could now see was a promontory. The ground dropped away towards sandy scrubland, and beyond that, the flat expanse of the ocean, a perfect blue line stretching across the horizon. Grace could even see the flicker of spray nearer the shore.

Brandon was breathing heavily again, his hands on his knees. Josh leaned over next to him.

"Do you need another break?"

Brandon shook his head. "Two minutes, and I'll be good to go."

Grace took the comm out of her pocket and was surprised to see that she'd received a message.

She stopped walking and stared at it.

"What is it?" said Josh.

"Someone is communicating with us, it looks like it's from another ship. They want to know our position."

"Tell them," said Chi, stepping up next to her. "Send the transmission now."

"I'm doing it."

"Your father was a very prudent man," Chi said as he watched her tapping the screen.

"What?" said Grace.

"Trusting you with those codes. He may just have saved us, and opened up this world for humanity."

"Are you going to tell us what this is about?" asked Brandon.

"We must get to safety first," said Chi, "or we'll be dead before anyone can rescue us."

"Is that someone coming to rescue us then?" said Dan. "I mean, should we even be trying to get across the sea in this dinghy?"

"Our enemies won't know of this," said Chi, pointing at the comm, "but they are probably following us even now. We must keep moving."

<hr>

RAY PUT his eye to the gunsight and looked at each of the young people.

There was the brash kid who hadn't received the immunity boosters. He was looking tired, bent over, and Ray noticed that he wasn't carrying anything. Then there was the Chinese boy who was carrying a large yellow pack, the young black guy, Joshua North, grandson of the famous Dr Zera North, after whom the planet was named. Then there was the engineer's daughter, intently studying what he assumed was a comm unit. Next to her was her brother, smaller and younger than the rest of them.

"Well?" said Mortis, looking over his shoulder.

"They're all there," said Ray. "I have a clean sight on all of them."

"Good," said Mortis, staring down at the group. His adaptive lenses were able to pick out each individual. He was pleased to see that all five were together.

"If I shoot one," said Ray, "the others will run."

"Well, you'd better shoot the one that needs to die first, hadn't you?" said Mortis.

Ray settled himself on the ground and brought the sight up to his eyes.

"And which would that be, sir?"

"You see, the one on the right, standing a metre from the rest of them now?" said Mortis.

"Yes, sir."

"That's the target."

"Yes, sir," Ray slowly moved his finger to the trigger.

"THIS DINGHY," said Josh, "I presume it will be simple to put together."

"We don't need to," said Grace. "We remove it from the bag, place it on the shoreline and pull a tag. That releases some compressed gas which inflates the thing, then off we go."

"Sounds simple," said Josh. "Let's see if it works after sixty years in storage."

"Okay," said Brandon, "I'm good, let's go."

As they moved, Grace heard the comm ping; they had another message, but she left it and they walked on further towards a gentle incline that would take them down to the beach. Dan was at her side, Brandon and Chi in front of her, and Josh just behind.

Grace had only taken a few steps when she heard a crack, and Chi's body jerked forward. At the same time, the corner of the pack carrying the dinghy exploded into tatters of yellow plastic. Chi stumbled and fell to the ground, the others stared at him.

"What the hell was that?" said Brandon, breathless again.

Chi grimaced. "Get down!"

Josh dropped beside him and saw the red blooming on his shirt.

"He's been shot," he said.

"How bad is it?" said Grace.

Josh looked back at her and frowned.

Chi turned to them, breathing heavily. "Get down and stay down."

"Where's that first aid kit?" said Josh.

"Leave it," said Chi, "listen to me."

"We've got to help him," said Dan. "Grace, help him."

"Quiet, all of you," said Chi, "and listen." He winced as he dropped the dingy pack on the ground. "Listen, please. That signal you sent will be what saves you. You've completed my mission for me, you and your father. You have opened the Einstein Rosen bridge."

"The what?" said Brandon.

"It's a wormhole," said Grace, staring at Chi. "You're saying we've opened a wormhole. But they're just a fantasy."

"They're not, although of course, we wanted people to think that," said Chi, "especially Mortis."

"You mean the *Aspira* had wormhole capability?" said Grace

"It was carrying the capability to set up one end of a wormhole," said Chi, "but that needed to be activated when we arrived. Your father's codes did that."

"So, are you some kind of government agent?" said Brandon. "Like a spy or something?"

"I am representing many governments, not just one, as I suspect our enemies have now realised."

"You're not Wong Chi-Ping, are you?" asked Josh.

"No, my name is Chen Wei. That message you've just received," he looked at Grace, "is your hope against these murderers."

"This can wait," said Grace, "we need to deal with this wound. Dan, get the first aid kit, now."

"No," said Chi, "it can't wait. Pay attention to what I am saying now, please. You are going to be rescued, and when you are, ask to speak to the Head of the Contact Group, have you got that?"

"Yes," said Grace, "the Head of the Contact Group."

"Tell them," said Chi, and paused as he winced at the pain in his side. "Tell them my real name, Chen Wei, remember that name, Chen Wei; and tell them I have confirmed intelligent life on the planet. Take the comm from my bag. All the evidence is recorded on it."

"Who are you really?" said Brandon.

"I was going to tell you all about this when we were safe. But there's no time. Have you got that message? It's important."

"We've got it," said Grace. "Now let us help you, so you can deliver that message yourself."

"It's too late," said Wei. "The candle is burning too fast for that."

They looked at him, mystified, and then Dan said, "I think we have another problem."

They followed his stare up the hill. At the brow of the promontory, one of the big cats stood staring at them.

"No," said Wei, "that thing cannot take you."

Brandon pulled out the knife he'd been carrying.

"Give me that, Brandon," said Wei. "I will buy you time."

"We're not going to let you face this on your own."

"We can't just leave you," said Josh.

"My friend, I am not going to survive this bullet wound, I can feel it. Only one strategy will save you. I must do my part, you must do yours."

"That thing looks like it will attack us," said Dan.

"Go!" said Wei. "Now, before more of those things come! Get rescued, and tell everyone what has happened here."

He levered himself up off the ground and moved towards Brandon, placing an arm on his shoulder. Brandon passed the knife to him and the sabre-tooth above them started to growl.

"Respect to you, Chen Wei," said Brandon.

"And long life to you, Brandon Kellerman, now go and survive."

Wei straightened himself and turned to face the predator.

"Go," he said, "and once I've killed this thing, I will catch you up."

Grace instinctively grabbed Dan's hand and ran down the hill towards the roar of the sea, Josh and Brandon followed her, leaving Wei to face the animal that now focused on its prey, the smell of blood filling its nostrils.

FROM THEIR VANTAGE point above the hill, Ray, Amelia, and Mortis stared down at the beast, pacing along the edge of the sandbank. They saw Wei stand, his head and shoulders just above the hill.

"Didn't you hit him?" said Mortis.

"I did," said Ray, "but the noise of the shot has brought a predator, and there may be others. We need to be careful."

"What about the rest of the brats?" said Mortis.

"They have run down to the sea," said Ray. "I don't have sight of them."

"That's a shame," said Mortis. "I was hoping you'd be able to pick off at least one more."

He watched Wei face the saber-tooth, and with his enhanced sight Mortis could just see the wound in the boy's side, and the knife.

So he has a weapon, thought Mortis, *this could be entertaining.*

The big cat crouched and then leapt at Wei.

Even injured, the boy moved fast. He skipped to one side and thrust the knife out as the big cat ran past him, catching its neck.

The move took him further down the hill, but Mortis could now see two more big cats running to the top of the bank. He smiled as they glanced down at their prey. There were three of them now, and Mortis assumed the calculations would be brief.

The end, when it came, was quick, and even from a distance Mortis, Ray, and Amelia could hear the noise of the creatures claiming their prize.

"Well, that was disappointing," said Mortis. "I was expecting more of a fight."

As he spoke, there was a noise like a billowing sail in the wind, filling the air above. Then something vast and heavy skimmed over the top of the trees to one side of them, blocking the sunlight for a moment before gliding down towards the feeding predators.

It circled above the ridge, flapping enormous wings and letting out a piercing screech that echoed across the land.

"Impressive looking bird," said Mortis. "When we eventually open a museum displaying the natural history of this planet, I want one of those, stuffed, in the entrance hall."

"We need to go," said Ray, "move back to higher ground."

"What about those kids?" said Amelia, pointing towards the coast.

"If we try to go down there," said Ray, "something will kill us. Night's drawing in, so we should head back to their shuttle and stay in there until morning."

Mortis stared at him. "But they'll escape again!"

"No, they won't," said Ray. "If they move up from the beach at night, they'll end up as prey for one of these creatures. If they walk along the coast in either direction, they'll get a couple of hundred metres at most before they reach sheer cliffs. This is the only way down to the shore for miles around. They're trapped. And besides," he added, "one of them is dead, one of them is sick, and they are only children; it's over."

"I need to be sure they're gone," said Mortis. "I need to be sure, Ray."

"We will be, sir," said Ray, "but if we stay here or we go after them now, we will end up as dinner for one of those cat things. I can't shoot everything that wants to eat us."

"Damn it," said Mortis. "Okay, we retreat to their shuttle until tomorrow."

19

———

"Come on, Dan, move," said Grace, keeping a firm grip on her brother's hand as they ran down the hill. She held Dan's hand and faced the sea, and kept running, holding tight to him. To one side of her, Josh jogged over the sandy ground while Brandon lagged behind them.

She didn't want to slow down, but couldn't bring herself to leave Brandon. She didn't want to admit that he was family now, but he was. Dan pulled his hand from hers as she looked back up the hill.

There was no sign of the creature that had attacked Chi, or Wei, as they now knew his name to be. Josh was just beside her, and Brandon was still catching up. His breathing was hoarse. When he reached Josh, his knees buckled and Josh took his arm, holding him up.

"Hang in there, we're nearly at the coast."

"I can't," panted Brandon, "I can't do this. This planet is killing me. What are we even going to do when we get to the coast?"

"We're going to get rescued," said Grace. "All we need to find somewhere to hide, just for a few hours until they come."

"Okay, I will try not to die." He straightened up, and spat on the sandy grass in front of him.

They walked again, the sound of the waves clearer now, pulling at the shore in an irregular motion as Zera's two moons tugged at the great mass of water that formed the planet's oceans.

Behind them, they heard a screech from high in the air.

"One of those pterosaur things," said Brandon, looking up.

"Maybe it's come to protect us again," said Dan.

"Maybe," said Grace. "Come on, let's keep moving."

The wind had picked up and they could see the ocean surging up the beach in the distance, the spray leaping onto the rocks at the edge of the bay.

"Over there," said Grace. She pointed left to a gentle slope leading down to a broad curve of sandy beach.

They made their way down the slope towards the shoreline, and Grace glanced down just as the spray smashed against the rocks again on the right, and the sight of the water and the sound of the fizzing foam plunged her into a vivid memory of back home and the headland at the northernmost point of Lewis.

Sometimes her parents would take them there, and she would stand, huddled against the raging wonder of the North Atlantic, leaning against her father, blinking against the wind, her mother holding little Daniel's hand. Their mother always called him Daniel, never Dan. The memory of those times broke her heart, and again tears came out of nowhere to run cold on her cheeks.

Josh came over to her and was about to tell her they should keep moving. When he saw the moisture on her face, he stepped back and stayed silent. Dan had turned back to walk with Brandon, and they were slowly catching up with Grace and Josh.

Far above them, the great winged creature circled around on the air currents, keeping watch over them.

Josh was still staring into the sky when he felt Grace touch his arm.

"Let's go," she said.

They pressed on and were soon standing on the crumbly sand of the bay, which curved around to form a protective arc against the main current of the seas. Behind the sand, most of the bay was cupped by cliffs rising from the beach, made from a rich, dark coffee coloured rock and topped with unruly tufts of grass.

Grace looked back up the ridge where they'd left Chi to his fate. There was no sign of the beast that had taken him, or their human enemies.

"We need to keep moving, find somewhere to hide for the next few hours. We're nearly there."

Brandon squinted as he looked out across the bay.

"They'll see us immediately if we're camped out on that beach. Maybe we should find somewhere near those cliffs?"

"We could try in there," said Dan, pointing to the far edge of the bay where the cliff face rose highest from the sand. They all stared at the dark rock and Grace could just make out a darker space, an opening in the cliff they had not noticed before.

"What is that," said Brandon, "a cave?"

"Let's go and see."

They picked their way over the sand. As they approached, they could see that there was indeed an opening in the rock, like a cave entrance. It was difficult to see too far in, but they could make out the sand of the shore extending into the cave and through to the darkness beyond. As they made their way into the damp darkness, the ground rose and became rocky under their feet.

"This will be fine," said Josh. "We should wait here." He glanced at Grace.

She looked at him but said nothing. He was probably right, but the sound of the sea and the memories of home had conspired to drive the energy from her.

Josh stepped closer to her and whispered, "Nearly there. You know, you've been the real leader here."

She turned to him to deny it, but he had already moved on.

At the back of the cave, there was a rocky platform. He led

them to it and climbed onto the ledge, helping Brandon up behind him. Grace and Dan clambered up onto the ledge next to Brandon, and she got out the comm unit again.

There was another message.

"There's a rescue ship, the *Obama*, coming for us now," she said. "It's using the comm as a homing beacon."

"Well, those guys can turn up any time they like," said Brandon. He yawned and then lay down on the rocky surface and closed his eyes.

"So, we wait here," said Josh. He pulled off the rucksack and dug around for one of the water bags.

"I saw a stream running down into that bay. I can fill this up and get us enough water to last us until they come."

"Okay," said Grace, "be careful."

"I will." He slid off the ledge and onto the wet floor of the cave.

Dan came and sat next to Grace, as she sat with her back to the cave wall.

She looked at the shoulder bag she'd held on to throughout all of this. It was spattered with mud and sand, and the buckle was scuffed.

She pulled out two of the protein bars she'd been carrying, and at the sound of the wrapper, Brandon opened his eyes.

She offered one bar to him and one to Dan.

"You're a star, Grace. That must be like a Mary Poppins' bag you've got there; you can find anything in it."

"Not quite," she said, "everything has its limits," and with that, she closed her eyes.

Josh stepped out into the afternoon light and looked along the bay and up to the hills beyond. There was no sign of life, but he could see the stream running into the sea. Further off, the waves chased up the beach; the wind driving the foam across the sand.

He jogged over the dunes and feeling the dull ache in his shoulder where Patrick's bullet had grazed him. When he got to the stream, he stared up at the sky and confessed his thoughts to the wind and the waves and to God.

"What do I need to do?" he spoke into the surrounding wind, "what can I do to save them? To save us all?"

He took the water bag, opened it out, and unscrewed the cap. They weren't rescued yet, and he knew that with Brandon sick, it might fall to him to look after them all until help arrived. Still, he felt unsatisfied. He looked up to the heavens again and thought of Grace, and her courage, her love. Then he found himself standing, bag in one hand, cap in the other, staring at the water by his feet.

"Come on," he said to himself and bent down to the stream.

He tried some of the water from the stream. It tasted clean and good, so he pressed the water bag into the stream and filled it, and as the bag filled, he thought about his father's mother, the great Dr Zera North, the astronomer who had confirmed the presence of the planet that bore her name. The world had celebrated her, but to him she'd always just been his grandma.

He wondered how she would have reacted to the knowledge that someone had murdered her family and that he, Josh, was fleeing for his life. Knowing Grandma Zera, she'd probably have told him to take responsibility and work out what he was going to do to help everyone in this situation.

He remembered one of the last things she'd said to him before she died.

You are a leader, Joshua; I see it in you.

She had only said it once, but the words had pierced his heart, and he knew, somehow, that this was his destiny. He knew that it was in him, but he was always the quiet one, the gentle one, the kind one, but not the leader.

It seemed to be the likes of Brandon who got to lead, or even

Grace, although he did not begrudge her the authority she'd earned. She had led them off that ship and got them down here safely.

He cried out once more, certain that his voice was drowned out by the sound of the waves.

"When do I get to prove who I am?"

He remembered that he'd been the one to face those sabretoothed predators, and he was proud of that, but still he yearned for more.

He screwed the cap onto the water bag, then walked back to the cave.

The other three were exactly where he'd left them. He put the water bag down next to the rucksack and glanced around the cave again. Now he could see that the roof of the cave rose above the entrance, and on the wall above the opening there were marks, designs and images.

He dug out the torch and shone it onto them.

"Hey, Grace," he called to the back of the cave, "come and look at this."

"What?" she said sleepily.

"Look at these images."

Grace climbed down from the ledge and wandered over to where he was standing. He shone the torch up at the designs.

"Cave paintings," said Grace, "like ones back on Earth."

"Parietal art, but not like anything I've ever seen."

"What do they mean?"

"I don't know," said Josh, "most of it's like this, the animals we've seen, but look at this one."

He pointed to a scene that showed a tower with a woman at the top of it. The figure was looking out over styled waves, across an ocean.

"She's waiting for someone," said Grace, "a partner, a lover."

"There's intelligent life on this planet," said Josh, "just like Chi said, and it doesn't surprise me."

"It doesn't surprise you," said Grace, "did you know already?"

"Yes."

"How?"

"Look at this," he said.

He took the pendant out of his pocket and showed her.

"I found this in Patrick's pocket. I don't think this is something anyone brought with them. He got this from someone here, a person."

"It's beautiful," said Grace, running her finger over the intricate hemisphere. "I don't know what to make of this, but I want to find out."

"After we've been rescued, I hope I get a chance to come back here."

"I hope I do too. We just need to survive first."

"I know, I'm sorry."

"None of this is your fault. How's your shoulder, by the way?"

She turned to him, and put her hand gently on the wound, over the stain of blood on his jacket.

"Aches a bit, I expect someone on this rescue ship will patch me up."

Grace paused for a moment, then without thinking, she put her arms around him and held him as tightly as she could, avoiding his injured shoulder.

They stood together like this, silent, motionless, exhausted, feeling the breath rise and fall in each other, listening to the ebb and flow of the waves on the shore.

Grace felt a delicious mixture of comfort and sorrow forming within her, and she was about to say something when she heard Brandon's familiar voice from the back of the cave.

"Hey, guys, I'm just saying if the tide comes in, we're screwed. You know that, don't you?"

Grace smiled despite herself.

"Thank you, Brandon," she said. "We'll bear that in mind."

They stepped back from each other and Josh said, "I'm not

sure this planet even has a tide in the sense that we would know it. It has two moons, so who knows what that means?"

"That rock ledge was dry," said Grace. "We'll be okay there."

They walked back and climbed up next to Brandon and Dan.

"When the cavalry turns up," said Brandon, "I'm hoping they have some of that immunisation booster juice. I mean a real dose, not just some second-hand stuff like Chi gave me, God rest his soul."

There was a little more conversation amongst them as the cave gradually fell into darkness and then they all drifted off to sleep.

WHEN DAN WOKE, he was not sure where he was. It was only after he heard the sea that he remembered.

There was rain now; he could hear it pattering onto the sand outside. The cave was dark except for the faintest glow from the cloud-covered moonlight outside, but that was enough for Dan to see the silhouette of a figure at the mouth of the cave.

He stared at the motionless figure. It was a woman, but taller, like a stretched version of someone.

He was not afraid. He knew that he should be shaking Grace, waking her up, but he was not afraid at all. For the first time in his life, it really dawned on him that he could not always expect Grace to be there for him, and that he could look after himself.

Next to him, Brandon snuffled in an uneasy sleep.

Without knowing why, he leaned over to Josh and nudged him.

"Hey, Josh."

"Huh?" Josh grunted and turned over. "What, what is it?"

"Look," said Dan, pointing at the cave mouth.

Josh stared at the tall figure, human but not human.

"It's okay," said Dan. "I know it's okay, you need to go with her."

Josh turned to Brandon, still snoring, and then Grace.

"Don't wake the others," said Dan. "Just go, go now."

"What do you mean, just go? Who is he?"

"She," said Dan, "she's female. And I just know you have to go, like I knew about the predator down at the lake."

Josh stared at the silhouette for a few more seconds and thought about the words he'd spoken hours earlier.

When do I get to prove who I am?

He looked at Dan and smiled. "Look after your sister, and Brandon, I'll be back soon."

Then he swung his legs over the ledge and dropped quietly to the ground.

He walked up to the figure, his heart beating furiously in his chest, and she reached out and took his right hand. It seemed to Josh the most natural gesture as they walked away from the mouth of the cave.

As Dan watched them go, a tremendous sense of sorrow fell on him. He wept quietly, and he didn't know why, but still, Grace stirred and woke.

"Dan," she said sleepily, "you okay?"

"Just sad," he said.

She was quiet for a moment and then reached out and gathered him close to herself.

"So am I," she said, "sad and tired, but it's nearly over."

"Some of it will never be the same."

"No, it won't, Dan. I'm sorry you had to suffer."

"Mum and Dad would have been proud of you,"

"They'd be proud of both of us."

Dan felt his sister's arms around him, and he listened to the waves rushing back and forth across the sand, until the rhythm of the water sent him back to sleep.

IN THE SILENCE OF SPACE, the ship that had docked with the *Aspira* uncoupled from the great craft and turned its prow to face the planet; a slight flare of its engines was enough to send it into a descent towards the surface, down to the northernmost tip of Zera's great continent.

20

———

Josh scrambled across the beach, still holding the Zeran's hand. He had to jog to keep up. The rain fell around them, soaking into the sand at their feet.

The Zeran took long steady strides, her feet planted firmly on the ground while Joshua slipped slightly with each step.

She was dressed in a tight-fitting one-piece garment that ended at the wrists and ankles, and she wore a pair of thin shoes like slippers. It seemed to Josh that these were not appropriate clothes for in this weather, but then, he was not his planet, so who was he to judge?

They hurried up to the top of the headland. He shivered as the wind hit them, driving the rain into their faces. She stopped, released Josh's hand, and turned to him. Placing her long fingers on her chest, and spoke.

"Gatherer."

The voice was pitched strong and clear. She stared at Joshua for a moment and then spoke again.

"Gatherer."

"Your name is Gatherer?" he asked.

"Yes, Gatherer," she repeated and smiled at him.

Josh slowly placed a hand on his own chest.

"Joshua, Joshua North."

"Joshua North," she repeated.

"Joshua, you can call me Joshua."

She nodded once, and led him at the same brisk pace back the way they'd come the day before, up towards the treeline. From there, they followed the edge of the forest east for about half an hour, towards a hill that spread out across the path ahead of them. Dawn was breaking and a pale orange smudge had formed above the line of the hill.

Gatherer did not break stride as they climbed. After a minute Josh was breathing heavily, and his shoulder ached again. She turned and looked at him and then stopped, letting his hand go.

"Thank you," he said, catching his breath and running his fingers across his hair where a sheen of sweat had formed.

"You are welcome."

He took one more breath and then stared at her.

"You speak my language, how is that? How are you able to understand me?"

"I understand some of your words, and will understand more as you speak and think."

"And think?" said Josh.

"I am beginning to discover who you are, Joshua. As I do so, I learn your language, and much else besides. With you it is easy, of all your kind, I understand your heart and your mind best."

She paused for a minute while he tried to get his breath back.

"The young one we also understand," said Gatherer. "He is open to us, but he is too young to give an account."

"You're talking about Dan."

"Dan. Yes, Dan. He is not yet of age, but you are, and you stood before the Sky Messengers."

"You mean those pterosaur things?"

Gatherer looked thoughtful.

"Yes, I suppose that is how you might know them. The Sky Messengers tell us that they have decided to watch over you."

"I thought they would kill us."

"No, you did not," said Gatherer. "If you had really thought that, you would have attacked the one that stood before you, or perhaps fled from it. But you didn't."

"You're right," said Josh, frowning. "I knew it meant us no harm, I don't know how."

"Because you sensed that it was so. The Messenger gave you an account of itself, and you believed it. Now, we require an account from your kind, and we chose you for that role. Are you ready to give an account?"

Josh frowned at her.

"I don't know what you mean by 'give an account'. I can only speak for my group, not for the people who want to murder us. I, we, need your help."

He stared straight at her. He hadn't looked at her properly yet, but now in the dawn light he could see her features: searching, enquiring eyes a little larger than a human would have, and she was smiling, expressing a kindness that seemed to warm his heart. Her hair was tied back into a bun and held with a clip made of dark wood, but a few wisps of it were free and blew in a gentle breeze, and she was fierce and beautiful in his eyes and he looked away.

Then he was surprised as an image of Grace come into his head, and he blinked, realising that he was not here to admire this alien woman, but to speak up for his friends. They were relying on him, and he needed the Zeran's help.

"Please," he said, "my friends and I, we are being pursued by some of our own kind. They are..." he didn't know how best to describe the people who wanted to murder him.

"We know of them," said Gatherer.

"Please help us, one of us also is sick, he needs medicine."

Gatherer nodded. "But first you must give an account."

"I don't know what that means."

"Come," she said and with that, she reached out her hand and they walked together to the summit.

Josh could see that the hill extended out into a horseshoe shape, with the sides sloping down into a small valley, at the centre of which was a dark round structure.

Gatherer led him down into the semi-circular space and towards the structure. Even in the faint dawn light, he could see that it was not made of sticks or mud or even stones piled together, but was in fact smooth and hard, like polished granite. It formed a perfect hemisphere above the ground. As they approached it, Gatherer led him around the edge of the structure until, quite suddenly, she stopped.

She studied a section of the wall which looked seamless to Josh, but when she placed the long fingers of her right hand on the surface, a door-sized portion moved back into the building and then to their left, revealing a lit tunnel with a pathway that led into the earth, extending far beyond the circumference of the building.

"Come." She led him down the path as the section of the wall fell back into place behind them. They walked below ground level into a tunnel which opened out so that for a moment Josh could not see the dimensions of the space he was in. The pathway was flanked by thin railings and lit by globes of soft white light, descended into darkness.

Even though Josh could not see the sides of the space, he could pick out an orange light, like a pale imitation of Zera's own sun, shining from far below. The pathway led down to a balcony that extended off in a curve in either direction around the edge of the space.

As they approached, he saw a wall bordering the inner edge of the balcony. It stood a metre high and was made of the same polished stone as the exterior of the building. Gatherer took his hand again and led him round to an opening in the wall, which gave access to a carriage in which there were clusters of seats. It reminded Josh of the monorail cars on the Aspira, except this space was larger and the seats were carved from Zeran wood. The carriage was lit by a series of glowing bulbs that hung from its ceiling, and the air smelt of cut grass. The walls of the carriage had narrow slits carved into them which admitted a little light from the outside.

"Sit, Joshua."

He took a chair that felt a little too large for him. Gatherer sat next to him, and the carriage descended, moving downwards at a steep diagonal, light flickering through the wall slits as they gathered speed.

Instinctively Josh felt for something to hold on to as the carriage picked up speed. There were no arm rests or handles and so he closed his eyes, held on to the edge of the seat. He wondered what this account was that he needed to give, and who he might need to give it to.

There was a white flash outside the carriage, and sunlight shone through slits in the wood panelling.

"We have just passed the sun grid," said Gatherer.

A couple more minutes passed before Josh felt the carriage slowing down. Finally, it stopped, and the door opened, and Josh could see the light of day, and hear sounds, conversation, people, the movement of feet. He felt as if he'd just arrived at a busy train station. "It feels like we're outside."

"This is our home," said Gatherer.

"So that's why we haven't seen all of you," said Josh. "You live underground."

"These concepts of outside and underground have no meaning for us," said Gatherer. "Sometimes we visit the surface and sometimes we are here. But it is all one to us. We are always in this place that you call Zera."

Gatherer led him out of the carriage and onto a bright and busy concourse. Other Zerans crowded around, some talking to each other, a few stopping to stare at him.

He was standing in sunshine in a broad city square. He looked up and thought he was looking at the sky on a summer day, although there was no single source of light.

On each side of the square, paths of level compacted earth ran off into the distance, flanked by the familiar Zeran trees, spiking into the air. Behind the trees, he could see two-storeyed houses spaced along each avenue, constructed of light wood with long rectangular windows.

Beyond the houses were some larger buildings, and he could not guess what their purpose was. They might have been meeting halls, temples, theatres or factories, or maybe something he could not even imagine.

"This way," said Gatherer, taking his hand again.

"It doesn't feel like we're below ground."

"But we are," said Gatherer, "you felt us descend. This is part of our space, and it is for us only. Whilst the surface is also ours, we share it with the flora of our planet, and animals of the land and the sea. It is theirs as much as ours, and in that space we," she paused, considering the right word to use, "we defer to them."

"Okay. So, you live underground and let the animals and plants of Zera live on the surface."

"We live where it seems right to us," said Gatherer, "and where it is right for the other life of the planet. To be underground or on the surface is as one space. The planet has made provision for us, as it does for every inhabitant: the Hungry of Eye, and the Ground Leapers, the Companions of the Hunt and the Sky Messengers, and all the other living things you haven't yet encountered."

"I don't know what you mean by these names," said Josh.

"There will be time for explanations," she took Josh's hand again. "We need to keep moving." She led him out of the square and along one of the tree-lined boulevards.

Some of the other Zerans were now looking at him, most with curiosity, some with suspicion.

"Tell me more about this account you want from me," he said.

"Of all the visitors of your kind, you are the one most open to us; and so you must give an account."

"Do you mean I should tell you why we are here?"

"Maybe that in time," said Gatherer, turning towards him, "but first, Joshua, you must give an account for the spilling of blood."

"You mean our friend Wei? Or Patrick, the one who attacked us?"

Gatherer frowned at him.

"No, although we should hear these stories as well when the time comes. The account you must give is for the spilling of the blood of my kin."

A Zeran male approached them, and Gatherer waved him away. He stared at Josh and shouted at him.

"What do you know of Singer's blood? What account do you give for your kind?"

"Say nothing," said Gatherer. She barked something behind her and pulled on Josh as if he were a dawdling child.

They stopped outside a larger, single storey building, set back from the avenue and surrounded by a garden full of purple and orange flowers. Unlike the other buildings he'd seen, this one was round. A thin streak of smoke rose above the roof from one of the rooms within.

Gatherer led him through this garden to a door of smooth, dark wood which opened when they approached.

"You are meeting one of our First Pairing," said Gatherer, "our leaders. Be silent before her; just answer her questions, and may it go well with you, Joshua."

Josh saw that there was another Zeran woman standing in the doorway. She was shorter than Gatherer and older, with grey streaks running through long hair braided with creamy red and pink shells. This woman now regarded him with fierce blue eyes. Josh felt as if she could see all his secrets and could judge him in an instant.

The woman turned to Gatherer and nodded. Josh noticed that, unlike Gatherer, she wore a knife in a scabbard on her belt. She stared at him and he felt naked, exposed.

"Come in, Joshua North. I am Savanatha, Wisdom Bringer, one of the First Pairing of the Northaven clan."

"Pleased to meet you," he said.

"Are you?" she said, then she whispered something to Gatherer, who bowed her head and walked away. Savanatha turned to Josh. "Come in."

He stepped into a tall, narrow hallway. Pieces of canvas covered each wall, some square and some perfectly round, some showing images of the sea, a forest, while others were just a single colour, dark green or blue or purple, and one showed a valley which might have been the place where they'd landed.

The thought reminded him of his friends.

"God help them," he whispered.

The woman turned to him.

"What did you say?"

"I was thinking of my friends," said Josh, "the ones I came with, the ones I left behind at the cave."

"That is not what I asked," said the woman, "I asked you what you said."

"I said 'God help them'."

"Indeed. So, you were praying for your friends. You were calling out to your God for them."

"Well, yes, I was."

"From now, answer the questions I ask you truthfully."

"I will," said Joshua, "but my friends are in danger. One of us has been murdered."

"We know, but the wise course of action for you is to be silent for now."

"But we need…"

"Silence," she said again, "come with me."

She led him along the hallway and into a bare room containing nothing but cupboards made of a light wood, and an old wooden table stained with use. There were six slim chairs arranged around it.

"Sit," said Savanatha.

Josh climbed up onto one of the tall chairs.

Savanatha went to a cupboard, opened it and took out a large glass jug and a wooden cup. She set the cup on the table in front of Josh and turned to a broad stone trough set against one of the walls. There was a tap made of silver metal, which she used to fill the jug with water.

"Here," she said, and poured some of the water into the cup.

He hesitated.

"It is only fresh water, we would not bring you all the way here into the holding just to poison you. You are thirsty, and therefore, your mind will not work at its best. I would not wish that disadvantage on you when the time comes for you to give your account."

He picked up the glass and drank the cool, clear water.

"Why did you come here in two craft?" said Savanatha.

"You mean our two shuttles?" said Josh. "It was because our enemies pursued my friends and me down here. We came in one shuttle; they came in the other."

"Why are they your enemies, Joshua?"

"They wish to kill us and claim the planet for themselves. But I can see that it belongs to you and all that lives here," he added.

Savanatha's face twitched with a smile.

"Now you are refreshed, we will go; and because I have decided that I like you, Joshua North, I will give you this advice. You will meet a woman today to whom you must give your account. When she comes near you, let her see you, let her hear you, let her examine you if she so wishes."

"Examine me?" said Joshua.

"Yes, let her see you, let her touch your pain if she wishes to do so. Do not stop her or resist her. Now, we should go."

"But what about my friends? I need to help them."

She raised a finger and touched his lips. "We know these things, you do not need to mention them again."

"I have to," said Josh, hearing his voice rise. "They are all I have now. If you want me to answer your questions, then you must help us."

Savanatha paused, then laughed, a clear, strong sound that echoed through her house.

"Defiant love!" And she laughed again. "I do like you, Joshua North. But now, centre yourself. Someone will watch over your friends, all of them."

She led him out of the house and back down the avenue to the concourse, where he could see a crowd had now gathered in the centre of the square. There must have been over two hundred Zerans, young and old, men and women. They murmured when they saw him.

The crowd formed a rough semicircle in the middle of which was a woman, separated from the others. When Josh came near to the group, she stared at him with fierce, bloodshot eyes. At her side were two children. Josh couldn't work out how old they were, but one, a girl, was about the same height as he was, and there was a boy who was smaller. For a moment, they reminded him of Grace and Dan.

Savanatha walked with Josh to the edge of the space.

"Walk forward three paces," she said, "and then stand still."

He did so and then heard Savanatha's voice behind him. She shouted a few words, clear and loud. The whole group shuffled and moved into an arc around them. The woman who had been crying came forward and faced him. She stood a couple of metres from Josh, and like Gatherer, she was more than a metre taller than him.

She released the hands of her children, kissed them both, and they ran to the edge of the group where an older Zeran couple stood.

The woman took a step closer to Joshua and stared down at him.

"The blood of the one I love is spilt," she said. The word 'spilt' came out so loud that the sound echoed around the square.

She removed a thin silver bladed knife from a scabbard at her belt and pointed it at Josh.

He stepped back a pace.

"Stand still," barked Savanatha, "and face her."

Josh's heart thumped in his chest, but he did what he was told, straightened his shoulders and looked her in the eye.

"The blood of the one I chose," the woman said, "whom I loved, is spilt, and I am torn. My children are torn, and I am told that one of your kind did this, Joshua North, and you will give me an account."

Joshua looked at her. He was afraid, but he also felt compassion for her and her children.

"I do not know what happened to your partner," he said, "and I am so sorry for you and your children." He looked at the woman and he thought about the violence she described, and a thought came into his mind.

It must have been Patrick.

"I do not even have his story," said the woman. "I cannot even make that whole with my own." Tears were on her cheeks and she clutched at a pendant that lay at her breast. The knife shook in her hand.

He looked at the little hemisphere that hung from her neck on a light silver cord, and he reached down to his jacket pocket where his hand closed on the pendant he had taken from Patrick's corpse. He drew it out and held it up in front of her.

"I found this."

The Zerans grew quiet, some of them moving closer to get a better look.

The woman let out a sigh like a heartbreak, reached forward, and gently took the pendant from his hand. She sheathed her knife and held up the blue hemisphere, then reached for her own pendant and carefully brought the two together.

The two halves fitted perfectly.

She held these two pendant halves together, closed her eyes and let out a deep, deep moan from the very core of her being, and all the crowd was silent. Then, finally, she turned to Josh and the rest of the crowd watched her, let out another cry, louder this time. The sound carried up into the air and filled the surrounding square.

"I found it with the one who might have killed him," said Josh, "but he is now dead, and I return it to you."

Everything was silent. Josh looked at this grieving Zeran woman in front of him, and then at the crowd.

"This is my account."

The woman in front of him shouted a question, but Josh could not understand what she was saying. He turned to Savanatha.

"What is she saying?" he said. "It wasn't me that killed him, it was Patrick, it was one of our enemies that did this."

"She asks," said Savanatha, "why she should believe you. She asks for proof that you were not the one who killed her partner, that you are not her enemy."

He turned back to the woman who stared at him, clenching the knife. At the edge of the crowd, the smaller of her children started to cry.

"I am asking you the same question, Joshua North," said Savanatha, "how do we know you are not in league with the one who killed Singer?"

Joshua looked at her and then back at the woman.

"I did not kill your partner, but the one who did also attacked me."

The woman just stared at him, and he could see the pain and the anger in her.

"Did he?" she said, speaking Joshua's language now. "These are just words. Where is the proof of what you say?"

The Zerans murmured to each other. Josh looked around at them, and then at Savanatha.

"How did he attack you?" she asked.

He looked at the woman in front of him.

God give me wisdom, he thought. His shoulder throbbed.

"Here," he said, "here is my proof."

Slowly, he took off his jacket. Then he eased off his shirt and finally he ripped off the dressing from where Patrick's shot had grazed his shoulder. The wound felt raw and cold, exposed to the open air, and fresh red blood formed on the wound.

The woman sheathed the knife and stared at the wound. Then she came forward and pressed her long fingers around the damaged flesh. Josh continued to look straight at her. Finally, she leaned forward and sniffed at Josh's shoulder where the blood had collected and was beginning to run down onto his chest.

"The smell of the weapon that killed Singer is in this wound," said the woman gently. "Have you suffered at the hands of my enemy, Joshua North? Speak the truth to me."

"I have, but not as your partner did. I am sorry." He tried to think of something else to say, but there was nothing. He reached for his shirt.

The woman stared at him as he eased his arms through the sleeves, the fresh blood in his wound sticking to the material.

She looked at him for a moment more and then she said, "I am *Venna*, and I accept your account, Joshua North."

She turned to the old man of the couple who was with her children and said something Josh could not understand. The old man reached into a pocket of his tunic and removed three square packets, they looked like little envelops, made of creamy coloured paper. He walked over to Venna and handed them to her.

She glanced at them and then returned all but one.

"Be still, Joshua." She spoke gently now as she opened the flap of the packet and removed a thin piece of material like gauze. With strong, delicate fingers, she pushed his shirt aside and placed the gauze onto the wound. The material stung when it touched his flesh, but soon turned to warmth.

"Be restored, Joshua North," said the woman. Then she turned from him and walked with the old man back to her children at the edge of the crowd.

From behind him, Josh heard Savanatha's voice speaking in words he could not understand, but then in his own language she said, "Bear witness, an account has been given to the one who by right demanded it, and the account is accepted."

The crowd answered with a murmur, and then Savanatha spoke again. "Come," she said, "as many of you as wish to witness this, it is time to demand that another account be given."

Then she turned to Josh.

"Put your shirt and jacket back on, Joshua North, and come with us."

21

———

Grace woke to the sound of the sea lapping at the floor of the cave, and the rattle of Brandon's breathing. Her head ached from where Patrick had hit her, and her throat was sore and parched.

She sat up and squinted at the light. It was well past dawn, and Dan lay next to her, still asleep, Brandon further over, snuffing and twitching, a sheen of sweat across his forehead.

But Josh was gone.

She looked up to the light and saw that the tide was now lapping at the sand just a few metres from the edge of the cave.

"Josh," she called, then she stretched her stiff legs and worked her way to the edge of the ledge.

"Josh!"

She took the comm from her bag. A new message appeared on the screen.

We are coming for you now. Make sure you are visible.

Dan stirred next to her. He opened his eyes.

"Hey," she said, holding up the comm, "they're coming to rescue us, we'll be okay."

Dan nodded.

"Do you know where Josh went?" she asked him.

He didn't answer.

"Dan?"

"He had to go," said Dan.

"What do you mean, he had to go?" said Grace. "Where did he go?"

She had lost count of the number of conversations she'd had with Dan over the years similar to this one.

"Someone came for him, one of the Zerans."

Grace stared at him. None of this made any sense, but she didn't have the energy to deal with it. She and Dan were going to be rescued, and Brandon would get the medical help he needed. She turned and called his name.

"Brandon."

"Huh?"

"They're coming for us."

"Who," he said, "those murderers?" He tried to raise himself onto an elbow.

"No," she said, "our rescuers, they're coming. Can you move?"

"Yeah," he said and groaned again.

"Come on, Dan," she said, "we need to put a big red cross or something on the ground for them."

"What about the others?" said Dan. "The ones that want to kill us?"

"We've got to hope that the rescue ship arrives first."

"Can't we just wait here?" said Brandon.

"They say we need to make ourselves visible," said Grace. "You can wait here if you want while Dan and I look for them."

"No," said Brandon, pushing himself up off the surface of the ledge. "I'm not staying on my own; we need to go together in a group." He laughed, "listen to me being all about the group now. Josh would be proud. Where is he, by the way?"

"He went off with a Zeran," said Dan.

Brandon stared at him.

"What?" he looked at Grace. "What does that mean?"

She shrugged her shoulders.

"I just don't know."

Brandon shook his head and laughed. "This place is crazy," he said.

They drank the rest of the water and Grace checked that she had Chi's comm as well as her own in her bag, and then they stumbled out of the cave into the sunlight.

They made their way slowly up the hill towards the bank above the shoreline. It took nearly an hour to reach the promontory, then Grace pulled everything she could find out of the rucksack and started scattering it all: clothing, bandages, their fire lighter, and binoculars into a rough cross shape on the sandy ground.

Brandon sat and watching them, Dan and Grace came and sat next to him as Grace stared up at the pale outlines of Zera's two moons, one light, one darker, still visible in the blue sky.

She blinked, then closed her eyes. Suddenly she was alone on the grass, listening to the wind, and then her mother was there, telling her how proud of her she was, for looking after Dan, and for figuring out how to enter the codes into the comm, and Grace told her about Chi, who was actually Wei and she nodded. Then her mother slipped away, and another voice entered her mind.

"Three of them, so one's missing."

She opened her eyes to see a sharp-featured woman, and a tired-looking man with cropped greying hair who was carrying a rifle.

Behind them was someone she immediately recognised.

"Callum Mortis," she said, as she stared at him.

Mortis pushed past the other two and walked up to her. He was panting, and she could see patches of sweat under the arms of his shirt. "The same," he said and grinned. "Always good to be recognised."

Dan, lying next to her, was stirring now, but Brandon stayed still, wheezing as he breathed.

Mortis leaned over her.

"Sick, is he," said Mortis, "this one?" He nodded at Brandon.

She stared at the old man, wanting to feel hatred and anger, wanting to feel anything, but there was nothing there now, she just felt numb.

"I thought so," said Mortis. "Honestly, I'm surprised he's not already dead. Now where is the other one, Joshua is it? Is he off collecting food and water? Or maybe he's watching us right now?"

Grace just stared at him.

"Why do you want to kill us?" said Dan in a small voice. "What have we ever done to you?"

"What?" said Mortis. "What did you say?"

"Why do you want to kill us?" said Dan.

"We don't want to kill you," said Mortis. "We just want you out of the way, that's all."

Brandon stirred, opened his eyes, and looked at Mortis.

"You," he croaked. He tried to say more, but fell into a coughing fit.

"Yes, it's me," said Mortis. "Not looking too well, are you, Mr Kellerman?"

"Can we just finish this please?" said Amelia.

"Oh, please do," said Mortis. "I'll watch from over here." He stepped back a few paces.

Ray sighed and then turned to them.

"This will be quick," he said, calmly, quietly. "I suggest you all close your eyes. If you hear a shot, don't move, just keep still and quiet, it will be over soon."

"Get on with it, Ray," said Mortis from behind them. "Do the sick one first, put him out of his misery."

Ray raised the gun. As he did so, a deep rumble came out of the sky and filled the surrounding air.

Ray paused; Mortis was about to speak, but then they all heard it. A whisper that became a hum and then the sound of an engine in the air.

Above them, out of the blue, a ship appeared. It banked

around over the sea and came circling in, deafening them all now, and landing with a roar on the broad expanse of sandy ground, kicking up grit as it touched down.

Ray lowered his gun as the noise of the ship settled to a ticking of cooling metal. Finally, a door on the side of the ship opened, and five figures, all in protective suits, emerged.

One of the suited people led the others down towards the group. A woman removed her helmet, and the others followed. She took a breath of Zeran air and said, "I am Captain Wu, of the Contact Group. This is Lieutenant Garcia and his team. Which of you has the comm we have been communicating with?"

"I do," said Grace.

"Is this all of you?"

"There's one more," said Grace. "We don't know where he is. But these–" She pointed to Ray, Amelia and Mortis.

Before she could say any more, Mortis butted in.

"Thank God you've arrived. We've been looking for these children. I assume you know what happened on the *Aspira*?"

"We do," said Captain Wu, "and you are?"

"I'm Callum Mortis, of course."

The captain looked at him, then whispered something to her lieutenant.

"After the disaster on the *Aspira*," said Mortis, "these children ran away, no doubt in fear, and came down to the planet. We've been chasing around trying to find them. They got confused and thought we meant them harm."

"Do any of you know what happened on the *Aspira*?" said Captain Wu.

"Malfunction in the final pod feed protocol," said Amelia. "We've done a limited investigation, but there's more work to be done."

"Indeed, there is," said Captain Wu, "and the bodies of the colonists?"

"Jettisoned into the atmosphere as per regulations," said

Amelia, "and," she pointed at Brandon, "this boy is ill, he needs immediate care."

"I'm just glad we found them in time," said Mortis, "and that you found us, Captain Wu."

"It's not true," said Grace. They all looked at her. "What he's saying is not true," she said more loudly. "They've been trying to kill us. We've been trying to escape!"

"You can see they're very distressed," said Mortis, "and I'm afraid there's more. I have to tell you we believe one of these children killed a member of our team when he came looking for them."

"You tried to murder us!" screamed Grace.

"The only ones who have done any murdering, are you and your little party," said Mortis. "Tell me what happened to our colleague, Patrick? What happened to him?"

"He attacked us," said Grace, feeling anger bubbling up inside her. "You're a liar and a murder."

"Patrick is dead," said Mortis, "because one of you stabbed him with a knife. Maybe you can tell Captain Wu here who was responsible for that?"

Grace stared at Mortis and then at the lieutenant.

"I think it's best if you deal with them now," said Mortis, "but there is one other matter I am compelled to clarify."

"In a moment," said Captain Wu, holding up a hand. She turned again to her team.

"Medical crew, get to work please," she said, "deal with the boy first, then check the others."

One figure spoke into a comm unit while two others went forward to Brandon.

"Now if I may," said Mortis.

"Yes, what is it?" said Wu.

"It's the question of ownership of the planet," said Mortis. "I know this might not seem like the time to do this, but it is important. I want you to bear witness to this, Captain Wu, as required by the agreed protocols."

He stood up straight and cleared his throat.

"On behalf of the crew and colonists of the *Aspira*," said Mortis, "and as the first citizens of age, I, Callum Primo Mortis, claim this land with my colleagues Raymond Douglas Merritt and Amelia Lucinda Gorst, under the Indigenous Rights Act whose jurisdiction is extended to all of Earth's planetary colonies. Under this provision, I claim these rights."

Grace listened in disbelief. How could he get away with this? What could she do?

Then a thought came to her.

"Wait," she said, standing up and looking at Captain Wu. "We arrived here first before any of them, so we claim the land, I claim it."

Mortis looked at her and smiled.

"It's true, you were here before us, but," he put on a sad look, "none of you are of age, you are all children, so I'm afraid it doesn't count."

"Chi wasn't a child, was he?" said Grace. "He was the first person of age here."

"Who is Chi?" said Mortis, raising his eyebrows. "And where is he?"

"He's dead," said Grace, "you shot him."

"No, we didn't," said Mortis calmly.

"Yes, you did!" Grace practically screamed out the words. She could feel tears coming, tears of frustration at the injustice of what was happening, tears for Chi, for her parents, for all the lives casually spent in the service of this man's greed and ambition.

"Enough," said Captain Wu. "We will deal with this from here. The priority now is your health and welfare." She turned to Callum Mortis.

"I provisionally accept your claim, Callum Mortis, as you say, under the auspices of the Indigenous Rights Act, and pending further investigation of what has happened here."

"Thank you," said Mortis, smiling, "thank you."

"No," said Grace, "he's a murderer, don't let him get away with it. He's probably murdered Josh." She was on her feet now. "What have you done with Josh?"

"Please calm down," said Captain Wu. "We are here to help you. Let us do that."

"But," said Grace, "he's a murderer!"

"As I was saying," said Mortis, "they are very upset."

He turned to Ray and Amelia. "Captain Wu, you have our full cooperation," he said. "Thank you for coming to rescue us, and for your acknowledgement of our claim."

Then someone else spoke.

"What is this claim that you dare to make, Callum Mortis?"

A female voice, clear and strong, spoke out from further up the hill.

They all turned to see who she was, and as they did so, she spoke again.

"You have no claim here, Callum Mortis, this is not your land."

A strikingly tall female was looking down at them. Grace could see that Joshua was standing next to her, and another tall figure, male, was standing on her other side. There were others like them clustered around.

All the humans present stared at the Zerans, trying to recognise them as humans, but they were not. They knew that what they were seeing was alien.

"No," whispered Mortis under his breath. "This is my land."

"Josh," said Grace under her breath.

He couldn't have heard her, but in that moment he glanced down at her, winked and smiled. Then the male Zeran spoke.

"This is our land, Callum Mortis, not yours, you have no claim here."

"What?" said Mortis, flustered now. "Who are these educated savages? I'm not putting up with this."

"You will be silent," the woman said, looking at him.

Mortis just stared at her, and as he opened his mouth again, she spoke. "Silence, Callum Mortis," she said.

Mortis closed his mouth.

The woman cast a long look across the humans before her.

"I am Savanatha," she said, "of the First Pairing and a leader of the community of this land. Joshua North, one of your kind, has given an account for himself and his own group. And in the spirit of friendship, we welcome you to our land."

She turned and looked at Captain Wu.

"Do you have authority here?" she asked.

"This is ridiculous," said Mortis. "I am the leader of humanity on Zera. If you want to address anyone, then address me."

Savanatha and Wu ignored him.

"I am Captain Wu Huan, of the National Space Administration of the People's Republic of China. I am seconded to the Contact Team of the Federation of Sponsoring Nations, and I have authority to speak for humanity here."

Savanatha turned to the male Zeran, who stood at her side.

"In the spirit of friendship and cooperation," he said, "we offer you this gift."

He walked down the hill towards Captain Wu and placed a small woven basket at her feet. In it was a hemispherical piece of black stone, carved with intricate patterns.

"Enough of this," said Mortis. "Captain Wu, are you going to restore the rule of law here or am I going to do it?"

Without waiting for an answer, he pulled a gun from his pocket.

"I will get a grip on this situation," he said. "Ray, come here and stand with me."

Ray looked at his boss and hesitated.

"Now, Ray," said Mortis.

Still Ray didn't move.

"Everyone will lay their weapons down," said Captain Wu, "now."

"Why am I always surrounded by weak people? Owen was weak, all of you are weak."

"Your son was not weak," said Amelia suddenly.

"What?" said Mortis, staring at Amelia, "Owen? My son Owen? Not weak? He was the weakest of all; a worthless, whiny brat. Useless, like his mother."

"You do not understand how strong he was," said Amelia. She was smiling faintly, as if she was seeing something in her mind, something far better than whatever was around her. "You," she continued, "you talk, and shout, and bully your way around, as if you are the big man, but you are weak. Your son was more of a man than you will ever be. You have nothing, and no one is listening to you anymore, do you understand? No one."

She took two paces towards him, and Mortis gaped at her.

"And this," said Amelia, "is my vengeance for what you did to your brave son, Owen," and she launched herself at him.

"Enough!" shouted Wu and signalled for her team to disarm Amelia, Ray, and Mortis.

Mortis staggered back. "She's jabbed me," he said, dropping the gun, "she's jabbed me with something."

Amelia tossed the inoculation gun to the ground. Ray let out a sigh, flicked on the safety catch of the rifle and laid it on the sandy grass at his feet.

"It's not as quick as the genetic virus," said Amelia, "but it will finish you just the same."

Wu's team gathered all the weapons, as one of the medical crew with Brandon looked up.

"Captain," she said.

"Report," said Wu.

"He's bad, we need to get him stabilised and back to Earth or we'll lose him."

As the medic spoke, half a dozen more people emerged from the ship.

"Medical teams," said Wu. "Brandon Kellerman and Callum Mortis are a priority, then the others. I want these two," she pointed at Ray and Amelia, "in the brig; we can treat the others in med bay." Then she turned to Savanatha.

"I fear that we have not given a good account of ourselves here," she said, "and I am sorry. I have to deal with these now." She pointed at the survivors and Mortis's party, who were being escorted onto the ship. "Others of my kind will return to speak with you."

"I understand. You should go now," said Savanatha, "and when others of your kind return, we expect them to do so in peace."

Captain Wu nodded.

"There are two more things," said Savanatha. "If you do not think you can save Brandon Kellerman, bring him back to us immediately. We have the means to cure him if you do not. Do not let him die."

"We will take him and assess him," said Wu. She hesitated and then said, "If we cannot cure him, we will seek your help. And the other thing?"

"When you return, bring Joshua North and Grace McAllan with you, they will have authority to speak for your kind."

"That will depend on how the Federation committee wishes to proceed," said Wu.

Savanatha looked at the captain.

"We appoint Joshua North and Grace McAllan as our representatives, you will deal with us through them."

Captain Wu paused for a moment, "I will make sure the Federation committee knows your wishes," she said.

"Hey," cried Mortis as they pulled him towards the ship. "You! Alien woman! I heard what you said about saving the boy. Save me! Save me from whatever that bitch has jabbed me with. Can you do that?"

"Yes, we can," said Savanatha.

"Do it then," said Mortis, "do it now."

"No," said Savanatha, "we will not. We could save you, but we choose not to. You have not given an account, and even if you did, I think it would not be accepted. Captain Wu will deal with you as she sees fit."

"But I am Callum Mortis," he said. "I made this trip happen."

Savanatha frowned at him but did not reply. She placed a hand on Josh's shoulder. Then all the Zerans turned and started to walk back up the hill.

Grace could see one of Captain Wu's team coming towards her, but before he arrived, she ran up the hill towards Josh.

"Josh," she called, "don't let them go yet."

Josh called out to Savanatha, and she paused and turned.

Grace ran up to her. "Wait, please. I have a gift for you as well."

"Ah, you are Grace," said Savanatha, smiling, "such a beautiful name. It pleases me to savour its meaning."

She closed her eyes and breathed in and out, slowly, then she smiled.

"What do you have for us, Grace?"

Grace reached around her neck and unclipped the St Christopher her parents had given her. She held it out.

"You have given us a gift," she said, "and in the spirit of friendship, I offer one back to you, a gift from humanity."

Savanatha reached out and took the St Christopher. She studied it for a moment, running her fingertips over the design, then she gently closed it in her hands.

"Thank you, Grace," she said, and she smiled. "Now I understand why there is such sorrow upon your group."

Josh looked at her and raised his eyebrows.

"It is clearer to me what has happened to you," said Savanatha, looking at both Grace and Josh. "Look at the image on this gift from your friend Grace."

Josh looked at the St Christopher, the image showed the saint barefoot, carrying a child across some water.

"This tells me not just of the longing of your kind to explore and travel, but that you would also take your children with you."

"Yes," said Grace.

"So now I see into your sorrow," said Savanatha.

"You do?" said Josh.

"Of course," said Savanatha. "You are little more than children yourselves. You must have travelled here with your family, those you loved, and who loved you, but they are gone, aren't they?"

Grace and Josh said nothing.

"I see that I am right," said Savanatha kindly, "and you are the survivors."

"I suppose we are," said Grace.

"There is one more thing," said Savanatha, "one more truth for you to know. You have called us Zerans, because, of course, you call our planet Zera. But we are the Alethi, naming ourselves after our moon, Aletheia, and those who bear her name, our brother Alethar, Queen Aletheia herself. We are the Alethi, and this land, this continent, is Aleth."

"Who is Alethar?" said Grace, "and Queen..."

"Queen Aletheia. Their stories are for another time. All you need to know for now is that this is Aleth, and we are the Alethi."

"Okay," said Grace, "thank you."

Savanatha nodded, and then Grace heard footsteps behind her; it was Captain Wu.

"We need to get you two on board for a medical review," she said.

"Goodbye, Joshua North, and Grace McAllan," said Savanatha, "and may you always be ready to give a good account. We will meet again soon."

She turned and walked up the hill, joining her people. Josh and Grace watched them as they disappeared into the forest.

"You should come with me now," said Captain Wu.

"Can you give us just one minute, please," said Grace.

Wu nodded and turned back to her crew and her ship.

"Are you okay?" Grace asked Josh, "how's the shoulder?"

"You know, it's so much better."

"What did you say to them? What was this account you had to give?"

"I just told them the truth," said Josh, "about us and the Transit Team, thank God they believed me."

"You heard what their leader told Captain Wu," said Grace. "They want us to represent them when humanity starts to talk to them."

"Well, let's hope her faith in us is justified."

"I don't want humans to ruin this place," said Grace. "Do you understand me?"

"I do," he said, "perhaps the Zerans know that, perhaps that's why they chose us."

"I won't let us do that to them she said, "I won't let humans damage their land or hurt them. We've made enough mess and we've only been here two days."

"I know you won't," he said, "I know what's in your heart, but I don't think you need worry, The Zerans will rely on us to look after their land."

"Their land," said Grace. "That's right."

He smiled and reached out a hand to her.

"Come on," he said, "let's see how Brandon and Dan are getting on."

She took his hand and held it as they walked back down towards the waiting ship.

THE SECRETS OF THE ALETHI - PROLOGUE

Book 2 in The Centauri Sequence, *The Secrets of the Alethi*, will be published in the Spring of 2025.

What follows is the prologue of that book.

Kasita's face smacked against the bow, and he tasted blood in his mouth.

Then, a shout from behind him.

"Hang on!"

It was Vidalo, shouting to them above the crashing waves, commanding and encouraging them as he had done for all of their journey.

Kasita grasped the forestay and shut his eyes. The rope bit his hand but he dared not loosen his grip, and as the boat reared, he glimpsed the stand of rocks again; a pale jumble of grey, jumping on the horizon as the boat thumped over the waves. He blinked away the salt spit of the ocean and risked a glance behind him. The others were still there, clinging on to whatever part of the boat they could find. He knew they were as desperate as him, and only Vidalo had the courage to rally them, willing them to hold on like limpets as the pitiless seas battered them.

"Hang on!" Again, the call, the urge.

Kasita felt something stir in his heart, some sense of achievement that they'd come all this way; twelve of them in two boats to start with, then ten of them, then five of them in one boat. The greedy waves had gobbled up the others, reducing their number to less than half of what it was. One piece of misfortune after another had taken each of them; a slip on a greasy deck, a handhold loosened, a moment of weakness and they were gone.

They had lost the other boat just south of the Redemption Isles, and he shook his head at the irony of the name.

At first, he'd thought of them all as a group, surviving together. He believed that the fates had chosen them for this ordeal, each one of them selected and imbued with destiny. But then he learnt again and again, and in the most brutal fashion, that reality does not respect the stories people tell themselves to make sense of the world.

Now he felt alone, even with the others around him; like a piece of flotsam on the water, one chance away from his own misfortune.

Kasita cursed the pointlessness of it all, even as the rocks grew before them with their promise of salvation and steadiness underfoot. He'd escaped the fire from the heavens, survived the journey to Balehaven, and crossed the Baleful Seas. He had endured all this, but it would not surprise him if, even with land in sight, he was right now sucked into the greedy waters to his death.

The forestay dug into his flesh and burned his palms again as the rope slid. He glanced up at the shapeless grey sky, and knew that there would be rain again soon.

"Hold!"

He jumped, gripping the line tighter still. This time, he hadn't been the subject of Vidalo's command. There was a scream behind him; the squeal of a sliding shoe on the deck, the hiss of the enclosing waves.

Kasita chose not to turn around to see who had gone into the deep. He had done that so many times and he didn't want to do it again now. Instead, he shut his eyes and felt the burn in his hands and tasted the bloody salt and the metal in his mouth. He let the cries and the curses wash over him, like waves over the bow. He didn't want to find out who Vidalo had screamed at, but he hoped it was Vark. Vark who had forgotten himself more completely than the rest of them, and who had taken to howling in his sleep.

Kasita reckoned they must be just a couple of hundred metres from shore now. There would be no rescue for them, not in this ship with its smashed rudder and its oars long since lost to the waters. All they could do was hope that the fickle tides would spare them the rock-faced coastline and instead toss them onto a beach.

The boat steadied for a moment, and he glanced behind himself. Three figures stared back, clinging to anything they could, skirting the edge of insanity.

Vark was still there, grinning at him, and Vidalo and Marchek, the sinewy old man amongst them; the one who he thought they would lose first.

Kasita turned back and cursed everything and everyone: the survivors on this boat, the god who put them there, the moons, the fire, the Haseraki and the Alethi, all of them; and above all, he cursed the greedy roiling sea, still tossing them like a juggler's ball, back and forth, towards the Alethi shoreline.

ACKNOWLEDGMENTS

The first inkling of this story came to me with that beguiling word, 'exoplanet', and the amazing advances made in this area of astronomy over the last thirty years. But my Survivors wouldn't have got off the ground without the help of many people who have been with me on this long journey. I am truly grateful to all of you.

Particular thanks go out to the editors and artists who helped me along the way. Ali Hull and Amanda Rutter, whose insights and support have been invaluable; to Julia 'Proofreader' Gibbs who weeded out a multitude of grammatical and spelling issues from the 2019 edition of my laughingly named 'final version'; to cover designer Esther Kotecha, and to Yen Quach and Naomi Trollope, all of whom helped me to visualise these characters and the worlds they inhabit - thank the Lord for great artists!

Grateful thanks also go out to Dave 'The Planet Builder' Angus who gave the planet Zera some geological rigour, to author and scientist C. John Arthur, who acted as my scientific adviser on all matters biological and genetic in the early drafts of this work. I am grateful also to Gareth Powell for an inspiring suggestion regarding Mr Mortis. My thanks as well to the innumerable people who have read the manuscript in its various iterations, including Andy Barnes and epic fantasy writer *par excellence* Michael J Harvey.

For this 2024 edition I want to extend a special thank you to my fellow writers at Resolute Books, especially those who read and critiqued the manuscript for this edition.

Last but not least an epic shout out to my friend and business partner, Ruth Leigh, who also acted as proof reader, and has provided more support and assistance than I can record here: madam, I remain your most obedient and humble friend!

Notwithstanding all the above, mistakes and omissions do, of course, remain my responsibility.

Andy Chamberlain
November 2024

About Resolute Books

We are an independent press representing a consortium of experienced authors, professional editors and talented designers producing engaging and inspiring books of the highest quality for readers everywhere. We produce books in a number of genres including historical fiction, crime suspense, young adult dystopia, memoir, Cold War thrillers, and even Jane Austen fan fiction!

Find out more at resolutebooks.co.uk

for the joy of reading

www.ingramcontent.com/pod-product-compliance
Lightning Source LLC
Chambersburg PA
CBHW051134190726
48290CB00006B/1841